THE HOLE OF THE PIT

AND

BY ONE, BY TWO AND BY THREE

ADRIAN ROSS

Oleander Press
16 Orchard Street
Cambridge
CB1 1JT

www.oleanderpress.com

© Oleander Press, 2010. All Rights reserved.
Introduction © Richard Dalby
Foreword © Barry Cross

No part of this publication may be reproduced, stored in a retrieval system, or transmitted, in any form or by any means without prior permission in writing of the publisher, nor be otherwise circulated in any form of binding or cover other than in which it is published and without a similar condition including this condition being imposed on the subsequent purchaser.

A CIP catalogue record for the book is available from the British Library.

ISBN: 9780900891861

Designed and typeset by Ayshea Carter
manganese@ntlworld.com

Printed in England

THE HOLE OF THE PIT
AND
BY ONE, BY TWO AND BY THREE

Adrian Ross
[Arthur R. Ropes]

With an introduction by
Richard Dalby

OLEANDER PRESS

CONTENTS

Introduction by Richard Dalby	7
Foreword by Barry Cross	15
By One, By Two and By Three (1887)	19
The Pipes of Pan (1899)	56
The Hole of the Pit (1914)	62

INTRODUCTION

'Adrian Ross' was a great name to conjure with in the early years of the 20th century. A founding father of 'musical comedy', this celebrated librettist wrote over two thousand lyrics and worked on around sixty popular musicals, including the hugely successful English versions of *The Merry Widow and Lilac Time*.

In his completely different earlier life, under his own name of Arthur R. Ropes, he was a multi-talented Cambridge don, a Senior Fellow at King's College during the 1880s, alongside M. R. James.

He composed two impressive works of supernatural horror fiction – both narrated by Cambridge scholars – which appear here together in one volume for the first time.

Ross and James were among the first writers of the late nineteenth century who moved away from the familiar traditional Victorian ghosts to the much stranger world of centuries-old demons, all extremely dangerous and horrifying, defying any clear description.

While the *Collected Ghost Stories of M. R. James* have been widely available for decades, it is now time for the collected horror fiction of 'Adrian Ross' to be available for the present 21st century generation.

***

Arthur Reed Ropes was born in Lewisham on 23 December 1859 and educated at Mill Hill and the City of London School. He then became a scholar at King's College, Cambridge, where he excelled in history, poetry and literature, and remained there for over ten years.

In 1881 he was awarded both the Chancellor's Medal for English Verse (for a poem titled 'Temple Bar') and the Members' Prize for the English Essay, followed in 1883 by a first-class degree in the Historical Tripos, winning the Lightfoot Scholarship for history and a Whewell Scholarship for international law.

His first collection of Poems was published by Macmillan in 1884. He was a Senior Fellow and lecturer in poetry and history at King's College from 1884 to 1890. He published *A Sketch of the History of Europe in 1889*, and also wrote a series of scholarly essays for the Royal Historical Society including 'The Causes of the Seven Years War' (1889) and 'Frederick the Great's Invasion of Saxony' (1891).

Montague Rhodes James, three years younger than Ropes, arrived at King's in 1882, and the two men must have seen each other a great deal during the following decade. They shared many common interests, especially history and literature, not least for the stories (both historical tales and '*contes fantastigues*') of the popular French writers Erckmann and Chatrian. Ropes translated and edited several of their works for school use in the Pitt Press series.

One of the best monthly magazines of this period which regularly featured supernatural fiction was Richard Bentley's *Temple Bar*, a worthy rival of Charles Dickens's All the Year Round. Besides J. Sheridan Le Fanu and Wilkie Collins, Temple Bar published several new weird tales by Erckmann- Chatrian and Rhoda Broughton (collected as *Twilight Stories*).

Traditional ghosts and 'grey ladies' frequently appeared in late Victorian magazines, but very few were genuinely terrifying. Ropes set out to write an original novella in six chapters, narrated by a Cambridge student only slightly younger than himself, in which the supernatural manifestation would be an ancient malevolent demon summoned up by sorcery.

'By One, By Two and By Three' was published in the *Christmas Number of Temple Bar* (December 1887), shortly before the author's 28th birthday.

Most readers and their families who enjoyed reading more benign ghost stories from magazines at their Christmas firesides were probably quite unprepared for the horrifying occult terrors in this story, which is certainly one of the best examples of its kind between Le Fanu's *In A Glass Darkly* (1872) and M.R. James's first two published ghost stories, 'Canon Alberic's Scrap-Book' and 'Lost Hearts' (both 1895).

I am grateful to fellow collector Barry Cross for drawing my attention over ten years ago to the original publication of 'By One, By Two and By Three' in *Temple Bar*.

His discovery of this story, extracted from the original magazine (omitting its title and date), with a letter from M.R. James dated '13 May 1926' loosely inserted, is detailed here on p. 15 Although it seems very likely that Ropes must have told James about his story in 1887, evidently the latter had completely forgotten all about it before reading the tale again over thirty- six years later.

Following the customary practice of the time, 'By One, By Two and By Three' was published anonymously, the true identity of the author remained a mystery nearly a century, until Bentley's archives of Temple Bar, with all the relevant details of contributors, were unearthed and published in the invaluable *Wellesley Index to Victorian Periodicals*.

'By One, By Two and By Three' was first reprinted in the March 1913 number of the American (not British) Strand magazine. The editor obviously took it from the 1887 *Temple Bar*, but did not divulge the source, and added a fictitious author's name – 'Stephen Hall'. As the American Strand was never distributed in Britain, it is unlikely that Ropes ever knew about this republication of his story, which may have been considered too horrific by more cautious British *Strand* editor.

His only contribution to the British Strand was a short piece on 'My Best Piece of Light Verse' in the April 1906 issue.

Ropes's entry in *Alumnis Cantabrigiensis* states that his move into the London theatrical world was a mere chance, after catching a bad cold while watching the University Boat Race. Confined to his home for a few days, he wrote the libretto of a vaudeville entertainment, *A Double Event*, which was produced (under the name 'Arthur Reed') at St. George's Hall.

He then collaborated with his Cambridge colleague, Frank Osmond Carr, a talented composer in the style of Sir Arthur Sullivan, on a burlesque called *Faddimir or The Triumph of Orthodoxy*. Launched at the Vaudeville Theatre in April 1889, Faddimir was much admired by the leading impresario George

Edwardes who commissioned Carr and Ropes to write the songs for a new burlesque of *Joan of Arc*.

Ropes now gave up his Cambridge career, and settled in London. He used the pseudonym of 'Adrian Ross' for the first time on *Joan of Arc*, which premiered at the Opera Comique in January 1891. This was an immediate success and ran for nearly eight hundred performances in London and on tour nationwide.

In 1892 Ross collaborated with Carr and James T. Turner ('James Leader') in writing another very popular farce, *In Town*, which is now widely regarded to be the first modern musical comedy.

In 1893 he wrote the lyrics for the equally successful *Morocco Bound* (with his celebrated song 'Marguerite of Monte Carlo'), again with music by Carr. This was followed by *The Shop Girl* in 1894, and *Go-Bang* (the name of an oriental country) in 1895, with Letty Lind starring as "A Prima Ballerina Assoluta, Famous from St. Petersburg to Utah". All these tremendously popular musical comedies ran for several months (plus many revivals) in London, followed by nationwide tours which also travelled to America and around the British Empire.

Ross also regularly contributed humorous pieces (both prose and verse) to *Punch*, *Sphere* and *The World*, and wrote under another pseudonym 'Bran Pie' in the *Tatler*.

'The Pipes of Pan' by Adrian Ross appeared at the front of the *Pall Mall Magazine* in February 1899, with three strange illustrations of Pan and other satyrs by Arthur H. Buckland. This poem is now reprinted here for the first time with these illustrations. The memorable ghost story by M. R. James, 'Lost Hearts', had been first published in *Pall Mall* in December 1895.

In 1901 Ropes collaborated with his sister, Mary Emily Ropes, on a children's book, *On Peter's Island*. In the same year he married Ethel Wood, a singer/actress who had appeared in several of his musicals. They had a son and two daughters.

During the great days of the Gaiety Theatre, Adrian Ross contributed many lyrics to virtually all their shows, sharing in all the greatest international hits of the Edwardes 'Gaiety' era of musical comedy. *The Orchid* (1903) and *The Cingalee* (1904) were two of his most successful comedies of this period.

When Edwardes began importing Continental shows, Ross (as a longtime translator of German and French classics, including Dumas, Verne and Erckmann-Chatrian) took over the function of adapting the lyrics of many of these shows into English. His first assignment was *Die Lustige Witwe*, and his lyrics to *The Merry Widow* (1907) became the standard English version of that comic opera, performed throughout the world for many decades and rarely equalled by subsequent adaptors.

Among the numerous other Continental musicals which Ross anglicised were *A Waltz Dream* (1908), *The Dollar Princess* (1909), *The Girl in the Train* (1910), *The Count of Luxemburg* (1911) and *The Marriage Market* (1913) all of which had a wide and enduring success in their English versions.

Ropes continued to use his *alter ego* 'Adrian Ross' on his only novel, *The Hole of the Pit*, which would have inevitably surprised any admirers of his musical comedies who bought this book expecting much lighter fare.

The book was published at a very inopportune time in October 1914, two months after the outbreak of war, by Edward Arnold, the regular publisher of all M.R. James's ghost story collections. Ropes dedicated the novel to his former colleague : "Montague Rhodes James, Provost of King's and Teller of Ghost Stories."

Although there are many Jamesian touches in the story, this novel is also reminiscent of the recently published books by William Hope Hodgson, notably *The House on the Borderland* (1908), and especially *The Boats of the 'Glen Carrig'* (1907), which is told in the same documentary fashion.

The story is told by young Cambridge scholar Hubert Leyton in quaint, but very readable, English. Ropes had long studied books and manuscripts of this period, but was careful to use unfamiliar words with due moderation, with words like 'somewhat' (for 'something'). This all gives great authenticity to the grim world of 1645, halfway through the English Civil War, soon after the Battle of Naseby. Most of the action takes place at Deeping Hold, a small castle held by Leyton's cousin, the ruthless cavalier Earl of Deeping, at an unspecified remote part of the English coast – probably near The Wash, on 10the edge of God-forsaken miasmal fen country.

The author never falls into the trap of describing the ancient all-devouring Fiend from the Pit too carefully. It remains a creature of amorphous vagueness throughout the narrative – a living tide of slime seething through the fen channels, with foul bubbles rising from the depths.

A different and more Jamesian creature is evoked by the Earl's partner, an Italian sorceress, in a graphic black magic ceremony in Chapter IX – with green glowing eyes, and formed with both the blackness and appearance of hair", it "flapped and and roared like a great sail torn loose in a tempest, and wrapped itself around the wench, leaving severe throat-wounds, not unlike the demon in the 1887 story. Coincidentally the line "By one, two, and three" appears in a verse in the following chapter.

The more traditional ghost of Margaret, the recently deceased Countess of Deeping, is also glimpsed fleetingly by Leyton and the throughout Earl the narrative.

The Hole of the Pit was advertised as "A Tale of the Great Rebellion, invitingly full of grisly horrors and of medieval superstition." The *Times Literary Supplement* reviewer commented (on 22 October 1914): "Mr Adrian Ross has dedicated *The Hole of the Pit* to the Provost of King's, and one may well imagine that the Curse which was loosed from the Hole was a sort of grey and amorphous elder brother of the engaging entity which haunted Canon Alberic's Scrap-book...There are some horrible episodes nicely told and not over-described."

The book was never exported to America, and no copies are recorded in any US libraries in the National Union Catalog. With the worsening of the War in Europe, it similarly soon disappeared without trace in Britain.

After the death of George Edwardes in 1915, Ross continued to write musical pieces for his successors at the Gaiety, Daly's and the Adelphi, while also working for other managements on other successful shows. He also wrote some of the earliest revues, including *Airs and Graces* and *Sky High*. He collaborated on several more musical hit shows, notably *Theodore & Co* (1916), *The Boy* (1917) and *Monsieur Beaucaire* (1919).

In 1922 Ross supplied both the libretto and the lyrics for the enormously successful English version of *Das Dreimaderlhaus*, produced in Britain (and around the world) as *Lilac Time*.

After forty active years of musical writing, his final farewell to the stage came with the English version of *Frederica, and The Toymaker of Nuremberg*, both in 1930. He remained busy working for the Performing Rights Society which he co-founded in 1914, becoming its vice-president in 1924.

Arthur Ropes died, surrounded by his family and friends, from heart failure, at his home, 68 Church Street, Kensington, on 11 September 1933.

His close friend John Parker (editor of *Who's Who in the Theatre*) described him as "a burly good-tempered man, bearded and bespectacled. He was remembered as a brilliant conversationalist with a fund of good stories, and an excellent companion."

***

His horror fiction was completely forgotten until editor Basil Davenport discovered 'By One, By Two and By Three' in the 1913 Strand magazine, and reprinted it in his 1953 anthology, *Tales to be Told in the Dark*, retaining the invented author's name of 'Stephen Hall'. This was seen by Herbert van Thal who included the story in his *Second Pan Book of Horror Stories* (1960).

I then reprinted 'By One, By Two and By Three' in my own anthology, *Twelve Gothic Tales* (1998), while Ramsey Campbell included The Hole of the Pit in *Uncanny Banquet* (1992). As these anthologies have gone out-of-print, now is a good time to bring these two classic vintage horror stories together in one volume, with 'By One, By Two and By Three' rightly credited to Adrian Ross / Arthur Ropes for the first time.

Richard Dalby
Scarborough, 2010

FOREWORD

In the late 1980s there existed a small bookshop in Swanmore in Hampshire close to where I live. This shop opened only at weekends and was a regular Saturday afternoon haunt of mine. The proprietor of the shop was well versed in books having been an assistant of Laurence Oxley at Alresford for some years.

My liking for supernatural fiction was well known locally and items were put aside for me. On one occasion I was shown a slim volume of a bound extract from an unnamed magazine containing the anonymous story 'By One, By Two and By Three'. There was also a loosely inserted letter from M.R. James dated 13 May 24.

The book was signed 'W.H. Hutton' on the endpaper. William Holden Hutton was Dean of Winchester from 1919 until his death in 1930. It appears that he had sent this bound copy of the story to James in order to try to establish its authorship.

In his May letter, James wrote: "My dear dean, Best thanks for a very good story. I can't place the author... though at first I had wondered if it could prove to be Rhoda Broughton who sometimes wrote a tale of this kind, as I don't doubt you know, and a practised writer, I judge. But there are no tricks of style that I can pitch upon. No. I must give it up; but I have enjoyed this story very much."

I attempted to research the origin of the story myself but eventually gave up the task and then sent a copy of MRJ's letter and the story to Richard Dalby, who was then able to track down the exact date and authorship details in the Temple Bar index, allowing this story to reappear for the time in the company of the equally impressive and memorable The Hole of the Pit.

Barry Cross

By One, By Two and By Three

(1887)

CHAPTER I

It was while I was at Cambridge that I first came to know Angus Macbane. We met casually, as undergraduates do, at the breakfast table of a mutual friend, or rather acquaintance; and I remember being struck with the odd cynical remarks my neighbour threw out at rare intervals, as he watched the argument we had started, about Heaven knows what or what not, and were maintaining on either side with the boundless confidence and almost boundless ignorance peculiar to freshmen. I seem to see him now, leaning back after the meal in a deep armchair, with his host's cat purring her contentment on his knee. He never looked at the semicircle of disputants round the fire, but blew beautiful rings of cigarette smoke into the air, or gazed with a critical expression, under half-shut lids, at the photographs of actresses forming a galaxy of popular beauty above the mantelpiece. Then he would emit some sentence, sometimes sensible, oftener wildly nonsensical; but always original, unexpected — a stone dropped with a splash and a ripple into the stream of conversation.

I do not think that he showed any very particular power of mind at the breakfast-party, or indeed afterwards. What made one notice him was the faint aroma of oddity that seemed to cling to him, and all his ways and doings. He was incalculable, indefinable; this was what made a good many dislike him, and made me, with one or two others, conceive a queer liking for him. I always had a taste, secret or confessed, for those delicate degrees of oddity which require a certain natural bent to appreciate them at all. Extravagance of any kind commands notice, and compels a choice between admiration and contempt; moreover, it generally (and not least at a University) invites imitation. No one ever either admired or despised Macbane, as far as I know; and no one could ever have imitated him. The singularity lay rather in the man himself than in any special habit. For Macbane was not definably different from other young men. He was of medium height, slightly made, but not spare; his face had hardly any colour, and his hair and moustache were light. His eyes were of a tint difficult to define — sometimes they seemed blue, sometimes grey, sometimes greenish; and he had a trick of keeping them half-shut, and of looking away from anyone who was with him. This peculiarity is popularly supposed to be the sign of a knave; in his case it was merely a part of the man's general oddity, and did not create any special distrust.

Our acquaintance, thus casually begun, ripened into a strange sort of friendship. Macbane and I saw very little of each other; we did not talk much, nor go for walks and rows together, nor confide to each other our doings and plans, as friends are supposed to do. On rainy afternoons I would stroll round to his rooms and enter, to find him generally seated before the fire, caressing his cat. We did not greet each other; but I generally took up one of the numerous strange and rare books that he contrived to accumulate, though he spent very little money. This I would read, occasionally dropping a remark which he would answer with some cynical, curt sentence; and then both of us relapsed into silence. Tea would be made and drunk, and we sometimes sat thus till dinner-time, or later. Yet though I always felt as if I bored Macbane, I still went to his rooms; and when I did not go for some time, he would generally, with an air of extreme lassitude and reluctance, come round to my quarters, there to sit and smoke and turn over my books in much the same way as I did when I visited him.

Angus Macbane never told me anything much about himself or his family; he was one of the most reticent of mortals. All he ever did in that way was to say once in an abrupt manner that some of his ancestors had been executed for witchcraft; and when I vented some of the usual commonplaces on the barbarous ignorance and cruelty of those times, he cut me short by remarking in a tone of profound conviction that he thought his ancestors thoroughly deserved their fate, and that their condemnation was the only oasis of justice in a desert of judicial infamy. From other sources, however, I discovered that Angus Macbane was an only son, whose parents had both died soon after his birth, leaving nothing behind them but their child. An uncle, a rich Glasgow merchant, had provided in no very lavish way for the boy's education, and was supposed to be intending to leave him a large share of his property. This was all I gathered from those people who made a point of knowing everything about everybody; and there is no lack of them at Universities.

Two striking peculiarities there were about Macbane, which stood out from the general oddity of the man. The first was his fondness for cats, or, to speak more accurately, the fondness of cats for him. He had always one pet cat — generally a black one — in his rooms, and sometimes more; and when he had two, they were invariably jealous of each other. But he seemed to have an irresistible attraction for cats in general: they would come to him uncalled, and show the greatest pleasure when he noticed or caressed them. He did not stroke a cat often, but when he did, it was with a certain delicate and sensitive action of the hand that seemed to delight the animal above everything. So marked was the attraction he exercised, that a scientific acquaintance accused him of carrying valerian in his pockets.

The other peculiarity was in his books. He had picked up, in ways only known to himself, a very fine collection of early works on demonology and witchcraft. A more complete account, from all sides, of 'Satan's invisible world' was seldom accumulated. There were books, pamphlets and broadsheets in Latin, French, German, English, Italian and Spanish, and some old family manuscripts relating to the arts or trials of warlocks and witches. There was even an old Arabic manual of sorcery, though this I am sure he could not read. Most of these works were of the sixteenth and seventeenth centuries, since which period, indeed, civilisation has ordained a 'close time' for witches; and any treatises on the black art dated after that time Macbane not only did not buy, but as a rule refused to accept as gifts. "Early in the eighteenth century," he once remarked, "men lost their faith in the devil; and they have not as yet recovered it sufficiently to produce any witchcraft worthy of the name." And indeed he had the greatest abhorrence and contempt for modern Spiritualism, mesmerism, esoteric Buddhism, &c.; and the only occasion during his Cambridge life on which I saw him really lose his temper was when a mild youth, destined to holy orders, called on him and asked him to join a society for investigating ghostly and occult phenomena. He turned on the intruder with something like ferocity, saying that he did not see why people wanted to be wiser than their ancestors, and that the old way of selling oneself to the devil, and getting the price duly paid, was far better both in its financial and moral aspects than paying foreign impostors to show the way to his place of business. "Though what the devil wants at all with such souls as yours," he added meditatively, "is the one point in his character that I have never been able to understand. It is a weakness on his part — I am afraid it is a weakness!" The incipient curate turned and fled.

A few sayings of this kind, reported and distorted in many little social circles, gave Angus Macbane an evil reputation which he hardly deserved. The College authorities looked askance on him, and some of them, I believe, would have been thankful if his conduct had given them a pretext for "sending him down," whether for a term or for ever. But no offence or glaring irregularity could be even plausibly alleged against him. He attended the College chapel frequently, and never lost an opportunity of hearing the Athanasian Creed. "When I hear all those worthy people mumbling their sing-song formulas, without attaching any meaning to them, and chanting forth vague curses into the air," he once said to me, "I close my eyes, and can sometimes almost fancy myself on the Brocken, in the midst of the Witches' Sabbath."

This devout assiduity was only reckoned as one point more against him; for Angus Macbane belonged by birth to the very straitest of Scotch

Presbyterians, and evinced no desire to quit them, or to dispute the harshest and most repulsive of the doctrines handed down from his ancestors. Yet to my knowledge he never went near any Presbyterian chapel, but preferred, as his worthy uncle said, "to bow in the house of Rimmon."

This uncle, as I gradually divined, was the one being whom my friend regarded with something like hatred. Mr. Duncan Macdonald was the brother of Macbane's mother. He was a big, red, sandy man, rich, unmarried, and not unkindly in nature; and an ordinary person with a little tact could have managed him, if not with complete satisfaction, at any rate to no small profit. It is true, the manufacturer was one of those self-made men who think that no man has any business to be otherwise than self-made; but by flattering his pride, he could easily have been induced to support his nephew in ease, and even in luxury and extravagance, if enough show were made for the money. But he was a Philistine of the Philistines, two-thirds of his life dominated by gain, and the rest by a rigid sense of duty. Material success and respectability were his two golden calves; and to both of these his nephew's every thought and act did dishonour. Angus Macbane could not have been made a successful man by any process less summary and complete than the creation of a world for his needs alone; and not even this would have given him respectability. He could not live without aid from his uncle; but he accepted from him a mere pittance, which, grudgingly taken, soon came to be as grudgingly given. Yet when he forced himself to compete for scholarships and prizes which would have made him partly independent, he missed them in a way which would have been wilful in any other man. His essays were a byword among examiners for their cynical originality, perverse ability, and instinctive avoidance of the obvious avenues to success. Thus he was constrained to depend on that scanty income of which every coin seemed flung in his face. With his developed misanthropy and contempt for ordinary men, he would at all times have been intolerant of the mere existence of such a man as his uncle; and that he himself should be hopelessly indebted to such a creature for every morsel he ate, for every book he read, was a sheer monstrosity to his mind — or so I should conjecture from what I knew of the two. Angus seldom willingly mentioned his uncle; and when he did so, it was with a deadly intensity of contempt in his tone — not his words — such as I never heard before or since.

CHAPTER II

An end comes to all things; and my time at Cambridge, which had passed as swiftly for me as for most men, and left me with the usual abundant third year's crop of unfulfilled purposes, came to its end in due course. Angus Macbane had 'gone down' before I did, with a high second-class degree in mathematics, chiefly gained, as I happened to hear from an examiner, by a very few problems which hardly anyone else solved. A serious quarrel with his uncle followed on this ill success; but from motives of family duty and respectability Mr. Macdonald continued to pay his nephew enough to maintain life. No relation of his, he felt, must come to the workhouse.

For a year or two I lost sight of Macbane; and when I saw him again, he was living in lodgings in an obscure street of a London suburb. I had learnt his address from another old college friend, Frank Standish by name, who had kept up relations with Angus. Frank was a complete contrast to Macbane; he was a tall, hearty, handsome, athletic fellow, successful in everything he undertook, and was now making his way as an engineer, and likely to do well. It was this opposition in their natures that had begotten their friendship. I have seen them sitting together at Cambridge, Standish chatting on by the hour, and Macbane watching him in contented silence. As someone remarked, it was like the famous friendship of a race-horse and a cat.

I was myself now an under-master at a large day-school, and my evenings were in general free; so one night I called for Standish at his lodging, and together we trudged off to find Macbane. Our path led through one of those strange uncanny wildernesses that lie about the outskirts of every great and growing town. Skeletons of unfinished houses, bristling with scaffolding poles, loomed on us at intervals through the rainy mist; the roads were long heaps of brickbats and loose stones, already varied with blades of coarse grass. The path we followed was seamed across with the ruts of heavy carts that had gone to and from the half-built houses; and we stumbled over posts and through plashy pools, along the ghostly highway, completely deserted now that the workmen were gone, and stretching its miles of raw ruin through the autumn mist. Standish whistled cheerily as he strode on through the desolation, and I was comforted to have him with me — I think I should almost have felt afraid but for his presence. We crossed the No Man's Land of chaotic brick and mortar, and found ourselves in a street of mean new houses. At No. 21, Wolseley Road, Standish paused and rang; a slatternly maid-of-all-work answered the bell, and ushered us into the presence of Angus Macbane.

He was sitting by a poor little fire, in a shabby armchair, with his black cat on his knee as usual, and a volume of demonology in his hand; and, save that the room was small, cheaply furnished and hideously papered, and the occupant looked thinner and wearier, we could have fancied ourselves at Cambridge again. But after the first greetings, I soon noticed that Macbane was changed for the worse since I had seen him last. He did not seem at all dissipated, nor had he acquired the air of meanness and shiftiness that marks the needy adventurer; but there was a genuineness, almost a desperation, in his cynical utterances, which they had not had before — a hopelessness of expression and an irritability which I did not like. The misanthropy at which he had played before was now in grim earnest.

He told us a little — very little, and that reluctantly — of his own way of life. He was doing nothing of any moment — a struggling unknown writer, spasmodically trying to secure some literary foothold, and failing always, whether by the fatality which attended him specially, or by the same chances as befall any author. Added to this misery was the consciousness of his dependence on his uncle, which was bitterer to him, I could see, than ever. He began to talk about Mr. Macdonald of his own accord, and that was always a bad sign.

"Do you know," he said, with a bitter laugh, "my worthy relative is coming out here before long? He writes me that he is due in London on business in a fortnight or so, and will pay me a visit to see if I am still given over to the same reprobate mind as before, and opposed to what he calls my duty. Won't you come and see the fun, you two? I think I know how to aggravate him now, perfectly well. I assure you, at my last interview with him, I made him swear within three minutes — and he an elder!"

"I say, Macbane," Standish put in, in his good-natured way, "don't carry that game too far. The old chap is good for a lot if only you don't rub him up the wrong way. If you rile him this time, ten to one he cuts you off with a shilling — and then where will you be?"

"If he only would die!" Macbane went on, not seeming to hear his friend's remonstrance. "Fellows like that have no sense of fitness. When I saw him last he reminded me of one of those big fat coarse speckled spiders, that you want to kill, only they make such a mess. I should so like to murder him, if I could do it by deputy."

He was joking, of course, but there was more earnestness than I liked in his manner. I looked at Standish, and he at me, before I spoke.

"If those are your sentiments," I said, echoing his light tone, "we had better come to prevent bloodshed."

"Yes, do come," Angus resumed; "and if you will kindly take off his head outside, I shall be greatly obliged to you. Bring a delightful rusty old axe, Standish, with plenty of notches in the blade. It will be so nice to be like one of those dear Italian despots, and get one's assassination done for one. Though there are better things than hiring a bravo, even. An ancestor of mine —" and here he stopped suddenly.

"Well, what did your ancestor do?" asked I.

"Oh," said Macbane coolly, "he raised a devil of some sort and got scragged by it himself."

As he spoke these trivial words, there came a faint sound at the door as of something scratching very gently on the panels. I turned to Macbane and asked —

"Is that your dog, Mac?"

"My dog!" he said with a shudder, "why, I *hate* dogs. I never have one near my room by any chance — except when the landlady sends me up sausages."

"Perhaps it is another cat come to make friends with you," suggested Standish. "There it is again. I will let it in, whatever it is."

He flung the door open, and the chill air rushed in from the draughty passage and stairs. There was nothing outside or in sight, and he shut the door again with a bang.

"I heard it distinctly," he said, in the aggrieved tone of one who fancies he has made himself ridiculous. "What could it have been?"

"Wind, perhaps, or a rat," said Macbane lightly. "There are plenty of rats in the place, and I am glad of it, for it is the only thing that prevents me from expecting the house to fall every moment. When it is going to fall the rats will all run out, and my cat Mephistopheles will run out after them, and I shall run out after Mephistopheles; and the landlady and the first-floor lodgers, and the landlady's cat that eats my tea and sugar, will all be squelched together, to the joy of all good cats and men — eh, Mephisto? Why, what ails the cat?"

For Mephistopheles was standing upon his master's lap, with back arched and tail rigid and bristling, glaring into the darkest corner of the little room, and hissing in a passion of mingled rage and fear. Then, before anyone could stop him, the cat made one leap at the window, with a yell and a great crash of glass, and was gone, leaving us staring at each other.

Angus Macbane spoke first, with a forced laugh.

"There goes my cat," he said, "and there goes one-and-nine for broken glass. Cats I may get again, but one-and-ninepence — never. A cat with nine lives, a shilling with nine pence — all lost, all lost!" — and he went on laughing in a shrill hysterical way that I did not at all like. During the pause that followed, Standish looked at his watch.

"It is pretty late now," he said, "and I have a lot of working drawings to prepare tomorrow. Goodnight, Macbane. If I come across your cat, I'll remonstrate with him for quitting us so rudely. But no doubt he will come back of himself."

As Standish said this, the rest of the large pane through which the cat had leaped suddenly fell out with a startling crash into the street, making us all wince.

"It was cracked already," remarked Angus; " and the glazier does not allow for the pieces. Goodnight, both of you. I fancy I have something to do myself, too."

I was surprised, and a little hurt, at being thus practically turned out by my friend (for I had expressed no intention of departing, and it was not really very late); but I was not sorry to go now, and have the solace of Standish's cheery company home. A curious undefined feeling of apprehension was creeping over me, and I wanted to be out in the night air, and shake off my uneasiness by a brisk walk.

We went downstairs, leaving Macbane brooding in his chair. As the landlady saw us out, I slipped a half-crown into her hand.

"Mr. Macbane's window got broken tonight," I said. "Will you have it mended, and not say anything about it to him?"

I knew that he would probably forget the occurrence if not reminded of it. Standish nodded approval, and we went out into the mist. We walked on in silence till we turned out of the lamp-lit and inhabited part, and then my companion remarked abruptly —

"That makes one-and-threepence I owe you, Eliot" — and relapsed into silence, not even whistling as he strode along.

We had reached nearly the middle of the long artificial desert, where a street was some day to be, when Standish stopped and caught me by the arm.

"Eliot, what is that?" he whispered.

We both stood still and listened. From the waste land beyond one of the skeleton houses came a fearful cry, whether of a child or an animal we could not tell — a scream of mere pain and terror, intense and thrilling, neither human nor bestial. Then there was a deep snarling growl, and the yell died into a choking gurgle, and suddenly fell silent.

"Come on," Standish gasped, and ran with all his speed in the direction of the sound.

I followed as fast as my shorter legs and wind would take me over the stiff slimy clay of the waste land, and after a few minutes found him bending over a little dark heap on the ground at the edge of a puddle.

"Have you get a match?" he said.

I nodded — I was too much out of breath to speak — and pulled out my match-box. I struck a light, screening it with my hand, and we both looked earnestly at the black lump at our feet.

"Bah!" said Standish, as he mopped the perspiration from his face. "Why, it's only a cat, and it sounded like a baby!"

It was the body of a large black cat, still warm and quivering, but quite dead. The throat was almost entirely severed, and the blood had streamed out, darkly streaking the thick yellow water of the pool. Of what had killed it there was no sign or sound, only, in the soft clay beside the puddle, there were marks which seemed those of the poor cat's feet, and other footprints like these, but larger. I pointed them out to Standish.

"I see what it was," he said, as we trudged laboriously back to the road. "The cat was out there, and some beast of a dog caught it and killed it — though what cat or dog should be doing there is more than I can say. What teeth the brute must have! Ugh! I hope he's not waiting round to take another bite!"

We got back to the road unbitten, and went on our way in silence, till I said —

"Standish, do you know, that cat was very like Macbane's?"

"Do you know, Eliot," was his answer, "that is just what I was going to tell you?"

And not another word did he utter, till I left him at his door and said goodnight.

CHAPTER III

Macbane was never a good correspondent, but he duly informed us of the date of his uncle's expected visit; and when the day came, I called for Standish in the evening as before, and we trudged off through another sloppy mist. Standish, good thoughtful fellow, had brought with him, in his overcoat pocket, a bottle of very fine old Irish whiskey, which he had long been treasuring up for some festal occasion, but now intended to devote to the mollifying, if possible, of Mr. Macdonald.

"Every glass he takes of this," he solemnly assured me as we went on, "will be worth a hundred a year to Macbane."

We did not go by the same dreary road that we had taken before. Frank declared, with a shudder, that the last cry of that cat was still ringing in his ears, and that he could not stand the ghastly place again. I was rather surprised at his unwonted nervousness, but readily acquiesced in it. So we went a mile or so out of our way, keeping along endless streets of shabby-genteel houses, which were sufficiently hideous, but not appalling; and about nine in the evening we reached Wolseley Road.

I was surprised and almost shocked to notice the change that had passed over Macbane in the few weeks since I had seen him last. He did not seem worse in health — on the contrary, there was at times a nervous alacrity about his movements which I had not remarked before. But his face and expression seemed to have darkened, as it were, and grown evil. His college cynicism had already turned into misanthropy; and now, I thought, it had developed into a positive malevolence. He still was silent and brooding, after the first greetings; but he no longer seemed dejected. Altogether a transformation of some kind had come to him, such that I — though not very impressionable — was rather inclined to fear than to pity him.

The conversation, as was natural, turned on the uncle, who might appear at any moment now. Standish and I joined in urging on our friend the necessity of attempting conciliation, of showing some semblance of submission. We had more than once induced him to do so before, though his perverse temper generally made him unable to do more than avert an instant stoppage of the supplies; but tonight he was obstinate, and even spoke as if he were the aggrieved party, and his uncle the one to make advances.

"If the old fool cares to be civil," he said fiercely, "then there's an end of it; and if not, there's an end too. I am tired of humouring him."

As he spoke, the 'old fool's' heavy tread was heard on the stairs, and in another minute he entered. He was a big, strong, red-faced, coarse-looking fellow, with sandy whiskers and grizzled hair, who nodded awkwardly to us, and gave a surly greeting to his nephew, who sat still in his armchair, looking into the fire with half-shut eyes.

Mr. Duncan Macdonald seemed disconcerted by our presence, and I offered to withdraw; but Macbane would not let us.

"You see, uncle," he remarked, still keeping his eyes averted, and using the familiar title solely, I am convinced, because he knew the uncle did not like it, "these gentlemen know all about our little affairs, and they had better hear your version of matters now than my version afterwards. Besides, one of them is going to he a literary man, and write a tale with Scotch characters in it; and you will be quite a godsend for him, as raw material for a study. If you want to swear at me, pray don't mind him; there is nothing that tells more in literature than a little aboriginal profanity, properly accented."

This was a bad beginning for an interview; and would have been worse still had Mr. Macdonald been able fully to understand his nephew's speech. What he did understand, however, obviously offended him; and he began to address Macbane in no very conciliatory tones, though at first with a forced moderation of language and strained English accent which were evidently the result of the young man's taunt. Then, as Macbane did not answer, but sat still looking into the fire, his uncle began to lose temper. His language grew broader and stronger, both as Scotch and as reproach. He addressed us with a sort of rough eloquence on the subject of his nephew's miserable laziness, shiftlessness, effeminacy — pointing at him, and showering down vigorous epithets on him. In the midst of his tirade, as he paused for breath, came a low sound of scratching at the door.

"There's that confounded rat again!" cried Standish, glad of any pretext for interrupting the miserable business. "Dead, for a ducat, this time!" He dashed open the door as he spoke, but there was nothing to be seen. Only the gaslight in the passage, flickering and flaring in the draught, sent strange shadows flitting across the walls.

Frank came back and sat down, and busied himself in uncorking his bottle of whiskey, and setting the kettle on to boil. I took up a book, so as not to seem to observe a scene which I knew must be so painful and humiliating for Macbane. The uncle again plunged into the stream of his invective, and

I kept my eyes on the nephew. I knew that he was really quite as passionate as the elder man, and I was afraid of what he might do if he once lost his self-control; but though a little shiver passed over him sometimes, he was quite silent, leaning back in the armchair, with his head resting on his right hand, and his left arm hanging listlessly over the side of the chair. Presently he began to move the hands languidly to and fro, with the fingers outstretched, and the palm horizontal and slightly hollowed, keeping it more than a foot from the carpet. It was a curious gesture, but he had many odd tricks of the kind.

At last Mr. Macdonald, having spent his store of abuse without any response, began, I fancy, to feel a little ashamed of himself, and became more conciliatory, letting fall some hints as to the terms on which he might even yet receive his prodigal nephew back to favour. The manner of his overtures was far more offensive than their substance, and to one who could make allowance for the man's coarse nature, there was even a trace of a feeling that might be called kindness. But Macbane was always far more sensitive to externals than other men, and his uncle's condescension, I could see, irritated him far more than his anger. He left off moving his hand to and fro, sat up and clutched the arms of his chair. Then, when the older man had done, he cast one deadly look at him, and shook his head as if he would not trust himself to speak.

"Winna ye speak, ye feckless pauper loon?" roared his uncle, with a string of oaths.

Macbane was silent, but that good fellow Standish interposed at what he thought was the right moment.

"Come, Mr. Macdonald," he said frankly, "I don't think you should talk like that. After all, Macbane is your own sister's son, and he is not well now, and you must not come down on him too heavily. Let us have a glass of toddy all round now and part friends, and we three will talk it all over, and make matters smooth tomorrow. We can't do any good tonight."

As he spoke, he got out some tumblers from the cupboard and wiped them clean. The Glasgow manufacturer seemed a little mollified; nobody could help liking Standish or his whiskey, and all might yet have been well if the devil had not seemed to enter suddenly into Angus Macbane. Standish had poured out a generous measure of the fragrant spirit, and was turning to take the kettle off the hob, when Macbane sprang up like a cat, in a white heat of rage, took the tumbler from the table and flung it right into the grate. The glass rang and crashed, and the flame leapt out blue like a tongue of hell-fire; and Angus stood at the table, quivering all over, with his right hand opening and shutting as if feeling for a weapon. Standish caught him by the arm and pulled him back into his chair.

"Are you mad, Mac?" he exclaimed. Macbane did not seem to hear, but sat glowering at his uncle. As for Mr. Duncan Macdonald, he turned purple with anger. The complicated atrocity of the insult — an outrage at once on kinship, hospitality, thrift and good whiskey — had smitten him dumb for a moment with surprise and rage. He clenched his fist and struck blindly at his nephew, who was fortunately out of reach; then he spoke in a husky but distinct voice, slowly, as if registering a vow.

"De'il throttle me," he said, "if ever you see bawbee of mine again." And he took up his hat and umbrella and turned to the door.

"Done with you, in the devil's name!" cried Macbane.

Without another word the uncle flung the door open, and shut it after him with a crash that shook the house. Then we heard him heavily stamping down the stairs and along the passage, till another great bang proclaimed that he had left the house. This last noise seemed to rouse Macbane from a sort of trance. He sprang up again and rushed to the door and threw it open, as if to pursue his uncle. We were going to stop him, for he looked murderous enough; but instead of dashing downstairs, he stopped, flung out his hand with a strange gesture, as if he were pointing at something, and muttered a few words that I could not catch. Then he shut the door and came back slowly to his old seat, as pale as a dead man.

In the excitement of the scene, we had none of us noticed the time; but now the cheap little clock on the mantelpiece struck twelve, and recalled the fact that two of us were far away from our lodgings. Standish and I looked at each other; we neither of us liked to leave Macbane alone yet. The man's expression as he flung the glass into the fire — still more his look as he pointed down the stairs — was black enough for anything; and if we went now, he seemed quite capable of going out and murdering his uncle, or staying and murdering himself. Standish winked at me, and went out quietly. In ten minutes he came back and addressed Macbane, who was sunk in one of his reveries again.

"All right, old fellow," he said cheerily; "your landlady tells me her first floor is vacant, and she will put us two up for the night. So cheer up, Mac. It is a bad business, but we will see you through it, never fear. Now let's brew some punch and be jolly tonight at any rate, as we needn't go."

Macbane woke up again at this, with a sudden feverish gaiety. He eagerly took the steaming tumbler Frank prepared for him, and drained it at a draught — he whose strongest stimulant was coffee. The whiskey did not seem to affect his head, however. More than this, he hunted out a soiled pack of cards from an obscure drawer, and proposed — he who hated all games — that we should play to pass the time. Dummy whist he thought too slow, and I proposed three-handed euchre, generally called 'cut-throat.' The name seemed to amuse our friend vastly. He insisted on learning the game, and we started at once. His spirits were almost uproarious; I had never seen him like this before. Yet his gaiety was very unequal. Sometimes he would cut the wildest jokes, till in spite of our uneasiness about him we shrieked with laughter; and again he would sink back in his chair, forgetting to play his hand, and seeming as if he listened for some sound. After some time he went to the door and flung it open, declaring that he was "stifling in this hole of a room." Then he sat down again to play, but fidgeted about in his chair impatiently. He was studying his cards, which he held up in his left hand, when I happened to look at the other arm hanging down by his chair.

"For goodness sake!" I exclaimed, "what have you done to your band, Macbane?"

He held up his right hand as I spoke, and looked at it. Palm and fingers were dabbled and smeared with watery blood, fresh and wet. For a moment we stared at each other with pale faces.

"I must have cut my hand over that confounded tumbler or something," said Macbane at last with an evident effort. "I will go and wash it off in my bedroom and be back in a moment."

He slipped out as he spoke, and we heard him washing his hand, muttering to himself all the time.

Then in a few minutes he came back, keeping his hand in his pocket, and resumed the game. But his former high spirits were gone, and another tumbler of punch failed to recall them. He made constant mistakes, played his hand at random, and at last suddenly threw all his cards down on the table, laid his head on them, and burst into a terrible fit of hysterical sobbing.

We did not know what to do with him, but Standish laid him on the hard sofa, and in a little time he seemed better, though greatly shaken, and managed to control himself. He thanked us in a whisper, and told us to go, and he would get to bed alone. We were still rather anxious about him, but there seemed no reason for staying with him now against his will. The natural reaction had followed on all the strain and excitement, and I, for one, was glad that it was no worse. So we left him beginning, in a slow and dazed way, to get to bed, and descended to try and snatch a little sleep in the genteel misery of the first-floor lodgings.

CHAPTER IV

We passed a rather disturbed night in our strange quarters. There were rats in the walls, the windows rattled, and altogether there were more queer noises than one generally hears in houses so new. However, we did get to sleep, and did not wake again till the grey dull sodden dawn was making ghastly the little strip of sky visible over the grimy roof of the house opposite. We rose and dressed quickly and went up to Macbane's room. I peered in, but he was still sleeping heavily; so we busied ourselves, as quietly as we could, in preparing breakfast, intending, if our friend did not wake, to go off to our own work for the day, leaving a message for him. We purposed, in a rather vague manner, to do something for poor Macbane. Standish hoped to work on the better feelings of his uncle; I had resolved to devote some of my little savings to keeping my friend out of the workhouse.

We were half through our scanty and silent meal, when a heavy tread was heard on the stairs, making apparently for the room where we were.

"What luck!" said the sanguine Standish. "Here's the penitent uncle, come back after the whiskey. Now leave me alone to manage him. There is half the bottle left."

The steps came up to the door and paused: then there was a single sharp rap, and in walked — not Mr. Macdonald, but a policeman. If Standish and I had been thieves or coiners taken in the act, we could hardly have shown more confusion. My first thought was that perhaps Macbane had done something wrong; and this suspicion was confirmed by the officer's first words.

"Beg your pardon, gentlemen," he said; "but is either of you Mr. A. Macbane?"

"No," said Standish; "Mr. Macbane is asleep in the next room. What do you want with him?"

"I want him to come with me to the station, as soon as convenient, sir," was the reply.

"What for?" persisted Standish. "Nothing wrong, I hope?"

"Nothing wrong about him; leastways, I don't suppose so, sir," said the man. "But there's been foul play somewhere. There's been a body found in the road out a mile off, and a card in the pocket with Mr. Macbane's name and address on it; and we want him to come and identify the corpse."

"Do you know the man's name?" I demanded, divining, as I asked, what the answer would be.

"His linen was marked 'Macdonald,' sir," was the cautious reply.

"And how had he been killed?" asked Standish breathlessly.

"Throat cut from ear to ear," said the constable, with terrible conciseness.

We looked at each other, and shuddered. Neither of us had any kind feelings for the man thus suddenly cut off; in fact, we had been thoroughly disgusted with his coarse and sordid temper, and had hoped — in jest, it is true — that he might break his neck over the dismal road he had to traverse. But this sudden, mysterious, hideous murder — for such it must be — struck us with a chill of horror. My first collected thought, I believe, was a feeling of intense thankfulness that we had not left Macbane alone the night before. Now, at any rate, no suspicion could attach to him.

The policeman looked curiously from one to the other of us.

"Perhaps," he said at length, "one of you two gentlemen would know him?"

"If it is the man I suppose," answered Standish, "we certainly do know him. Mr. Macdonald is Mr. Macbane's uncle, and was here last night. We both saw him leave before twelve o'clock, and have not seen him since."

"Then, sir," said the policeman, "perhaps one of you will wake Mr. Macbane and bring him along as soon as he can come, and the other will go to the station at once, for there is never any time to lose in these cases."

I went into Macbane's bedroom, and Standish took up his hat and followed the policeman out. I touched my friend on the shoulder. He gasped, yawned, then sat up, rubbed his eyes, and stared wildly round him, till his gaze rested on me. Then the recollection of what had happened seemed to come back on him in a flash, and he laid his head back on the pillow.

"Is that you, Eliot?" he said. "I have had such a horrible dream. Thank you for waking me. Must I get up now?"

"Yes, you must, Macbane," I replied gravely. "I will tell you why afterwards."

"Moralities and mysteries!" said he, in his cynical way. "Well, I shall soon hear, if I am a good boy, and don't take long over my dressing. Reach me my trousers, there's a good fellow."

As I did so, I saw that his right hand was again streaked thinly with dried blood, and I could not help an exclamation.

"Ah!" said he, as I called his attention to it. "That thing has been bleeding again, I see. Well, I can soon wash it off." And he sprang up in his nightshirt, and ran to his washbasin.

"Look here!" he cried, as he plunged his hand into the water. "Shouldn't I make a lovely Lady Macbeth? 'Here's the smell of the blood yet. Oh! oh! oh! All the perfumes of Araby —' How does it go? 'Yet who would have thought the old man had so much blood in him?'"

"For God's sake, be quiet!" I screamed. "Your uncle is lying at the police station with his throat cut! Be thankful you had nothing to do with killing him!"

Macbane turned faint and sick, and sat down on his bed again; but he bore the news much better than I had thought he would. To be sure, he had no love for his uncle, and could not be expected to sorrow for him; but the shock did not seem somehow to affect him greatly, except by a mere physical repulsion at the horrid manner of his uncle's death. He soon got up again, and went on dressing, listening meanwhile as I told him all I yet knew about the matter; and as soon as he was ready, we went out together.

The police-station was soon reached, and we were admitted into a back room where Mr. Macdonald's body lay on a table, covered with a piece of sacking. There was no difficulty in identifying the corpse. The throat was cut, or rather, as it seemed to me, torn almost through with a frightful wound; but the face was uninjured, and still bore an expression of sudden horror and surprise that was very ghastly. We did not care to look on the sight long. When the covering had been replaced, the constables told us all they knew. Some workmen, coming to their work at one of the unfinished houses in the new road, had found the body, lying on its back in a pool of clotted blood. There were no marks of a struggle that they noticed. They had put the corpse on a short ladder left in one of the houses, and carried it to the police-station. The nearest surgeon had been called in, and had pronounced that life had been extinct for some hours. A purse and gold watch were found in the pockets. As to the hand or the weapon that had done the deed, neither the surgeon nor the police would offer any suggestion; and we could not help them. Only, as we left the station, the police-sergeant remarked that he thought he had a clue to the murderer.

"Do you hear that, Standish?" said Macbane in a mocking tone. "*He* thinks he has a clue."

We walked back to Wolseley Road and left Macbane there; and then Standish and I trudged off to our work — for work must be done, whoever has died. And all that afternoon and evening, whenever I was within sight or sound of a main street, my eyes were greeted with sensational placards, and my ears deafened with the shouts of newsboys, reiterating the same burden — "Third Edition! Awful Murder in Craddock Park! A Glasgow Merchant Murdered!" and over every placard I seemed to see the vision of the dead face, and that gash in the throat.

The inquest was held a few days afterwards, and of course we all attended it. The story of the quarrel with Angus Macbane came out, in its main outlines, from his evidence and ours; and I could tell from the Coroner's pointed questions, that he suspected our friend. But there was no reasonable doubt that Duncan Macdonald had been killed within an hour after he left the lodging-house; and it was perfectly clear from our evidence and the landlady's that Angus Macbane had been in his room long after this, and practically certain that he had never left the house at all that night. The medical evidence, when it came, was conclusive; the distinguished surgeon who had made the post-mortem examination gave it as his opinion that the wound in the throat could have been inflicted with no species of weapon with which he was acquainted; and as far as he could venture to form a hypothesis, death had been caused by the bite of some animal armed with exceedingly large and powerful cutting teeth. This unexpected statement caused quite a sensation in court; and Standish jumped up.

"By Jove, I forgot the cat!" he said to me; and then, advancing to the Coroner, he informed him that he had an addition to make to his former statement. He was sworn again, and told the story of the mysterious death of poor Mephistopheles in a straightforward way that evidently impressed the jury. I confirmed his tale in every particular.

There were no more witnesses, and the Coroner summed up. He began by stating that all the evidence that could be collected still left this terrible affair in a very mysterious state. So far as he could see, however, there was happily no reason for regarding it as a murder. There had been no robbery of the body, though robbery would have been perfectly easy; and though there might have seemed some *prima facie* grounds for suspecting one person of complicity in the act — here the worthy Coroner glanced at Macbane, who smiled slightly — yet it had been proved by reputable witnesses, whose testimony had not been impugned (here Standish blushed, and I think I did, too), that the person in question could not possibly have been present on the scene of Mr. Macdonald's death at the hour when it took place, and had apparently confined the expression of his ill-will to mere words, which it would be unfair to invest with any special significance — and so on, in the usual moralizing vein of coroners. The medical evidence, he went on to say, pointed to the theory that the death of the deceased was caused by some savage animal; and the further statement of two of the witnesses seemed to indicate that some such ferocious beast, perhaps a dog, was loose in the neighbourhood. It would be for the jury, however, to review all the facts, and return a just and impartial verdict upon the case.

The jury deliberated for some time, and finally determined that the deceased died from the bite of some savage animal, but what animal they were unable to say. A rider to the verdict directed the police to use all possible diligence to track out and destroy so dangerous a beast, and suggested that a reward should be offered for its capture or death. This was done by the local authorities, but with no result; and as weeks went on, and no fresh victim fell to the "ravenous beast or beasts unknown," men ceased to go armed, or to apprehend attacks, and the Craddock Park Mystery was forgotten.

Mr. Duncan Macdonald had left no will; and though he had torn up a testament providing for his nephew, he had not yet executed his threat of disinheriting him. So Macbane, as the only near relative, came in for the manufacturer's very considerable fortune. He sold out his uncle's share in his business, and his first act, almost, was to purchase an old, half-ruinous place, called Dullas Tower, which had been (as I gathered from the scanty letter he wrote me about it) the ancestral seat of the Macbanes before the family fell into poverty and ill repute in the old witchcraft days.

I was prevented by my school duties from seeing Macbane, now that he had gone north; and about this time Standish got a good appointment on an Indian railway in course of construction, and had to sail at once. Thus we three friends were parted for long, and it might be for ever. I was sorry enough to lose Standish; I think it was rather a relief to see no more of Macbane. He was stranger than ever, now that his sudden prosperity had come upon him — alternately gay and sullen, exalted and depressed, and disquieting enough in either mood. I occasionally sent him a line, and at still rarer intervals received an answer; but, on the whole, I thought he had dropped out of my life permanently, and I was not sorry to have it so, now that he needed no help. I did not dream of the strange way in which we were once again to be brought together.

CHAPTER V

It was some months after Standish had left for India, and I had already received one letter from him, when I was startled by a brief paragraph among the Indian telegrams in *The Times*. It ran thus — "I regret to state that Mr. F. Standish, the young and talented engineer superintending the construction of the Salampore Junction Railway, has been killed, it is supposed by a tiger."

This was all terribly simple, brief and direct, as messages of evil are now. I was greatly shocked and grieved at this sudden death of my old friend; for though I was not likely to see him again for many years, and college friendships fade sadly when college life is over, yet we had been much together before he left, and my remembrance of him was still warm and affectionate.

As soon as I recovered from the blow of the news, I wrote at once to Lieutenant Johnson, a young officer whom Standish had mentioned as being stationed near his quarters, and as being an acquaintance of his, to ask for some particulars of my friend's death.

The answer was forwarded to me about the end of August. I was not at the time in London, but had been invited by an old friend of my family to stay with him and have some shooting (though this was mere pretence on my part) at his place in Yorkshire. Lieutenant Johnson's letter was sent on from my lodgings to Darton Manor, where I was. It was a good letter, showing in its tone of manly regret how familiar and dear Standish had grown in the short time of intercourse with his new neighbours; but what I turned to most eagerly was of course the account of my poor friend's death. It was brief and rather mysterious. Standish had gone out for an early walk in the cool of the morning, taking his gun with him, as was his custom. He had walked along the line of the new railway a little distance, and then turned off into the country. As he did not come back at his usual time, two of his servants had gone out to look for him, and found him lying on his back in a path, quite dead. His throat was fearfully torn, but there was no other wound on him.

There had been no struggle, and the gun was still loaded. Footprints of some animal were observed in a patch of soft ground near by, but it was not certain whether this was the beast that had killed Standish; for while the footmarks were like those of a small panther, the wound seemed rather as if inflicted by the teeth of a tiger. A large hunting-party had beaten the neighbouring country without finding any dangerous wild animal.

This narrative set me on a very gloomy train of thought. The details of Standish's end were horribly like those of Mr. Duncan Macdonald's — the suddenness, the stealth, the mystery, the ferocity of the attack were the same in both cases. Yet, what possible connection could there be between the Craddock Park mystery and the death of an engineer on the Salampore railway? Still, I could not keep this haunting feeling of some impending doom from shadowing my mind. Four men had met in that little room in Wolseley Road on that memorable night in November; two of the four had already perished by the same mysterious and horrible death. Was it possible that the same end was reserved for the other two, and, if so, who would be the next victim? It was a wild idea, I felt; but I simply could not get it out of my head, and it made me very gloomy and depressed at the dinner-table that night.

My kindly old host noticed this, and his genial nature could not rest satisfied till all around him were as cheery as himself. So when our *tête-à-tête* dinner was done — we had been very late in dining that day — he resolved to have up a bottle of a certain very rare old wine, which he kept under special lock and key for great occasions. This precious liquor he was now resolved to devote to clearing away my melancholy.

He would never trust a butler with the key of his cellar — least of all would he let a servant touch this priceless vintage. He was going to fetch the bottle himself, but of course I interposed and insisted on going for him. With a sigh of resignation, he gave me his bunch of cellar-keys, carefully instructing me as to their particular uses, and the treasures to which they respectively gave access. Then he dismissed me, and I went down to the cellar.

The cellar of Darton Manor was far older than the house. It was hewn out of the rock on which the hall stood, and was large and lofty. I think that when the old castle, whose walls are still to be traced in the Manor garden, was standing, the vaults beneath must have been the storehouse of the garrison. When the modern house was built, two windows were cut up through the rock to give light to the cellars ; but the present owner had protected these openings with double gratings, and put an iron-plated door, with a strong and cunning lock, to defend his precious wines.

I took up a candle, lit it, and went down the winding stair that led to the cellar. The vault below was so lofty and so far beneath the floor of the hall, that the staircase, cut in the rock, seemed as if it would never end; I felt like one descending into a sepulchre. The clash of the keys swinging from my hand was the only sound in the chilly silence, except when noises came, muffled and faint, from the house above. At last I reached the heavy door of the cellar, and, with some labour, unlocked it and swung it back. Then I drew out the key, as I wanted another on the bunch for releasing the precious bottle I had been sent to fetch. For a moment I stood in the doorway, holding my light high, and gazing round me into the great cavernous room. I could not see all of it; but the long rows of casks and the racks of bottles were very impressive in their silent array of potential conviviality. Then I glanced up at the windows, whose gratings were now and then made visible by a flicker of summer lightning across the sky; and as I did so, I suddenly heard a crash as of glass, far up in the house above. Then, as I still listened, came a faint sound of footfalls rapidly growing louder, as if something was coming down the winding stair with long leaps.

I did not stop to face whatever this might be; I did not pause to think what I should do. In a blind and fortunate impulse of overpowering terror, I flung the heavy door to, plunged the key into the lock and shot the bolt home. How I managed to do it in the one instant left to me, I never could understand; I had found the door hard enough to open before. As I gave the key a last turn, something came against the iron outside with a thud that almost shook the hinges loose. Then there was a moment of quiet, and I, listening behind the door, could catch a quick, hoarse, heavy panting, as of some beast of prey. Then came another great shock, and another; and at every blow the good door creaked and shook, but held firm. Next there was a grating, rending sound, as if teeth and claws were tearing at this last obstacle between my life and its destroyer — and still I stood silent, transfixed with horror, as in a nightmare, expecting to feel the fangs of the unseen Thing close through my throat. How long I stood thus, tasting all the bitterness of death, I cannot tell. It was years in agony — it may have been only minutes of time. To feel that something fiendish, brutal and merciless was slowly tearing its way to me, and to know nothing of It save that It was death, this was the deadly and overmastering terror. My trance cannot have lasted long. With a start, I awoke to the consciousness that life was still mine, and that a chance of escape yet remained. The frozen blood again coursed through my veins, and my dead courage revived. I sprang to the nearest large barrel that lay on its side and rolled it close against the door, to keep the panels from giving way. Then I took up an iron bar that I found lying on the floor — perhaps a lever for moving the casks — and stood ready to give one last blow for my life. The sound of tearing ceased; I heard one deep snarling growl of disappointed rage; and then the quick steps seemed to recede up the stair. I stood there delivered, for a moment.

Only for a moment, however. My candle, which was a mere stump, suddenly flared, flickered and left me in total darkness, made darker by the little patch of sky seen through the nearer window, across which still ran an occasional flicker of summer lightning. In trying to strike a light, I dropped the match-box on the rock floor. While I was groping for it, I suddenly looked up and saw two eyes.

Two eyes, I say, but they were rather two flames, or two burning coals. For a moment I stood glaring, fascinated, at the orbs that glared into mine. Then, as the Thing turned what seemed its head, and the eyes were averted for a moment, I saw, or thought I saw, a dim phosphorescent mass obscuring the faint light of the window. Then the eyes were on me again, and I heard the sound of tearing and wrenching at the outer grating — for there were two, one above the window and one inside. The outer bars were old and rusty — strong enough to resist any common shocks, but not to hold against the unknown might that was rending at them. I heard them creaking, cracking, and then — *Oh Heaven!* The whole grating gave way, and I heard it ring as it was hurled aloft and fell far out on the stones. Next instant the strong glass of the window flew in shivers on the floor — and there were those awful eyes looking into mine now, with only a few bars between us. Then the wrenching began once more at the last barrier. It bent — it shifted — I thought it was giving way, and in a frenzy I rushed forward, whirling the iron bar round my head, and struck with all my force through the grating. Another horrible growl answered the blow, and the bar was seized and dragged from my grasp. It was found next day, deeply indented, on the ground, a hundred yards away.

But now that the prey seemed given over disarmed to its teeth, the devilish fury of the Thing seemed to triumph over the devilish cunning that had directed it. It gave up the persistent assault on the grating, and writhed against the bars in a transport of hissing rage, biting the air, grinding its jaws on the tough iron. And yet — this was the horror of it — I could see nothing distinctly — only a phosphorescent shadow, twisted and tortured with agonies of rage, and turning upon me sometimes those eyes which seemed to redden with the growing frenzy of the Thing, till they were like blood-red lamps. I think I had lost all fear for my life now. I did not think of danger or resistance; but so mighty was the sheer horror of that bestial rage, that I grovelled down in the darkest corner of the vault, and hid my eyes and stopped my ears, and cried to Heaven to deliver me from the presence of the Thing.

Suddenly, as I crouched there, the end came. The noise ceased. I turned and saw that the eyes were gone. I stood up and stretched out my arms, and a cool air blew through the shattered window on my streaming forehead. Then every tense fibre of my body seemed to give way, and I fell like one dead on the floor.

I was wakened from my swoon by a thundering at the door, and the sound of voices — human voices once more. I staggered to the door, pushed away the cask, and after long wrenching — for my hands seemed to have lost all strength — got the lock open, and stumbled into the arms of my good host. Above him, on the stairs, were two or three of the men-servants, their pale frightened faces looking ghastly in the light of the flaring candles.

"My dear boy!" he cried. "Thank God you are alive! We have been so frightened about you."

I told him faintly that I had fallen in a swoon. I could not yet speak of what I had gone through, and, indeed, it now seemed like a hideous dream.

"Well, do you know," he said, as he took my arm, and helped me up the stair, "we had such a scare upstairs! Just a few minutes after you had gone, when I was wondering whether you would find the right wine, smash came something right through the dining-room window, and over went the big candlestick, and we were in the dark. And when we got a light again, you never saw such a scared set as we were; but there was nothing to be seen. Did you have a visit, too?"

"Something did come down here," I managed to articulate; "but don't ask me about it — not tonight. I want to sleep first."

"I think we all want that," he said briefly, as we reached the lighted hall again; and I, for one, felt as if I had come up from the grave alive.

CHAPTER VI

I slept late into the following morning, and should have slept later still had I not been aroused about ten o'clock by the butler, who held in his hand a yellow telegram envelope. As soon as I could shake off my drowsiness in part, I tore open the missive, and unfolding the paper, found to my surprise that it was from Macbane. He knew my address, indeed, from a letter that I had sent him; but knowing his ways, I never expected even a note from him, much less a telegram. When I read the message, my surprise was not diminished.

"If safe, and wishing to see me alive," it ran, "come at once. If unable, forget me. Nearest station, Kilburgh."

What could this mean? Could Macbane know anything of my mysterious danger of last night? And if so, was the doom that had missed me impending over him? Or was it merely that he was ill and desponding, and thought himself dying? Turn and twist the message as I could, it puzzled me; but one thing was plain — Macbane was, or thought himself to be, in deadly need of me, his only friend, as far as I knew: and if I did not go, it was possible that he might lose the last chance of any friendly human care in his solitary life. I resolved at once, shaken and weary as I still felt, to start for Dullas Tower. I rose and dressed hurriedly, and snatched some breakfast alone — for my good old host was too much exhausted by the excitement of the last night to come down yet. While eating, I was studying a railway guide, and discovered that by driving to the nearest station at once, I could catch a train which would enable me by devious junction lines to make my way to Kilburgh (a little place in a wild part of a Lowland county) by the evening. While the horse was being put into the dog-cart, I scribbled a note to my host, explaining the reason for my speedy departure, and promising to return as soon as possible; and then I stepped into the cart and was driven off, arriving just in time to catch the train.

My journey was of the exasperatingly tedious character known to all who have ever tried to go any distance by means of cross-lines and local lines and junctions. Twice I got some food during my long intervals of waiting at stations; and all the time, whether travelling or resting, I was possessed with a haunting perplexity, a shadowy fear. Through my brain incessantly beat, keeping time to the pulsating roar of the wheels, a text, or something like one — I know not how or why it suggested itself — "One woe is past; behold another woe cometh." The mysterious peril of the last night seemed already to have happened years ago; the dim terror of the future would be ages in coming; and between them, and in the shadow of both, I was still going on and on, slowly but endlessly — a dream myself, and in a dream.

It was about eight in the evening, I think, when I reached Kilburgh station; but my watch had stopped, and I could not be sure. As I stepped out on the platform, I was conscious of an intense sultry heat in the dense night air, and a sudden little gust of wind smote on my cheek like a breath from a furnace. The train went on again, plunged with a doleful wailing shriek into a tunnel, and was lost to sight; and when its rumble died away, the utter stillness was strange after the noise and rattle in which I had passed the day. I cast a hasty glance round me, and could just make out the lights of a few houses in the valley below the station, and the dark outlines of hills around, some of them serrated with black pines, and the sky dense with cloud, and with a denser mass of gloom labouring slowly up from the west. There was the weight of a coming storm in the air.

I asked the station-master where Dullas Tower was, and how I was to reach it.

"Dullas Tower?" he said meditatively; and then, with a sudden flash of comprehension- "Oh, it's the De'il's Tower ye'll be meaning, sir — Macbane's?"

I nodded acquiescence; this popular corruption of the name seemed ominous, but somehow natural.

"Then ye've a matter of ten miles to go," he said deliberately; "and gin I might offer an opeenion, ye'll do better to tak' Jimmy Brown's bit giggie. The man frae Macbane's tauld him to be ready the morn."

Guided by the cautious 'opeenion' of the station-master, I found Brown's trap waiting outside the station. He was English, as I could tell by his accent; and this perhaps accounted for the slight tinge of contempt in the worthy official's reference to him and his vehicle. His horse, as far as I could tell by the station lamp, seemed a poor one; but it showed a remarkably vicious temper when I tried to get in — kicking and backing, and seeming possessed by an irrational desire to do me some bodily harm.

"Whoa, then, will ye, ye beast?" called Brown, as he caught hold of the rein and dexterously foiled the brute's instant attempt to bite him. "You're a harm to others and no good to your owner. You're just like Macbane's muckle cat, that killed two men, and the third was Macbane."

I had gained my place on the seat at last, but this remark nearly shook me off it again.

"What do you mean by that?" I almost screamed at the man.

He turned a puzzled face up to mine, as he climbed into his place and took the reins.

"Oh, I don't know, sir," he answered, as we rattled off. "It's just a saying the folks have about here. It's some story about an old Warlock Macbane that had the Tower long ago, I believe. Nothing to do with this one, sir — of course not. I got into the way of saying it from hearing it often, that's all."

I did not answer him, as we drove on between high banks of earth and rock, with now and then a tree nodding threateningly above us. I was faint and tired, and unable to think in a connected manner. The grim old proverb, like the Scriptural or quasi-Scriptural phrase, transformed itself into a dreary refrain, which rang in time to the beat of the horse-hoofs on the dry road: "*Killed* two *men*, and the *third* was Macbane — *killed* two *men*, and the *third* was Macbane" — it seemed a part of me, a pulse in my very brain, till it grew meaningless with incessant repetition.

We drove on westward, tolling up hills, rattling down them, always moving towards the storm, as the storm moved towards us. Now and then I heard the muttering of thunder — now and then a livid gleam of lightning glanced across the face of the cloud, or a moaning gust of hot wind swept up the dust, and fell silent again. I took little note of the scenery on either side; and indeed I could see but little of it in the darkness. The lightning, growing brighter and nearer, occasionally revealed some bare cliff-face. some solemn black row of pines, some thread or sheet of water — I hardly saw anything. It was all a part of my dream still, and it seemed natural to me when a black grove of tall trees, and in the midst a denser black mass, with one or two lights twinkling in it, rose up before us, and the driver told me this was the De'il's Tower.

As we came up to it, and I roused myself from my lethargy a little to observe my journey's end, I could see that part of the building seemed ruinous and broken down; the walls ended in a slope bristling with bushes. One grim-looking tower at the corner loomed high above us, apparently uninjured, and half-way up it shone a faint light.

I alighted, paid the driver, who seemed in a hurry to get away, rang, and when an old woman came to the door, asked if Macbane was at home. She said in reply that he was ill, and could see no one; but when I gave my name she conducted me through a long passage — part of it almost ruinous, part in better repair — to the foot of a winding stair. Here she told me to go up and knock at the first door I came to, and stood at the foot of the steps with her candle to light me up. When I reached the door — which was some way up — I could hear her hobble away, leaving me in darkness, only relieved by an occasional gleam of lightning through the narrow slits that let in light and air to the staircase. I knocked gently, and a voice said "Come in." I felt along the iron-studded door till I found and turned the handle of the latch. As I entered I saw Macbane sitting back in an old chair with a shaded lamp on the table beside him, and some books and papers in its circle of light. The room was small and circular, and was, as I conjectured, half-way up the tower that had given its name to the building. A window, made visible from time to time by the lightning, opened on the outer air; and I noticed with a sort of dull wonder that there seemed to be a set of strong bars defending it — perhaps a relic of old times when the room was a prison; I cannot tell.

My friend did not rise from his chair to greet me. He motioned languidly to a seat near him, and for some minutes I sat and looked at him, and he stared at the door. I noticed a new and alarming change in him, since I had seen him last. Then, his look had been almost malevolent, instinct with a positive hatred for men; now all passion, all life, good or bad, seemed extinct in him. He looked worn and wasted; but it was the settled stony hopelessness of his face that struck me most: and the pity that I had felt for him in his old days of poverty now revived tenfold.

After a long pause, only broken by the muffled growls of the nearer thunder, he spoke.

"I hardly thought you would come," he said; "but now you are here, you had better read this. There is not much time to explain," — and he pointed to a yellow and torn old manuscript lying on the table.

I was perplexed by this — for why should I have been sent for in hot haste to read an ancient document of this sort? But I did not inquire or object. It all seemed part of the inexplicable dream in which I was moving. I took up the roll and began to look into it.

It was crabbed and quaint in writing and style, and it would only be perplexing to give its antique phraseology and obsolete Scotch law-terms and phrases, even if I remembered them. But the substance of it was plain. It was a record of the trial and condemnation of Alexander Macbane of Dullas Tower for witchcraft, early in the seventeenth century. After many preliminaries, over which I passed hastily, the narrative came to the confession of the wizard. This was apparently volunteered, and not extorted by any torture; but such cases were by no means rare at that time, I think. The peculiarity of this confession was that it was clear, consistent, rational even (if so wild a tale could be called rational), and did not involve anyone besides the wizard himself. Actual torture was applied, it would seem, to make Alexander Macbane implicate an old crone tried at the same time, but in vain. "The devil," he had said, "was no fool; he had better servants than these poor women." These particulars, petty though they may be, struck my attention at the time; and I have never been able to forget them since.

Briefly put, the gist of Alexander Macbane's confession was as follows. He admitted that he had, by certain magic processes which he refused to reveal (because their very simplicity might lead others to use them), secured the services of a strange familiar. This Thing owned him as master and did his bidding, though only in one way — it could slay, and nothing more. He had killed by it two men, kinsmen of his, one his enemy and one his friend, who had in fact (a marginal note stated) died in a sudden and strange manner. But that which he had regarded as his servant (the confession went on to say) had become his master, and he a bondslave to its devilish power. It was jealous of all he did; it had cut off any beast for which he showed a fondness, and it had driven him to cast off all his friends, and to give up all friendly feeling for men. One man, whom he loved, he had bidden it slay, or else it would have slain himself. The Thing needed to have victims pointed out to it at certain intervals, or it turned on its master. Being asked how he knew the intentions of his familiar, the wizard answered that he could not tell how, but he divined its thoughts, even as, he felt sure, it read his. To the inquiry what form his demon assumed, he said that at first it was invisible to him as to others, but could be felt; and that gradually it took visible form as a beast black and catlike, with a great mouth.

The judges here asked the reason why Alexander Macbane had turned against his demon; the answer, given in quaint but still pathetic language, was that he had married a woman whom he loved, and had been happy with her for some months, and now he knew that he must choose between her and himself as a sacrifice to his familiar. In making his confession, he knew that he was devoting himself to death the same night; but he was resolved to do this. Better, he said, was it to die horribly thus, than to live alone with his sin and its punishment.

"And so," the record concisely ended, "the said Alexander Macbane, being remanded to his prison, was there found dead the next day, with his throat rent through, and the bars of the window broken. Whereby it was thought that he had said the truth as to himself."

As I read the last words, I dropped the roll; for the lightning glared into my very face, and a moment after a ringing crash of thunder burst over the building as if sky and earth were coming together. Then the roar leaped and rolled through the clouds, and died muttering far away; and through the rush of rain and wind I heard Macbane's voice.

"You understand now," he said, with that dreadful hollow sameness in his tone. "I am glad any way that you will be left, and not I; I always liked you better than Standish. Perhaps it was a tiger after all that killed him, poor fellow. You are quite safe now; it is coming for me tonight. I thought it would have killed me last night, when I called it back —" A crash of thunder drowned his last words.

"Macbane!" I cried, finding my power of speech at last. "It shall not be! Whether it is real or a dream, I do not know; but you shall not die that way. I kept the Thing out; cannot you do it? Never give up hope. Cannot you save yourself?"

Macbane smiled hopelessly. "Listen," said he, and held up his hand; and in a pause of the rain I heard, low and distinct, *a scratching on the door.*

"Open it, Eliot," he said calmly. "It must come, and the sooner the better. Then go down and wait; for it will not be a pleasant thing to see."

I sprang to the door, but not to open it. With frenzied speed I locked and double-locked it, and drove the heavy bolts into their sockets. But no rush came against the door — no tearing or grinding of teeth. I could hear nothing — not even a breath; and the stillness was more terrifying than any sound.

"It is no use," said my friend. "You could keep yourself safe; you cannot save me. It will have help tonight."

A gust of wind swept round the tower as he spoke; and mingling in its wail I seemed to hear — or was it but my fancy? — the long deadly howl of the Thing that I felt was so near us. For a few moments there was silence. Then, with a crash, the lightning fell close to the tower, and a great pine, shattered by the stroke, rushed down right against the window, and its top crashed into the room, rending away the iron bars like rotten sticks. The wind of the fall extinguished the lamp; but in the darkness and the roar of thunder I could *feel* something pass by me with a mighty leap: and next moment a fainter flash showed me a picture which was but for an instant, but in that instant was branded in on my memory.

Macbane stood upright with arms folded, gazing calmly forward and upward — and before him crouched, as if for a spring, a black mass with blood-red burning eyes — the same eyes that had glared on me the night before. So much I saw; then, suddenly, the world was one blinding flame, one rending crash around me, and I fell stunned and senseless.

When I lived again, the dawn's grey glimmer was dimly lighting the tower; and outside the blackened and shattered window a bird was singing. As I opened my eyes, my glance fell on something lying in the centre of the room. It was Macbane's body. I crawled to him and looked into the dead face. There was no wound or mark on him, and there even seemed a faint smile on his lips; and near his feet lay a little heap of grey ash.

The Pipes of Pan

(1899)

THE PIPES OF PAN

WHEN the woods are gay in the time of June
    With the chestnut flower and fan,
And the birds are still in the hush of noon—
    Hark to the pipes of Pan!
He plays on the reed that was once a maid
    Who broke from his arms and ran,
And her soul goes out to the listening glade—
    Hark to the pipes of Pan!

Though you hear, come not near,
    Fearing the wood-god's ban;
Soft and sweet in the dim retreat,
    Hark to the pipes of Pan!

When the sun goes down and the stars are out,
    He gathers his goat-foot clan,
And the Dryads dance with the Satyr rout—
    Hark to the pipes of Pan!
For he pipes the dance of the happy Earth
    Ere ever the gods began,
When the woods were merry and mad with mirth—
    Hark to the pipes of Pan!

THE PIPES OF PAN

Come not nigh, pass them by,
    Woe to the eyes that scan!
Wild and loud to the leaping crowd,
    Hark to the pipes of Pan!

When the armies meet on the battlefield,
    And the fight is man to man,
With the gride of sword and the clash of shield—
    Hark to the pipes of Pan!
Through the maddened shriek of the flying rear
    Through the roar of the charging van,
There skirls the tune of the God of Fear—
    Hark to the pipes of Pan!

Turn and flee – it is he!
    Let him escape that can!
Ringing out in the battle-shout,
    Hark to the pipes of Pan!

Adrian Ross

The Hole of the Pit

(1914)

TO
MONTAGUE RHODES JAMES
PROVOST OF KING'S
AND
TELLER OF GHOST STORIES

CHAPTER I

Of the Messenger that came to me from Marsham

This is the story of a strange and terrible judgment of the Lord in the deeps; and it has seemed good to me, and to the one other who knows, to set down in order that which happened, for the instruction and warning of our children, to show them the certain end of evil-doing. For there is need of much exhortation to keep the young from the taint of that recklessness of unclean living that has of late years corrupted our people, in spite of the plain signification of God's wrath by plague and fire, and by discomfiture before our enemies.

It was, as I remember, the autumn of the year of Our Lord 1645, and I was but twenty-seven years of age, when those matters happened which I now set forth. But in truth I had always been older of look than my years, from my very schooldays; and seeing this and my strong love of books, my good parents had bred me for the Church at Cambridge, and looked for me in time to take a living in the gift of my cousin, the Earl of Deeping. But my father and mother both dying in one month of the smallpox, I was left to my own will; and much misliking the ways of Archbishop Laud, and inclining towards the doctrines of those that were called Puritans, I scrupled to enter upon an office wherein I must do violence either to my own soul or to the authority placed over me. I returned, therefore, to my father's estate, where I could make shift to live as became a gentleman, though little more. Of my wisdom in holding aloof from the quarrels of religion I was the more persuaded when our unhappy divisions broke out into civil war.

The Earl of Deeping, though impoverished by his father's and his own riot and excess, raised a troop of idle fellows from the countryside, with the help of a few desperate ruffians, the leavings of his service in the German wars, and rode off to join Prince Rupert, sending word to me to follow him with my tenants, which I would in no wise do. Nor could I yield any more to a zealous letter from Mr Oliver Cromwell (whom I had known at Cambridge), afterwards so great, summoning me to play the man on the Lord's side. For in truth I could never see that either party was on the Lord's side, whether the ravaging rakes of the King's army or the slaughtering saints of the Parliament. And had I gone to the wars on either party, I might well have followed the ill example of the good Lord Falkland, ever doubting the right of my own side, groaning "Peace, peace," and finding peace at last, after the manner of an ancient Roman, by riding to my death.

Thus doubtful, and being besides of a studious and retired mind, and timid withal, nor loving to look on bloodshed, I kept my house as far as might be, and counselled others to do the same; and the place where I dwelt being far away from any field of fighting, and in especial, three full days' ride from the lands of my warlike cousin, the Earl of Deeping, we were left not merely alive, but unharried by either party. Only once, having occasion to ride a day's journey from my house, I fell into the midst of a score of troopers in armour, who pulled me off my horse and very fiercely demanded of me on which side I was, when as yet I had found no means of knowing on which side they were. But I told them that I was all for peace, and giving them my name, their officer pulled out a list of the gentry of those parts, some marked (as the phrase went) as malignants to be despoiled, and some as quiet men to be spared, among which latter the Lord General Cromwell, as he then was, had written my name. So all passed off well, and at no more cost to me than ale or cider for the troopers and an hour's talk as I rode with the officer, a devout man, and of good parts, but too fond of citing Scripture away from the plain meaning.

In the summer of the year 1645 came the news of the Naseby fight, and the utter overthrow, as men thought, and as it proved, of the King's party. Now one of those who fled from that field, after having borne himself bravely but not prudently, was my cousin, the Earl of Deeping, with the wrecks of his troop. He would not follow the rags of the King's army, for he had quarrelled with Prince Rupert on some point, being, I am told, too eager a plunderer even for the no ways squeamish stomach of the Prince. Therefore he made for his own place, Deeping Hold by Marsham, and there that which was to befall, befell him.

On a day in September I sat in my library, and had purposed to read through Dr John Owen's 'Display of Arminianism'. But, to my shame be it said, I soon tired of the divine; and indeed, the discords of our times had spoilt my early relish for controversies of doctrine. In setting Dr Owen again on the shelf, I pushed back a volume of some commentary, and seeking to draw this out, I thrust in two more. So, with the sudden anger that makes children beat the footstools and chairs for tripping them, I flung on the floor first the other volumes of the commentary, and then those that I had thrust to the back. There was much dust on them, and looking into the shadow of the shelf before I set the books in their place again, I saw a little leather book, flat and thin, and stamped on the cover with the arms of our house. Taking it up, I opened on a genealogy of the family of the Earls of Deeping and other their kinsmen, written in a fair hand, with the shields very well blazoned in colours and gold; the whole, as I judged by the last names, some eighty years old, for my great-grandfather ended his branch of the tree. All these names I knew, or nearly all, but as I cast my eye over the pages, it lighted on a string of rhymes in the middle of a leaf:

> 'When the Lord of Deeping Hold
> To the Fiend his soul hath sold,
> And hath awaken'd what doth sit
> In the darkness of the Pit,
> Then what doth sit beneath the Hole
> Shall come and take him body and soul.'

I had not beforetime come upon this rhyme of the Earls of Deeping, but it called up remembrances of stories and songs that I had heard and half forgotten on my nurse's knee.

Never had I seen Deeping Hold, in the sea-marshes at the mouth of the river Bere, nor the village of Marsham, on the hill-sides above the creeks. But I had heard legends of a curse hanging over the Lords of Deeping, which had fallen once, if the story might be believed, and was to fall again and no more. And on the one day when I, a mere boy, had seen my cousin the Earl as a tall young man, with fair hair and a small pointed beard, riding with my father, I had wondered at the wildness of his blue eyes, and had thought of the stories my nurse told me. Then I read the rude verse again, and even as I lifted my eyes from the page, my serving-man knocked at the door, and entering, said that Eldad Pentry, from Marsham, desired to see me. I bade the man bring him in, and there came the strangest fellow that I had seen. Of low stature, lean, and with lank hair, and a face of no nobleness, his eyes were yet great and shining, and wide open and staring ever, as if set on something far away behind that which was for him to see. But for these eyes, the man had been merely mean-looking. He was dressed plainly enough in a sad-coloured suit, much stained with dust, and from his belt hung I great old rusty sword of a bigness fitter for Goliath of Gath than for this starveling. I gave him greeting, and asked of his errand.

"I have received of the Lord a message for thee, Hubert Leyton," he said in a strange and harsh voice, never thinking to doff his hat, whereby I knew him to be a fanatic of some sect, of whom that time had great plenty. "Arise and come with me, for there is a work for thee to do in the land of Marsham."

It irked me to have the man mouthing his texts like broken meat, and I bade him, with some sharpness, I fear, to tell me his tale with less Scripture and more sense. He cast his strange eyes upon me, as if he saw somewhat beyond me, where was nothing but the books and the wall.

"I will not be angered by thee, for thou art a chosen instrument," he said, in the same harsh and drawling tone. "Listen, and thou shalt hear what hath brought me hither, and wherefore I, a man of peace even as thou art, have girt my sword unto me."

It seemed to me rather as if he had girt himself unto his sword, a jest made of old time by the learned Tully, and doubtless by many others after him and before. But I was silent, and Master Eldad enlightened me further.

"When the Man of Blood was smitten before Israel," he said, by which I presently knew that he spake of the battle of Naseby, "that son of Belial, thy cousin, fled from the battle and came to Marsham. And finding his castle swept and garnished, he entered in with forty other devils worse than himself, and a woman worse than the forty—"

But here I broke in with a question.

"A woman!" said I; "but what of the Countess?"

His face worked, and he winked with his eyes, and for the first time doffed his hat.

"The Lady of Deeping had been ailing for long," he answered, and I noted that he spake of her without Scripture. "A week ago she died, no man of us knows how."

"God rest her soul!" I said, not weighing my words.

"It is a Popish prayer," he answered, frowning, "but I could well-nigh say 'Amen' to it. Yea, and much more, God avenge her death on the wicked!"

"What mean you, man?" I cried, for his whole face lowered with sudden wrath and hatred. But at my question his brow was blank again.

"Nay, I know nothing," he muttered. "Yet, if two kites be alone with a dove, it needs no seer, Master Leyton, to know that which will be, or that which hath been. And this woman of the son of Belial, this Jezebel, this Delilah—"

"Aye, what of her?" I broke in, for he had called the roll of all the ill women in the Bible.

"She may well be a witch and poisoner" he said, "being from the land of all abominations, where the Scarlet Woman sitteth on the seven hills."

"An Italian," I guessed, and he bowed his head. "'Tis an ill story, but how can I better it by going thither with you, Master Eldad?"

"Thus canst thou help us, Hubert Leyton. When thy cousin the Earl came to Deeping Hold in the sea-marshes, he strengthened himself there with forty desperate swearing drunken villains of his troop, and mounted cannon on the walls, and gave out that he would hold for the King, though

Noll himself were to come. And straightway he sent to us at Marsham, bidding us bring corn and sheep and cattle, ale and cider, butter and cheese and eggs, also bacon and hams great store, to victual the castle for siege. And we, being distressed, besought his good lady to intercede for us, the which she did; but after her dying he was as one beside himself, and vowed he would take by force all that seemed good to him, nor would he listen to us. So I said to the others, 'Lo, we are in a strait, and we are but a feeble folk and cannot contend with men of war; let us therefore seek one of his own kindred to plead for us, for he is such a son of Belial that a man cannot speak to him.' And all they said that the counsel was good, and bade me go. Now, therefore, arise, and come with me, for we have far to go, and the man hath said that if we bring him not all that his soul desireth by the seventh day, he will burn our houses upon us with fire."

I knew that the threat was no idle one; the ways of the German wars were well known to us, and my Lord of Deeping had learnt his warfare there, and was like to outstrip his schoolmasters. Yet the business liked me not, for I knew my cousin to be one that feared not God, neither regarded man, and his own life was little to him, and another's less than nought. Yet was he, as I knew, proud of his name and his heritage, to both of which was I now heir as the next in blood, though neither have I taken, for what reason this story will show. Therefore I sat still, communing with myself, and Master Pentry sat also with his great eyes fixed on somewhat beyond me. But after a while, seeing that I was yet in two minds, he rose up and took the great Bible from a desk by the window, and cast it down before me with a clap like a musket-shot.

"Open the Book, Hubert Leyton," he said; "and the Lord shall show thee what thou shalt do."

I have ever thought but little of this divination out of the Scriptures, after the manner of the heathen and their uses with Virgil, though indeed there be many very apt prophecies cited from both, as with the late King Charles. But Master Eldad moved me, I could not say wherefore, and at his speech I opened the Book at a venture, and my sight lighted on the ninth verse of the first chapter of the Book of Joshua, so that the man and I read together:

> 'Have I not commanded thee? Be strong and of a good
> courage; be not afraid, neither be thou dismayed...' etc.

"That is for thee," said Master Eldad, sharply; "now read what shall be for me." With that, he flung over the heavy leaves, and his eyes and mine fell on a verse in the Lamentations of Jeremiah:

> 'They have cut off my life in the dungeon, and cast
> a stone upon me. Waters flowed over mine head;
> then I said, I am cut off.'

I started at that, and looked back over my shoulder at the man; but he was smiling, though grimly, and his eyes were set far away.

"Thus it is ever with me, when I seek an oracle out of the Book," he said. "I know what shall happen to me, and yet I go; wilt thou then turn back?"

I put my hand in his, that felt hard and dry like parchment, and said, "Master Pentry, I will go with thee."

CHAPTER II

Of our Ride to Marsham and what we found There

I would have had Master Eldad to stay that night in my house, but he would not, saying that we should return but one day before the week's grace granted by the Earl was ended, and that my cousin would show no mercy, nor would his troopers. So after dinner, I laid up in my mails a suit richer than I was wont to wear, that I might not seem too much the poor scholar in my kinsman's house, of which I was heir, and like to be owner some day; also I took my laced shirts and other matters, Eldad watching me with a sour smile, and muttering I know not what about 'the changeable suits of apparel and the mantles', so that I told him that I cared as little for such vanities as himself, but I would not appear as a sloven to my cousin, or even to the Italian woman. Master Pentry bowed his head, as his way was, and said no more, till presently they led up our horses; but his was sore tired with the journey, being little better than a cart-horse, if the truth were told. Therefore I had out for him the horse my serving-man rode, a strong beast, but slower than mine, and so we departed. I wore an Italian rapier of a new fashion, slender and light in the blade, and apt for tricks of swordmanship; for I had been at some pains to study fence at Cambridge, to clear my wits from overmuch reading. Master Pentry had the sword of Goliath of Gath, and a great pistol. But we met with no call to use our weapons, these parts, as I said, being remote from the war; so making what speed we could, not to weary out our horses, we lay at country inns on our way, three nights, and on the morning of the fourth day we were near Marsham.

Now up till then Master Eldad spake little, and that for the more part Scripture; and when I asked him of the Earl and the Italian woman, he could tell me nought more than I knew already, save that my cousin looked older, and his face fiercer than heretofore, as was like enough. The strange woman Master Pentry had never seen, but those who had met her reported her as of no great bigness or beauty, which made him the more believe her to be a witch. Only concerning my cousin the dead Countess he spake freely, telling me of her good deeds in the village, and how, while her lord was at the wars, she had spent her days in prayer and pious works, with scarce another by her but Mistress Rosamund Fanshawe, her kinswoman. I asked him of this lady, and whether she yet dwelt in the castle. He told me, Aye, and that she was young, and well enough, and kind to most, but, he feared, of a carnal, worldly and unbelieving heart; the which I took to mean that she laughed once or twice and sang snatches of songs to cheer the Countess, and soon wearied of Master Pentry's expounding of doctrine.

Little more than this did I draw from my companion, till we came, about three hours after dawn, to a hill, not steep, but very long, up the which we let our horses pace to breathe them, for our road had lain upward for miles. When we came to the top, Master Eldad touched his beast with the spur. I did the like, and we rode forward swiftly till we passed through a fringe of low trees and bushes that had long stood out as a jagged black edge against the blue sky. Then he drew rein and turned to me, saying, "Look now!"

And well he might bid me to look, for a fairer prospect had I never seen, nor yet a stranger. Under us the grassy hill fell away steeply, with the white road crossing to and fro like a riband laced across a maid's gown. Then came slopes of cornland golden with harvest, green meadows and fair orchards, with high roofs of thatch peering up among the trees, and deep small dells cut through the hillsides, with little brooks at the bottom, and a church with a square tower, which, Master Eldad told me, was the parish church of Marsham, now without a parson since the death of the last vicar, the Earl of Deeping having other work to do than appointing priests.

So far, the prospect, though fair enough on a morning of sunshine, was such as, thank God, a man could still see on many roads of our England, where even civil war had not roused up Croats or Pandours to burn and plunder foe and friend. But now came in the strangeness of that countryside. Through the plain below us, as we hung on the hillside, was thrust what seemed a grey leafless tree, like an oak smitten with lightning. Then, as I looked again, I saw that the trunk of the tree was a river, flowing at the bottom of a grey cleft, and the branches were winding creeks, now empty, but to be full at high tide. Casting my eyes outward yet further, I beheld a waste of grey sea-marsh, seamed and scarred with darker channels, and patched with green wherever a knoll gave foothold to the coarse grass. Further still, all was grey, the channels grew wider, and a thin mist hung over the salt flats, that seemed to melt away into the distance like a wizard's vision; and I could note nothing clearly, save that on the very edge of the world, as it were, I caught the dazzle of the open sea.

Methought that there was something fearsome in the look of the place, with the grey salt desert lying at the edge of the fair meadows and fields, and reaching up its inlets like the arms of some fabled Hydra or monster of the sea. The strong sun, and the merry wind that sang through the bushes, made that grey waste but seem the more gloomy, even as the sunlight doth when it rests on a thundercloud labouring up across a summer sky. But from these fancies I was called by Master Eldad's voice at my shoulder.

"See'st thou, Hubert Leyton," he said in his harsh slow tones, "the house of the son of Belial?" And he pointed a lean forefinger out towards the part where the mist hung thickest over the marsh. For a moment I saw nothing; but presently, as the wind shifted, I caught the sun winking on a weathercock, like a sudden golden flame out of rolling smoke; and with this to guide me, I made out a belfry turret, and then a broad round tower at the end of a blur of shadow in the mist, and lastly a gabled hall and a huddle of buildings along one side of the shadow. All round it were grey steaming wastes of wet marsh, and seams of dull water, and the glare of the mist wearied my eyes.

"This must be Deeping Hold," I said, turning to Master Pentry. "How does it keep its place in this shifting sand and shale?"

"Because thy forefathers," he answered with a grim smile, "though no great readers of Scripture, were wise enough to build their house on a rock, after the first had been swallowed up. Deeping Hold stands on a rock in the marsh. There is but one other space of sure ground, and that is beyond the castle, where I point my finger."

At first, following his guidance again, I saw nothing, but as my eyes grew used to the shimmer of the mist, I noted a low sharp point of dark rock, with what seemed the ruins of some rude building hanging to its side, at a mile, as I judged, from Deeping Hold. Wondering what dwelling could have been on so narrow a foothold, I asked Master Eldad of it.

"The old women of these parts say that this was the house of some Popish saint or eremite of ancient time," he answered, sneering. "And they will tell you that when an Earl of Deeping, being rebuked by the holy man for ill-living, slew him and brake down his monkish cell, a judgment came on him, and he and his were swallowed of some fabled Leviathan monster. Lo, there was Deeping Hold aforetime, they say."

He swept his arm around and pointed again to a spot where a corner of wall, as it were the horn of a tower, clung to the edge of a steep above the marsh; and below was a clean sheer fall of rock, as if some immeasurable tooth had bitten a great morsel out of the hill. Then came the heaped boulders of a landslip, half hidden by weeds and bushes, and then a grey slope of shale; and a little way seaward one of the broader creeks at the river mouth ran up near the shore. The channel was well-nigh dry now, but strange of shape; for in the midst of it was a black spot, of some twenty yards across, as far as I could judge of its bigness, and the grey mud around it was like a steep funnel.

"Aye," said my companion, as he saw that my eyes rested on the ruin and the space below it; "that black spot they call the Hole, and fable that it hath no bottom, and that down there the Leviathan sleeps with the old Earl and his castle in his belly, till it be time for him to swallow another. But these be old wives' fables. We have wasted over-much time in gazing and babbling. Come!"

I shook my reins, and together we clattered down the steep road, but warily. Yet in spite of his scorn, my mind was full of his story and of the ancient rhyme that jumped so with its purport. And at each turn of the road, when we caught the slowly narrowing view of the shore, and the marsh, I lingered awhile to carry my eyes to the Hole, that lay black and ominous under that shred of the old castle. This I could do easily, for I was much the better mounted, and ever overtook Master Eldad before the next bend of the way. Lastly, a ridge overgrown with brambles took the Hole from my sight, and for that morning I saw it no more, nor, to speak the truth, did I think of it again, for this was to be no holiday time for me. We were got to the foot of the hill now, and rode through a deep lane with brambles bristling up the sides, the blackberries now red, and great foxgloves lingering here and there, and nothing to see but the green banks and the blue sky above, till the earth seemed a peaceful and happy place. Here Master Eldad turned to me as we rode boot to boot for the narrowness of the way, and spake, his harsh voice, so near to my ears, jarring me strangely.

"I must needs gather together the men of the village, Hubert Leyton, that they may meet thee and take counsel what is to be done. If thou wilt rest at mine own house, there is near by a place that we have built for coming together, and there we may meet today."

I had gathered from Master Pentry that he had appointed himself as a minister or preacher to the men of Marsham, and that they had built for themselves what men style a conventicle, not caring to use the parish church, though now left vacant. For himself, he had exercised, so he told me, the calling of a tailor; but thinking it unfit for a messenger of the Gospel to serve man's carnal vanities, he lived, poorly enough, of the gifts his flock made shift to spare him, and the produce of his garden. So I looked for no banquet with him, and could but hope, frugal scholar as I was, that some farmer might be moved to mend my host's cheer.

"From yonder corner," said Master Eldad, as we climbed out of the hollow lane, "I will show thee my house and the tabernacle hard by"; and as he spake, we came to a turn from which the village showed near at hand, clustered round the church. I halted and looked thither, and methought all was strangely still, without crow of cock or low of cattle, as is the wont of villages. Nor did men seem to be stirring about the place, nor maids singing, and a cold fear fell on me that we had come too late. As I shivered with that dread, Master Pentry, who had been peering under his hand for the sunlight, called out sharply and strangely at my elbow.

"It is gone! It is gone!" he cried. "Hasten! Hasten!" and so put spurs to his horse and pushed on towards the village. I followed, marvelling what he might have seen so to distract him, for he rode like a madman, tossing his arms and raving. But I saw full soon. Skirting the silent village, he came, and I with him, on a space where I could see there had been two buildings, of the stone of those parts, grey or iron-brown in colour. But the foundations alone were left, or not even these; for in one place a scorched hollow showed where a wall had been, and the stones and roof-beams, charred thatch and shards of tiles were scattered over the earth like scraps of broken meat thrown for fowls to peck at. Master Eldad threw himself from his horse and grovelled on the ground within the foundations of what I judged to have been his conventicle. I lighted down also, wondering what had wrought this ruin; but on looking closer at the stones, I smelt a sharp savour that told me well enough the villainy that had been done. Here had been gunpowder at work, and none but my worshipful cousin had laid it. I am no knight-errant greedy of adventure and thirsting for danger; and I will own that my first thought was of what welcome I was like to find from my kinsman when I should go to him as an ambassador of peace. The careless cruelty that could waste two barrels of good powder to lay low a couple of poor hovels, that a truss of straw and a flint and steel had destroyed as easily, would not grudge a drachm or two to send a ball through my head. But I shook off the thought and went to Master Pentry, who had come partly to himself, and was muttering some of the verses wherein David curses wicked men, the which I have ever relished least of the Psalms.

"Come, Master Eldad," I said, taking him by the arm and raising him, so that he stood staring before him; " 'tis a devilish deed, but you shall have your cottage again; aye, and your meeting-house, if I pledge mine for it. God grant that they have done no worse harm. Let us to the village to see."

"What worse could they do?" he asked. "The house of the Lord is broken down and burnt with fire..." — and so rambled off into cursing again.

"Why, there be human temples of the Lord also," I answered, drawing him towards the horses, "that these villains may have shattered or defiled. Come and save them, if there be yet time."

My words seemed to mean but little to Master Eldad; and indeed it was a sore blow, and one that might well have dazed him: moreover, I have seen more than once that a man eaten up with the zeal of religion is wont to think but little of the earthly good of others. Still, he roused himself and got on his beast, and I doing the like, we rode together into the hamlet of Marsham.

There we drew rein before the little inn, the "Apple Tree", whose sign hung out bravely, but with black holes through half its apples. The door was barred against us, and we knocked in vain with our hands and the pommels of our swords. Lastly, Master Eldad lifted up his voice, hearing, as I conceive, some sound within.

"John Saunders, John Saunders!" he shouted, "how long wilt thou leave thy minister outside the door? Come and let us in; there is none here but Eldad Pentry and a friend."

Methought that if John Saunders were above ground, that summons should bring him; for Master Eldad's voice was not one to be forgotten nor disregarded. And in truth, I heard a stirring within, and after a while, the bars were undone and the bolts withdrawn, and John Saunders, the innkeeper, stood in the doorway. He was a fat man, and had been ruddy of face and jovial as a heathen Bacchus; but some mighty terror had left him pale, with his great cheeks hanging like bags. He started when he saw my horse and clothes, as if afraid that I was some enemy; but Master Eldad lighted down and took him by the shoulder.

"Speak, thou coward!" he said, roughly enough. "What has happened?"

John Saunders began a rambling story, that I could make but little of; and ever as Master Pentry broke in with some swift question, the innkeeper lost the thread of his tale, and was fain to go back to the beginning again, so that I despaired of learning aught of him. But as he maundered on, I heard a hinge creak across the way, and saw a red head peer out, and then a body follow it. Next, a woman's white face showed in the dark patch of a broken window-pane, and one by one the villagers came out, but timidly, like a cat that has been chased into a hole by a dog, and will hardly venture out for her milk.

Soon Master Eldad and I were in the midst of a ring of pale faces; and on learning from my companion who I was and for what come, they took courage to tell us all that had befallen them, but brokenly, dwelling on small matters, and going over the story again and again, as is the way of country folk and such as have commonly but little to speak of, and much desire to speak. It seemed that the Earl of Deeping, after that he had set the people of Marsham a day to provision his castle, sent some of his men to spy out what was being done to that end; and these fellows, coming to the "Apple Tree" and paying for liquor, and talking civilly enough (for they were skilful knaves), drew out of the tapster all concerning Master Pentry's journey. Now my cousin the Earl, not hearing that Master Eldad had gone to seek me (nor, had he heard it, would he have believed it), fell into a great and devilish rage (as I learned afterwards, and could even then guess), thinking that the man he hated most of all was gone to fetch the soldiers of the Parliament; and perhaps Master Pentry had done so, were there any such within call. Therefore, without giving any warning to the villagers, or seeking to find out whether they were privy to their minister's plan, the Earl came up the river a little before high tide with thirty men, being his whole garrison but a few, in three flat barges and a skiff, and set his troopers carrying off corn and flour, butter and cheese, eggs and bacon and hams from the houses; Saunders they robbed of his whole provision of ale and cider. Next they fell to catching and chasing the fowls and geese, and driving cattle and sheep and swine down to the barges. The men of the village were afield, save the innkeeper, who dared not say a word, the blacksmith, and an old man or two, who could do naught but curse the robbers, and be laughed at. Of the women, most fled from the place; but the maid at the inn, a wanton jade and fond of talking with soldiers, went with the villains of her own foolish freewill; and the blacksmith's daughter, a well-favoured lass, striving to save her geese from them, two of them took her also to the barges, and her father, making after them, and striking one with a hammer, was beaten down with the butt of a musket and lay speechless for an hour.

So, having taken what they would, and beat in the bottoms of the boats that none might follow, these robbers rowed out with the tide to Deeping Hold; but first the Earl himself went up to Master Eldad's cottage and conventicle, with two of his men that were most with him, each bearing a barrel of powder. In a little while they went back laughing, and as they were at the barges, there came two great thunderclaps, one on the other, and a rocking of the ground, and a great flame and branching pillar of smoke. That sound and sight brought the villagers back in hot haste; and indeed, some of them were already warned by the fleeing women. But as they came on the hills above, they could see the flash of arms on the black barges dropping down with the tide through the grey maze of channel and quicksand that none knew like the men of Deeping Hold.

Since that time, now two days gone, the Marsham men had kept their doors bolted, and their women, and what of their cattle was left, hidden away when the tide rose, lest the Earl's troopers should harry them again; but nought more had been seen of them. So much we learned from the village men and women, with what tears and curses I need not now write.

CHAPTER III

Of my Voyage to Deeping Hold

When the tale of the robbery was told, and an ill tale it was, it behoved us to see what was yet to be done. But first, it being now close on noon, and little fear of the Deeping men till the tide was half risen, Master Eldad and myself must put up our horses, and eat and drink. The villagers had lost much of their stores of victual, but some was overlooked by the plunderers, or hidden hastily by the women when they saw the boats, so that we ate well enough for folk who did but seek to be fed, while our beasts had room and to spare in the cattle sheds. Then we gathered together again in the churchyard, which was higher than the rest of the place, and showed a clear gap through the trees down to the river and the easiest landing-place. Also a watch was set on the church tower, to give us the greater safety, and so we stood and talked together.

Master Pentry, as was his wont, spake first, and with much Scripture, strangely wrested from the true meaning at times. His counsel was to keep no terms of truce with the son of Belial, and to cut him off root and branch with all his house; nor, indeed, did I wonder at his wrath and thirst for vengeance, but I saw not how the thing was to be done. For arms we had none, save his sword and mine, and his pistol; and the rest would be fain to use their pitchforks and scythes without beating them into swords and spears, for the blacksmith was no armourer. Nor (having read something of wars) could I put faith in his prophecy that the Lord would deliver them into our hands. For the Lord has been known to let the worse cause win the field, as was shown by the changing fortunes of our own Civil War, or even more of the war in Germany, in which either side triumphed in turn, and at last both sank into a baffled peace. Something of this I said to the men, being asked for my counsel next to Master Eldad, who had not waited for the asking; and it was thought good that we should try the course of peaceful treaty before we took up arms. For though our case was well-nigh desperate as against the Earl's ruffians, yet was theirs little better when a Parliament ship of war or troop of horse found time to search them out, nor could they look for aught but hanging as thieves and outlaws, making pretence of the state of war for their private plundering, to whom all generals have with reason shown scant mercy.

So, when I had spoken, and none cared to say further, it was agreed, none disputing save Master Pentry and the blacksmith, that an ambassador should be sent to the Earl under flag of truce, to offer him safe conduct out of the country for himself and his men, and safe keeping for his castle and household stuff, saving only payment for the destruction of Master Pentry's house and conventicle. But, should he reject the terms, we were to declare our purpose of seeking aid from the Lord General Cromwell, whom I knew well, and who had showed me a singular friendship.

Now this last matter was known to my cousin, for he had heard of the letter whereof I spake before, and would therefore know that if I stirred in the quarrel, there was the more likelihood of the Lord General taking it up; also (though I knew it not then) the Earl had in one of his raids plundered some of the General's baggage, and slain a servant of his after a beastly and barbarous manner.

For the choice of our ambassador there was no disputing, seeing that all, without exception, laid the office on me; nor could I well refuse, as having been the first mover of such a course. For indeed I knew that to none other than one of his own quality would my cousin so much as give ear, being of an unmeasured pride and arrogance; nor would any low-born envoy escape a bullet, though he had a hundred white flags. Therefore it behoved me to take the post of honour, none coveting it, and myself least of all.

First, then, I wrote a letter to the Lord General Cromwell, setting forth the ill deeds of the Earl of Deeping, and beseeching him by the friendship he had for me, and the wrath he bore against murder and oppression, to send a troop swiftly to Marsham, and root out that nest of robbers. This letter I gave to Master Eldad, charging him, if I were kept prisoner or slain, to write on the foot of the letter what had happened to me, and send the whole by a sure messenger on my horse to the nearest post of the Parliament army. So Master Pentry took the writing and duly did with it as I charged him; though (as will appear) I might have spared my pains to secure my life or revenge my death, for all was otherwise ordered.

This being done, there was naught remaining but to repair to Deeping Hold, and there see my cousin. For that I must wait till the high tide was past, and go out with the ebb by boat. Though there was a way across the marshes at low tide to a landing near the castle, yet was the path winding, slippery, and beset with quicksands, where any man not knowing the places as well as the face of his nearest of kin might well be mired and lost; nor could even the skilful be over sure, for it was the nature of those sands to change with a great tide or heavy storm. But in a boat I could scarce come to much harm, being used to handle oars, and strong to swim; for in those parts the sea was like to prove less treacherous than the land.

So we came down to the river together, and found an old boat belonging to one of the men, that the Earl's troopers had overlooked, since it lay in a little creek among the willows. It was small and scarce seaworthy, but we made shift to caulk the seams. Hither they brought my mails, and a staff with a white kerchief tied to it for a flag of truce, and laid them in the boat with the oars, and as all was ready, being now past noon, the tide came in. It was a strange sight to see, for the spot where we were might have been leagues from any coast, as it seemed to me looking down the little creek into the steep trench of grey shale, with the swift river gliding dumbly at the bottom. There was no great wave such as is seen in the Severn river, but a wide hiss and whispering rustle from the marshes, that grew louder and nearer, and then a little wave, grey with mud and crested with thick yellow foam, wrestling up against the current, with others following it, crowding on each other's backs like children at a show, till it passed us; and when I looked round, the river-bed was filling with the dense water, till the grey broken slopes were hidden, and the ripples were leaping at the green rim.

We waited still, till the tide slackened in its flow, and the ridges of yellow foam and lines of slime ceased to strive onwards and caught in the reeds and grasses, and then began to hang on the slopes of the creeks. The time had come, and I stepped into the boat, and the Marsham men pushed it out into the brimming creek. Then, ere I launched out into the ebb, one man after another gave me blessing or warning, the women weeping loudly, and Master Eldad gripped my hand, and standing on the bank, put off his hat and spake earnestly, praying that my journey might be for the glory of God, and the saving of the oppressed. "And fear not thou, Hubert Leyton," he added, resting his strange eyes on me, "for it hath been revealed to me that thy life shall be given to thee for a prey. Launch out into the deep, and follow the main channel till thou come to the place of the beacon; then shalt thou go by the left hand under the shore."

But here arose a clamour of voices, shrill with fear. "Not that way!" cried one. "That channel leads to the Hole."

"No man goes thither!" cried a woman. "Know you not the story?" Master Eldad shook his hair disdainfully, and looked on them as if he were a very Goliath among the pygmies.

"Heed not old wives' fables," he said. "Go in the fear of the Lord, and thou shalt tread on the lion and the adder; the young lion and the dragon shall thou trample under feet!" — and with that he leant on the pole that he held, and sent the boat out into the river, where the ebb and the current together were swirling down with petty whirlpools of grey thick water and coiling streaks of foam. I set the oars on the tholes and steered the head of the boat down stream; and what with looking over my shoulder to keep in mid-channel, I saw but little of the village folk, and heard only a babble of voices, with here and there some frightened speech of 'the Hole', and again 'the Hole', and Master Eldad harshly rebuking his flock out of the Scriptures.

The stream and the ebb-tide together bore me swiftly down with small labour, save to steer with a stroke or two of either oar when the channel wound. I could see little but the green banks, now edged with a widening riband of wet grey, for the tide had fallen somewhat. It was not long till I glanced over my right shoulder, and saw, standing up from a heap of stones, a stone pillar with a great iron basket half eaten away by the salt winds, and it came into my mind that this must be the beacon whereof Master Pentry spoke. Turning my face to the bow, I saw that the main stream made a sharp elbow on the right hand, but a wide channel went to the left, near the shore, which there ceased, and out beyond was the green and grey tangle of the marsh. This, then, must be the way that my friend had bidden me take, to save a great bend of the main river on my way to Deeping Hold; and somewhere in that channel, too, must be the black deep that the Marsham men feared as 'the Hole'. Something of their fear made a coldness in my blood, for I could not but remember the strange rhyme in the old book; but for all that I turned the boat's head into the broad channel as I passed the basket of the beacon, that looked like the blackened rotting skeleton of some strange beast. The ebb ran but slowly over the shallows, and I pulled at the heavy oars with the sun hot on my face. But the brisk wind that I felt now and again mightily refreshed me.

Little by little the current grew feebler and died away, the wind dropped, and the sun felt warmer than before, so that I was fain to pause and wipe my brow; and at the moment I was aware of a strange smell in the air, as of some dead thing washed up by the sea, cold, foul, salt, and sickening. I looked round me on the water, and saw no such floating carcase such as I thought to see; the channel whereon I floated was dark and strangely still. I cast my eyes up shorewards. There was a band of grey shale, and then a heap of boulders, like the ruin of a cliff, and up against the blue sky a broken horn, as it were, that I knew to be the sole fragment of the old castle; and all at once it came upon me that I must be verily rowing across 'the Hole'. With something of fear, and something of eagerness, I stood up in the boat and looked down over the sides. There was nought to frighten a man, save the evil odour; and this seemed to rise from a certain grey glistering slime, whereof streaks and patches lay on the thick water, or coiled lazily towards the side, and now and then a bubble rose and hung long ere it burst. To one so near the water as I was, the blackness of the Hole did not so much appear as from the height above; but even there I could see that it made a round of some eighteen yards across, as I judged. I was now as near as might be to the middle of this strange place, which I thought, from the slime, to be above the mouth of some pit of bitumen, such as we read of in the story of Sodom and Gomorrah. I looked down, therefore, drawing back my body to trim the boat, and bending my head over the side, till my face was near to the water, which in that spot had no slime, and was clear, and black with depth alone. My sight seemed to travel down into the unfathomable abyss, till light failed; nor did I wonder that the villagers fabled that pit to be bottomless. Yet as I gazed into the darkness, as into a great black agate stone, I seemed to see somewhat moving, and looking more narrowly, it was as if a grey tendril, coloured like the slime, were winding upwards through the blackness and rising swiftly towards me, so that I cried out sharply, as a man will when he wakes from a dream, and at the cry the grey thread wavered and seemed to coil downward out of sight.

I said to myself that this was but a streak of the slime of the pit, and that it behoved me to do my errand to Deeping Hold, where I was like to find more danger than in the Hole. Nevertheless, I could well conceive how the dread of that place came to be fixed in the minds of the men of Marsham; for to speak truth, the smell of the slime and the writhing of that grey riband in the black water made me more afraid than I would own to myself. So, bending to the oars, I rowed on, and in a stroke or two was clear of the dark circle of the Hole, and among the dancing ripples of the channel; and with small labour I won through to the main river, the which, as Master Pentry had told me, made a great elbow and met me further out in the marshes. Now I felt the current again, and was swept swiftly on between wet banks of sand or shale, and growing islands covered with grey grass, or dotted with harsh samphire. In no long time I caught the winking flash of the weathercock on the castle belfry and then a glimpse of a roof and the hard lines of the walls. Methought that if I could see, I might also be seen, so I took the white flag that had been given me, and set it upright in the bows of the boat.

Nor was I too soon; for as I came round another bend of the stream, I could see a good piece of the wall, and the flash of a steel cap and of a pike; then two or three men came together, and one ran along the wall and vanished, as if gone to tell of my coming. I could see well enough now, for as I had little but guidance to do with my oars, I sat looking to the bow and rowing forward, like a boatman of Venice. So the ebb and the stream swept me on, and the castle loomed larger, till I came out into a wide inlet, and Deeping Hold lay before me on its island, clear of the marshes.

The castle was of no great size, being pent in by the water. The island of rock on which it stood was some fifty yards across, and shaped like a pear, with a mound at the point, on which was reared the keep. The turreted wall was low, and followed the shore of the islet, which rose to four feet or so above spring-tide mark, and the wall added twice as much again. In places the rock had been scarped down to the water; in others a slope of grey shale was heaped against the wall. The whole castle was of one colour with the rock whereon it stood, grey, with stains as of rust; and indeed it was built of the stone hewn out from its cellars and storehouses. At the broader end of the islet stood the mansion, built in the days of Queen Bess, when men feared no more for private enemies; and this house was fair enough, though not great, with oriel windows and a belfry turret with gilded vane. So much I saw well, as the ebb-tide and the river stream bore me down slower in that wide water. The sentinels were watching me curiously, screening their eyes from the dazzle of the sun on the ripples, until I came within short musket-shot; then one of them, levelling his piece, but more in sport than in threat, gave the challenge:

"Who goes there?"

"A friend," I answered, and came on towards the wall, though I saw no place to land.

"Are you for the King or for the rebels?" he called again.

"For neither!" I answered shortly, somewhat scornful to find such military punctilio in a den of robbers. "I come for peace, as this sign shows."

"So you sail under the ensign of the dishclout?" he said, grinning evilly; "and who and what may your worship be?"

My gorge rose at this insolence from a common sworder, and I spoke, I fear, too sharply for my peaceful mission.

"When thou hast done with playing at soldiers," I answered him, "thou canst tell thy master the Earl of Deeping that his cousin Hubert Leyton would speak with him." The knave on sentry growled somewhat in his red beard, but another by him laughed.

"He touched thee there, man," he said; "what need to ask watchwords of one man, and none other within miles of him?" Then he spake to me, who was now close under the wall, fending my boat off from the rock with an oar.

"If you row round the keep, sir, you shall see the gate and the harbour, and I will conduct you to the Earl," he said, civilly enough, and went down from the wall. The other walked to and fro again, cursing at all canting Roundheads and foreign traitors, and I set to my oars again, for the water was too deep for poling. As I came round the keep, a little window, made of an old loophole cut wider for convenience, was opened, and a head put forth, so that I, looking up unthinking at the sound of the casement, met the eyes of one looking down. It was a maiden, as I deemed, of some twenty years of age, with dark hair curling loosely round the head, as the way then was, and grey eyes (but I minded me not of their colour then) set in dusky circles of weariness and grief. The splash of my oars had startled her, even as the creak of her window caught my ear; so for a brief space we paused, each looking on the other, till I remembered the reverence due to a woman, and put off my hat, waving it, as the fashion of courtesy then was, but, I doubt not, awkwardly enough. She bowed her head, flushing suddenly, and then withdrew it, and I to my oars again, wondering who this might be. But of a truth I had not far to seek, for Master Eldad had spoken of but two women at the Hold, nor could this be one of the stolen village girls; further, he had talked of the Italian as little and not well-favoured. This that I had seen, therefore, must needs be Mistress Rosamund Fanshawe, kinswoman to the dead Lady of Deeping.

So I came round the keep, and saw a little harbour made out of a jutting ridge of the rock, helped with masonry, wherein were moored the barges and boats of the garrison, commanded by two culverins and the loopholes of a barbican tower, through which a way went under a portcullis. Here were more men, some busy caulking the barges, some fishing from the rocks, some idling, in buff jerkins and breeches, and some with boots and hose off. As they gaped on me, methought that I had never seen so many villainous faces in all my life before. For here you had not plain honest English wickedness alone, but the flower of the rascals of all nations. Here was a shock-headed Irish kerne, wrangling over a catch of fish with a burly German, all of his face beard that was not scars, and each flaying the English he strove to speak. A Spaniard, his lip as it were skewered on a stiff moustache, was gambling with a dark Italian, whose hand ever strayed towards his dagger hilt when the dice ran against him. But each paused in his work or his sport to stare on me and break some jest on my face and garb, nor did any so much as offer to help me tie up my boat. I made shift to do that for myself, and without seeming to mark the knaves, took my mails and went boldly up to the gate, that stood open, and within it was the man who had bidden me row round thither.

He was tall, and had been goodly of face, but for a scar that seamed his cheek; his hair was yellow, though his skin was tanned with sun and wind; also his dress was rich, though somewhat worn, and not tawdry as that of some of the men. He wore a long sword at his side. He spoke well, yet with a foreign twang, so that I judged him to be some Norlander, belike a Swede, and so it proved; for, indeed, even as many English and Scots served under the great Gustavus, so not a few Swede and German soldiers of fortune came to help the one or the other of our English factions.

"Welcome to Deeping Hold, Mr. Leyton," he said, with a soldierly courtesy that sat well on him. "New faces are not so many here that we can be churlish to any friend. May I name my own unworthiness to you as Eric Guldenstierna, once of Upsala, shortened by my men to Gulston of Nowhere, a comet of my lord's troop, or what Noll Cromwell has left of it."

I gave the man my hand in greeting before I thought, so frank and manly was his bearing. Then I had nigh plucked it back, for there came on me the remembrance that surely this Swede must have helped my cousin in all his late wickedness, and in how much more and worse before, God knows. Yet I mastered myself, and took my hand back no quicker than need. If mine eyes told aught of the struggle, I know not; Gulston, as I will call him for brevity, laughed shortly, not as one that is merry, and turning, led the way across the castle court, part paven, part living rock. At the door of the house, that stood open, a black Moor in a gay dress was sunning himself, who rolled white eyeballs on us, and loitered within to announce my coming to the Earl.

CHAPTER IV

Of my Embassy and how I Fared

The black was long in doing his errand, as is ever the way of his kind when they see not the whip, and to pass the time I fell to talk with the Swede. The man was well-spoken, and had seen much; and his soldierly bluntness sat well on him. Yet it was a marvel to me that in all he said there was a scorn of what simple men think goodness. He had no praise for any of his own side save for Prince Rupert, and would laugh even at him as a fool, that cared not to knock his wavering weakling of a master on the head and take his crown.

"As for your war here," he said, laughing in his yellow beard, "you English know not the meaning of the word. Noll Cromwell can order his battle indifferent well, and his saints have swords as long as their sermons; yet where will you find a real soldier in either host, save one or two of us from Germany or the Low Countries? Here you shall march the Ironsides through a village, and not a cottage burnt or a maiden missing."

I answered him that such was surely but the proper Swedish discipline of the wars, as it had been taught by the great Gustavus himself.

"O aye," said Gulston, mocking. "When we began, we were a sort of Roundheads ourselves, save that we sang not our psalms through our noses. But the King was a fool, though a good fighter, and out of the battle old Wallenstein was my man. Had he not gone star-gazing on to the pikes of some rascal Irish, he had been our leader. Wallenstein would never hang a man for a burgher's purse or a matter of a girl or two. You have no soldiers here, nor will have."

I answered him, I fear with some sharpness, that if we had no such warriors among us, we grew indifferent good hemp to reward them with according to their deeds; but he laughed again.

"I forgot," said he, "that men say you are yourself half a Roundhead—and not the half that fights. But I would have you keep your sermons to yourself when you shall meet the Earl and the Signora. To speak the name of hemp might be of ill omen to your worshipful and peaceful self."

I let his taunt pass, for I was curious to hear more of the Italian woman; so I asked him if he knew aught of her.

The Swede shook his locks and laughed sourly. "Nay, what I know is soon told," said he, "and what I know not, but think, is never told at all. Fiammetta Bardi is her name, and her father was hurt to death by a crowd in Ratisbon. Some called him a wizard, some a scholar. All I know is that my Lord and a few of us took her from the chance of a bath in the Danube, and she has companied with my Lord since then."

"Know you aught," I asked him, seeing that it were waste of breath to inquire further of the Signora, "of the end of my cousin the Countess?"

"I know she is dead, for she is buried by now," said Gulston; "and I know she is buried, for that I was by; all else the Earl and the Signora can tell you, if they will. And now will I take my leave, for I see the raven messenger returning."

With that he put his hand to his hat in a mocking salute, and strode off across the court, and the black, coming forth with somewhat more of alacrity in his manner, took up my mails and asked me to follow him within.

The house, as I have said, was not great, for the builders of it had lacked both space and wealth for that. From the entrance I came into the dining-hall, now empty, where the afternoon sun sent a dusty shaft of light through the western window to the great table. The upper lights of the window were set with painted glass bearing the Earl's shield, argent with a castle gules, that I knew well, though I have not borne it. Two great chairs of carven oak stood on the dais at the head of the table, as was the wont, for the lord and lady of the castle; and as the light fell on the seats I had a strange vision of a shadow in a trailing robe, with a stain of red on the breast, so that I started and cried out sharply, "What is that?" and with the word I knew myself for a fool, for it was but the play of the light on the wood, and the colour of the red castle in the shield. But when I looked at the black, he was shaking like a man with the ague, and his face went grey with fear.

"Massa see her?" he said, stumbling in his speech; "Pompey see her many times!" and with that he fell to crossing himself and gabbling of jargon that I judged to be prayers mingled with heathen charms, as is the manner of Africans; nor would he leave his mumbling, though I told him to lead me to his master, but took me to a door at the further side of the hall and pointed to it with a shaking finger; and then, as I signed that he could go, he crept from the place, still muttering his spells.

This vision, though I knew it was but a shadow, joined with the fear of the black, had shaken me strangely, so that I lingered for a while at the door. But the memory of the poor men of Marsham came back to me, and the words of Master Pentry's oracle, and I knocked and was bidden enter.

The room I came into was but small, and somewhat dark, being wainscoted with oak gone black with age. An oaken table stood across the midst, and beyond it a fire was burning bright on the hearth. Two only were in the room, a man and a woman, with their faces turned to the fire; but as I came in, the man rose to his feet, and I knew my cousin the Earl, though changed. He was broader and greater than when I had last seen him, and his hair had touches of grey; but that which chiefly moved me was the wildness of his eyes, which shifted restlessly from my face to the corners of the room, and changed without seeming cause from a flaming wrath to a desperate deadness. Yet he came forward and gave me his hand with a show of friendliness.

"Welcome, cousin!" he said in a voice that would fain sound hearty. "Welcome, whatever brings you here. Let me present to you the Signorina Bardi, a scholar like yourself, and able to discourse of such curious learning as Cambridge men delight in."

As he spoke, the woman had risen from her seat, and while my cousin ran on, I had leisure to cast my eyes over her, which I did with the more exactness that I was curious to know the truth of what Master Pentry had told me. As he had said, she was of no great bigness or beauty, under the middle stature, and lean, but supple and well made, as the close robe she wore gave opportunity to judge. Her face had no colour, and her eyes were narrow and near together, and slanted somewhat after the fashion of Easterns. Their hue was greenish, as I came to know afterwards, but she seemed loth to open them to the full. Her hair, which was rolled in a gilded net, was great and red, as in the paintings of Venice, but more dusky, whereby I judged that the colour was of nature, and not of art as travellers say it is with the fair Venetians, who were born dark. She was clad in some dark red stuff, with embroideries about the neck, and wore no ornaments that I could see, save for one great red jewel hanging at her neck, that glowed like a hot coal in the flicker of the fire.

I made shift to bow, and salute her with a word or two in the Italian, at which her lips, that were thin and dusky red, parted in a smile, and her face changed, so that for a flash she seemed beautiful. Her voice also was most musical, with a singing sound in it that made even her English (that she spoke very well) a delight to hear; and in listening to her I almost forgot what she was, and what it was most like she had done or procured to be done. My cousin the Earl looked on us with a snarling smile.

"So she hath bewitched you too, Cousin Hubert?" he said, and I felt my cheek grow hot as he laughed. "Never blush, man, to follow the head of your house, but sit and empty your budget of news. Stay, it is ill telling a dry story," and he took up a flagon of Spanish wine that stood at his side, and filled me a Venice goblet to the brim, and another for himself, after the Signora had put it away with a dainty wave of her long fingers. "Give a health to the King, man, Puritan or none, and drown your conscience!"

"There is no need," I said. "To the King, and may he be happily and righteously restored to his due honours!" With that I drank off the wine, which was somewhat too hot for my palate.

"A right Trimmer's toast!" he mocked; "I will give you a better. To the King, and damn him for a fool that cannot lead and will not follow!"

"Nay," I said, smiling (for I would not anger him at the start); "I think I am the better Cavalier of the two, so far as wishing goes, though I own you have fought well for the King."

"Aye," he answered, showing his teeth like a dog, "none has fought better, though I say it; and what is my reward? To sit here in mine own house like a badger in his hole, waiting for the men to smoke me out and the dogs to worry me." At that the woman sighed with a sort of scornful weariness, and he turned on her. "And there will be dogs enough to worry the cat that houses in the badger's den, *cara mia*!"

Now I saw my way to speak of my mission, and thrust into the opening.

"There is no need," I said quickly, "to think of such a base and wretched ending to the Signora's wisdom and your valour. You are more a lion than a badger, cousin; and I am the mouse in the fable, that may get you out of the snare."

He gave a great rough laugh. "A right mousy plan, I doubt not," he cried; "some cowardly pettifogging device of feigned submission to save my neck if I will sing psalms through my nose. Here's damnation to all facing-both-ways knaves," and he filled his goblet and drank it off.

I am by nature and breeding of a quiet temper, and slow to take offence; but at this rudeness my gorge rose.

"My lord," I said, as calmly as I might, "if you know what I would say before I speak it, it is plain that I am not needed here, and I have but to accept your own similitude, and leave the badger to the dogs, that may find argument more suited to his comprehension."

He chafed at that, and felt for his sword that lay sheathed on the table; and I stood warily, cursing his madness and my own folly, yet ready to draw if need were. But as my cousin's eyes roved round the room, they met those of the Italian woman, and I wondered; for it was like the change in a demon that knows the sorceress, or a wild beast that sees the tamer. The fire sank in his eyes, and his hand fell from the sword-hilt; and when he spoke again, he was like a child that has been chidden for rudeness.

"I crave your pardon, cousin," he said; "I am a luckless man, and trifles anger me. Drink with me in token that you forgive me, and will be my kinsman and good friend again," and he filled my goblet and his own with the Spanish wine.

I touched my lips to my glass and set it down, while he emptied his at a draught. "Come, man, no heeltaps!" he said; "or I shall think that you bear me malice."

"No malice," I answered, "but your wine is too noble for my poor pate, and I would fain have all my wits to serve you."

"Well, well," he said with a wry smile, "I will drink for you," and was about to fill again, when the Signora looked at him again with her eyes narrowing.

"No more, *Filippo mio*," she said in her soft singing voice, and he pushed the flagon away sullenly, and bade me say on.

"Thus is the case," I began, weighing my words ere I spake. "Here are you with a company of desperate men, cooped up in a corner of the marshes, till it shall please the Parliament men to think of you and root you out. A hard task they will assuredly find it, but the end is certain; also, the more pain you give them, the less mercy will they show. Nor am I sure that your soldiers might not give you up to save their necks, when they saw the game lost; and so should you perish meanly by mere treason. Now, if you will but send away your fellows to their countries, or to the King's forces that yet hold out, you may stay here quiet, no man troubling you; or if you would not seem to submit, you may go forth to the Low Countries, where is no lack of honourable employment for a soldier, and look to find all as you left it here, when the King is restored."

Thus far my cousin had heard me patiently, only drumming with his fingers on the table; but now he broke in with an oath.

"'Sblood!" he cried; "I gave my word to bide quiet, but this is too much! What shall happen to my house and my lands while I starve in the Low Countries? Find all as I left it, forsooth! Nay, I shall find more than I left by half-a-dozen little crop-eared puppies born to the fat Roundhead that will own Deeping Hold!"

"Not so," I made haste to answer; "for I will be your bailiff, cousin, and keep your house. Your tenants have sworn to hold what covenant I make with you, and I will send you your rents by a sure messenger. A trimmer I may be, but no man can say that I broke my given word, or wronged any of a farthing. And if the Parliament should take the house away from me, as I see not how they can, I will make shift to send you somewhat from mine own estate."

He looked at me with narrow eyes. "And to what end is all this policy?" he asked, sneering. "Wherefore not stay safe at home and lick Noll Cromwell's jack-boots for my succession?"

"Cousin Philip," I answered him, though it was hard to speak quietly, "the poor men of Marsham have trusted their cause to me, and I am bound to them in honour; also, I am of your blood and kin, nor do I greatly care for the Earl of Deeping to be knocked on the head in a paltry scuffle for a common robber. Nay, though I have no cause to love the Signora Bardi, it would irk me to have so much learning and wit sunk in the mire or smothered in the smoke."

This I said to get the Italian on my side; and assuredly I lied not, for the barbarous superstition of witchcraft had brought many poor women to burning, that were less witchlike than the Signora.

I could see that this moved her, for her eyes widened, though nothing else stirred in her face; and subtle as she was, I could read her mind by my own. The vision of the stake and the faggots, that were then no vain terror, daunted even her high spirit; and on the other side were the fortunes and chances of camp and city, of war and policy and plotting, and the power to be the spider in the web of Machiavelli.

So for a space we both abode with our eyes fixed on the Earl, that sat in his great chair, with one leg thrown over the other, drumming with his hand on the table, and his eyes roving around the room. Methought he too could see the wisdom of my counsel, for his brows were frowning with thought rather than anger; and indeed, he was one of good parts, save when his wildness came upon him. At last he leant forward, and his lips parted as if to speak, and I looked for him to assent to the plan that I had opened to him; and so it had been, but that in the very beginning of his speech his mood changed. His wondering eyes were fixed in a stare on the window, and his face was frozen with fear. What he could have said died in his throat, and there came only mutterings that I could not well catch; but I seemed to hear him say — "Why dost thou come again? I did not slay thee! Has thou no pity in death?" and other such murmurs, as if he spake to one that we could not see. Thinking that my cousin was smitten with some madness, I turned towards the window, that bore the arms of the house painted on the glass; and for a moment there seemed to me to be the similitude of a white figure with a stain of red on the breast, as the evening sunshine fell on the glass. Yet I knew it to be but the white and red colour of the window, as in the dining-hall before; nor could I think why so common a trick of the eyes should have moved my cousin, that sat bowed in his chair and muttering. Presently he straightened himself, and his eyes were set and staring, yet not now at the window, nor in fear, but rather desperate, as of a fiend more than of a man. I looked for him to fly out on me in a fury, but he did but strike sharply on a silver bell that stood by his chair, and the sound tinkled out through the empty hall beyond. Nor did he say a word more till the black Pompey entered; to whom he spake low in his ear for a minute, and dismissed him, and we sat silent as before.

Lastly, I could endure no longer. "Cousin Philip," I said, "I have told you all my plan; may I not have an answer before I return to those who sent me?"

He made as if he heard nought, and I was about to ask him a second time, when there fell on my ear the heavy sullen strokes of an axe or hammer on wood, at which the Earl stirred in his chair, and an evil smile came upon his lips.

"You have your answer, cousin," he said, sneeringly. "I have bidden to break up your barge of state for kindling, that we shall lack here in the autumn mists. I am minded to abide here till what ending may be; and seeing that there is no great affluence of company here, I would fain have your learned society to help pass the time. I will not lightly part with mine only kinsman; and though the cheer may be rough, yet a soldier's welcome is yours."

He had spoken smoothly, yet with a jeering tone; and it angered me that all my policy had but ended in making myself a prisoner to my cousin and his ruffians. I sprang up, facing him, and my hand fell to my rapier hilt; but he never moved.

"Methinks," I said, "you have forgotten that I am an ambassador under flag of truce, and that I must give an answer to those that sent me hither."

"O aye!" he sneered; "I had forgotten that you were the herald of His Majesty Eldad Pentry, by the grace of Beelzebub, botcher and gospeller to the rats of Marsham. Be content, most punctilious cousin; in not many days I look to deliver them mine answer in person, and you shall be by to hear it. Till then, and perchance afterwards, you must be my guest; and as it grows near to supper-time, I will bid Pompey show you your chamber." At that he smote the bell again.

Now, I could not leave him thus, but began again entreating him to consider my counsels, and save himself and others from a certain doom; and growing desperate as he answered not, I turned to the Italian woman, and besought her to join her voice to mine, thinking that she had more power over him than I. But at her first words his eyes flamed with anger, and he smote his fist on the table.

"What, you too?" he said, after the manner of Caesar to Brutus in his dying. "You must needs have me forth to the Low Countries, that you may leave me for a richer gallant or poison me for hire. No, by God! I have you both here, and you shall end with me. Not another word, cousin, or I call Gulston and a file of musketeers to set you up against the wall and shoot you for a Roundhead traitor. If I am a broken man, yet am I still Lord of Deeping Hold, and with men to do my bidding, and store of powder to send all aloft when the end comes. And for you Fiammetta…"

With that he turned and looked on her, and she at him; and her eyes were as those of a snake that bewitches a bird to flutter into its mouth. Yet did not my cousin's eyes droop before hers as beforetime, but shone strangely as a beast's in the night, till I saw her tremble as though with sickness of fear, and turn away her gaze.

Thereupon Pompey came in, and the Earl, smiling at the Signora, bade him take up my mails and lead me to my room.

Nor would I yet yield, but as I strove to speak, the woman beckoned sharply to me to go; and I saw that she was wiser than I, for of a surety my cousin had a devil.

So, with a salutation that he marked not, I followed the black through the empty hall, where the light had now climbed above the chairs, and across the court; and in my head, despite my anger at the treason of my cousin, and my scorn of myself that I had been so easily entrapped, there was ringing the old rhyme of the little book:

> 'When the Lord of Deeping Hold
> To the Fiend his soul hath sold —'

and I fell to thinking of the black deeps of the Hole, and the grey riband winding up from it.

CHAPTER V

Of Mistress Rosamund Fanshawe, and my Talk with Her

I followed the loitering Pompey across the court with steps as slow as his own; for I was sick at heart for the ill-success of mine embassy, and meseemed that through my own folly had ill matters been aroused. Yet, cast about as I would, might I not think how I should have spoken better or done more wisely. Of a surety my plan was such as had commended itself to mine enemy the Italian woman, whose fortune was bound up with my cousin's; nor had he seemed to take it so amiss till he had the vision of somewhat in the window, and thenceforward had he been as one possessed of a devil. Yet could I not feel angered with him as I might with a stranger; for it was borne in on me that there was a doom on the man to be froward and perverse, even as with Pharaoh, whose heart God hardened that he should not let Israel go: and it was given to me as though spoken in mine ear that I should wait and behold the end, nor meddle further with the unsearchable judgments of God.

Wherefore, when I had reached my lodging, which was a little chamber in the thickness of the keep, barred like a dungeon, but furnished well enough for one that cared not for soft living, I changed my apparel without help from the black, and looked from my window over the marshes, whence the sea had now fallen, though it was ever lapping at the foot of the tower. The sun was setting over the hills, big and blood red, and the pools of the marshes seemed red as though a great slaughter had been made there; but overhead there hung one great cloud, shapen like a monster that stretched long trailing arms and claws across the sky. The evening was strangely still, but for the measured pace of the sentinel, and the clank of his pike as he struck it on the stone in turning at the end of his walk. So, wearying of mine own thoughts, I came down the worn stone stairs to the court, thinking that I might speak with someone, though it was not yet supper-time.

I judged that the men of the garrison were at their supper, for the gates were shut fast, and none stirring in sight but a sentry on either wall; also two windows in a room of the castle were litten, and the sound of loud talk and rough laughter came from them, and once a woman's scream, but of no great terror; so I lingered, thinking that perchance I might light upon the Swede or other of the better sort: nor was I mistaken, for presently Gulston strode out from his quarters, that were hard by the guard-room, and greeted me civilly enough. So we stood talking of the wars in Germany, which I judged safer to speak of than our own troubles, and I was able to entertain him with stratagems of war out of Livy and Polybius, and found him apt and eager to hear, though unlearned; and by his voice could I tell (for his face was not read in the shadow) that his contempt for me was shaken, when he heard a mere scholar discourse of the ordering of battles with knowledge; yet I was careful always to defer to him as to one of great experience, and indeed, his speeches were often most pertinent. We were upon the proper mingling of pikemen and musketeers, when I heard steps descending the stairs of the keep, and broke off to see who came; but the Swede only laughed.

"'Tis but the spectre at the feast," he said, sneering in his wonted manner; "the white ghost in the black gown, that sits and never speaks or drinks, and hardly eats — I mean my dead Lady's cousin, Mistress Rosamund. Perchance she may throw you a word, for that you are not one of us. For myself, I grow weary of the sight of her, though full often we see her not for days together. I will present you."

But it so fell that I needed not his offices, which, I doubt me, would have been of little value with Mistress Fanshawe. For as she lingered in the door of the keep, seeing us in her way, a drunken ruffian of the garrison, who had been sent with supper for the sentinel, came reeling out across the court, and whether taking her for a handmaid or being too far gone in liquor to distinguish, caught her by the arm and strove to kiss her. She broke away from him, crying out with disgust rather than fear; but he followed, and since the drink was rather in his head than his legs, he penned her into a corner of the wall, and was at point to renew his attack, when I ran to help her, and taking the knave by the collar swung him aside. With that he vented an oath or two, and drawing his sword, made for me; so that Mistress Rosamund cried out for help, but the Swede stood still mocking.

I drew also, not knowing the man's skill of fence; but when I saw the roughness of his sword-play, I scorned to do him hurt, but practised a trick that I had often served my unskilled fellows at Cambridge. Keeping him off for a few passes, I made as if to leave my breast open to him, and as he ran at me, I turned his blade under my left arm and locked the hilt to my side, while with my right hand I offered my point at his throat, so that he let go his sword and reeled backwards, and his heel catching on a stone, he fell and so lay gaping. With that, Gulston laughed with somewhat of surprise, and came to me.

"Rarely done, my Puritan!" said he, "of a truth, for a man of peace, you have some skill of your weapon. But why did you not kill the knave?" And then, kicking the man, that was yet dazed with drink and his fall — "Giles Warner, get up and give me your sword!" — which when the man did, Gulston smote him on the jaw with the hilt, so that his teeth rattled, and bade him sheathe his sword and never draw it again till he had learned to know hilt from point, and so drove him to the guard-room, leaving me alone with Mistress Fanshawe.

She had stood still in the shadow after that first cry, seeing (as she has told me since) that the man had no skill to hurt me; but now she came to me and laid her hand on my arm, and the first words she spake startled me, for that they were as an echo of the Swede's question. "Why did you not kill him?" she asked me, sharply, and I could see her eyes shine in the shadow of her hood.

The fierceness of her speech moved me strangely, for her voice was low and sweet, and it seemed not fitting that she should speak with such anger and loathing; insomuch that I stammered, and could find no words to answer her at the first. Nor did I know by what passion and grief she had been so far wrought. Yet I made shift to say somewhat of the man being but a poor drunken sot, nor deserving of death for his rudeness; but she brake in as one distraught — "Oh!" she said, "were I but a man, I would kill them all, all! But you are cold like the rest of them, and have no heart to revenge a wrong!"

"Perchance," I said, for I would not have her think me better than I was, "I had found it in my heart to hurt him, had it not been all too easy" — and, indeed, I had but needed to oppose my point that he might run on it. "Yet am I glad that I spared him even out of scorn," I went on; "for it is ill shedding of blood for a private quarrel, when there is One that hath said, 'Vengeance is Mine, I will repay'."

"Oh!" said she, brokenly, as though a sob came in the midst of her utterance. "You men are all the same, and when a woman is wronged you can but counsel patience, and fling her a jest or a text as small money to a beggar. I am sick of you all."

Now this her flying out on me, though assuredly it was but the working of a brain overwrought, did strangely move me, for that I felt that if the one other in the castle — I will not say righteous, but not altogether given over to iniquity — were so to misconceive me, it boded the worse for both of us. Moreover, I knew not wherefore, it cut me to the heart to have her deem me cold and careless of her need, and the more so that I knew myself to be of a timid spirit. But as I was at point to speak to her in mine excuse, the great bell from the turret rang the hour for supper, and gathering her skirts around her, she made haste to the hall, nor could I have speech with her till we were within.

My cousin, the Earl, was already leading the Signora to the high seat at his side, where the Countess was wont to sit, and where the sunshine had made a phantom with blood on the breast but a few hours agone. Mistress Rosamund looked on her as she sat, and methought there was bitter scorn in the eyes of both. But the Earl greeted me friendly, and presented me to Mistress Fanshawe as an honoured guest, and would have me sit next to the Signora, and made much of me as a kinsman and scholar; nor was the Italian lacking in flatteries and pleasing speeches, whereof she had skill beyond the wont of women, so that it was hard for me to remember that I was kept prisoner in breach of faith; also I could see Mistress Rosamund's eyes dwell on me in scorn as she feigned to listen to the blunt speech of Gulston, that was our only companion at table. Our cheer was but rough, savouring of camp cookery, though served well enough by Pompey and two of the troopers that were the Earl's servants; and only the Swede, that was used to hardness of life, ate and drank heartily, as who might look to go long before he found another meal. There was good Gascony and Canary, though my cousin favoured the Spanish wine, and drank more than he ate; while the Signora took a morsel daintily, and Mistress Rosamund but feigned to eat. The which my cousin marked, and suddenly, with a friendliness that was perchance not all feigned (for his moods ever shifted like the wind), reached over and filled her glass with Gascony, bidding her drink to the health of her cousin and his, and his honoured guest: also he called Pompey to give me wine that I might answer the pledge, and drank to me himself, and bade the Signora drink also. But she excused herself daintily, saying that it was for my kinswoman to pledge first before her, that was but a poor stranger. For the Swede, he had not waited for nice considerations of precedence, but had nodded to me and drained his goblet in one motion so soon as he saw the Earl's lips at his glass.

I could see that Mistress Rosamund was angered by the feigned humility and reverence of the Italian, and her face flushed from its paleness to see the eyes of all fixed on her. Yet she mastered her anger, and raised the brimming glass with a hand that shook not.

"Methinks, Mistress Bardi," she said, coldly, and dropping her words slowly as a physician might some bitter medicine, "that forasmuch as you have been so far able to overcome your humbleness as to sit in my dead cousin's seat, you might well venture to drink before my lord's poor kinswoman. Yet will I not cross you in this, but will even pledge my good cousin according to his desert, and wish him many more such merry evenings as this."

The Earl frowned and muttered somewhat, and the Italian looked at

Mistress Fanshawe with narrow eyes; but Gulston brake into one of his great laughs, and called to us to clink glasses after the German custom. At that Mistress Rosamund rose, smiling, and stretched forth her goblet across the table, and I likewise; but whether by mishap or of a purpose, I know not, nor would she ever tell me afterwards, she shocked her glass on mine with such strength that both were broken, and the red wine made a great splash like blood on the cloth.

At this the Earl sprang up, with his face writhen like a madman's, and brake out in a flood of oaths and foul words that I would not chronicle, had I even heard them clearly, and snatched at a knife that lay before him as though to slay Mistress Rosamund, that stood still with the neck of the goblet in her hand, and blenched not; yet before I could speak or go to her help, the Signora caught his wrist and signed to Gulston, that came to his side and took the knife from him; and indeed he was already in part come to himself, and ashamed that he had been so overcome with passion at his own board — perchance more ashamed than for many a worse fault, for he was hospitable after the wont of spendthrifts.

"Cousin Hubert, and you, mistress," he said, looking on the girl, that answered nothing, "I am much distempered of late, and a little thing moves me. I crave your pardon if I leave you suddenly" — and at that his eyes fell on the stained cloth again, and a strong shuddering took him, so that the Swede was fain to help him from his seat to the door, and the Signora followed, while Mistress Fanshawe and I looked on each other across the table and stirred not. Pompey, as one that had seen such matters before, took up my lord's flagon of Spanish wine and followed to his apartment, and the two serving-men began to clear the board, for supper had been ended. Nor did Mistress Rosamund move or speak till they had swept off the shreds of glass and taken away the cloth, leaving us alone.

"I am sorry for you, cousin," she said; "for though my lord is tonight wrought above his wont, yet may you look for other such passions in days to come. It were better that I should keep my chamber, for I have the unhappiness to anger him. Pity it is that Mistress Bardi was quicker than you, or he had rid the company of my presence for good, and left you to talk of Italian poets to her, that takes great delight in your learning."

The scorn wherewith she said this cut me to the heart, and I stretched out my hands towards her passionately. "In the name of God," I cried, "why must you so misconceive me? I am as a man thrown into a dark dungeon, where I hear snakes stirring and hissing, and know not which way to step. God knows that I sought not this journey, but came with a single mind to help the poor men of Marsham in their need, and now have I worsened all matters by my meddling; yet I meant well. I am a prisoner here like yourself, cousin, and no flatterer or parasite, nor willing to humour the wicked for hire; yet what am I to do? I must speak them fair, or I shall endanger not mine own life merely, but other and better lives; coward I may be, but I am a true man, and if you shall think basely of me, I must go mad!"

Now while I spake, at the first she looked coldly on me as before, and her scorn made me the more vehement beyond my wont, till I was nigh weeping; but as I despaired of winning her belief, I could see her face change wonderfully, and her eyes grow greater and darker, and her breast heave as though she were stifling for lack of air. I looked for her to break into weeping, and so perchance it had been with any woman less noble to endure. Yet she did but stretch out both hands to me, that I took gladly in mine own.

"Cousin Hubert," she said — and it pleased me that she had noted my name — "forgive me that I doubted you. In this house of murder, where men mutter in corners, I know not friend from foe, and scarcely living soul from ghost or devil, and methought you were but another spy like the Swede."

At that I beckoned to her to be silent, for the door of the Earl's apartment opened stealthily, and Gulston came out; and whether he had heard her latest words I know not, but when he saw he was observed, he came forward carelessly, humming a song, while Pompey drew the curtain behind him.

"What, still quarrelling?" he said, lightly; and indeed, for aught he saw, we might have been as well enemies as friends, for I doubt not that the disorder of my wits showed itself in my face.

Now at his speech it came into my mind that it were well to leave him in his error, if so he thought, for I judged him to be rather cunning than deep in his malice. So on the moment, I answered him according to his bent, deeming that he would not believe that a mere scholar would be subtle enough to feign.

"Indeed," said I, "I would not quarrel for a woman's temper, though it cost me a bumper of good Gascony. I was but telling Mistress Fanshawe that my lord had much excuse for his passion, and that it had moved me to anger even at Cambridge to see needless waste of good wine, that we might come to need sorely when the castle lay under siege —" and other such stuff that I mind not, nor is it worth recounting, but it served my turn. At the first, Mistress Rosamund's face, that I could see dimly in the candle-light, and the Swede saw not, being behind her, grew hard and scornful that I should dare to chide her, and I feared that she might return to her ill opinion of me. But in no brief space her eyes lightened on me, and she smiled a little as though to show that she understood my policy. Then, speaking coldly as before, but with greater scornfulness, that I knew to be feigned, she bade me keep my ratings for college knaves, and mine excuses for those from whom I hoped for favours, and so flung out of the hall as one in a fury, leaving me with Gulston.

"Said I not true?" he asked me, fingering his yellow beard. "'Tis a very shrew tonight, though I marvel that she should have been so moved by you. Had we such a maid in camp in Germany, we should soon tame her, but my lord is over kind with women, and the wench has a touch of likeness to his dead lady, though I will vouch for her that she is no saint. You shall do well to shun Mistress Rosamund, if you would bear an unscratched face." From which I guessed that the Swede had sought to pass the time with dalliance, after the fashion of his kind, and had met with the welcome that I could guess; nor did I love him the more for my thought.

"Nay," I answered smoothly; "I am not angered, but grieved to see one so young and goodly in so froward a mind, and I would seek to win her to a temper more submissive and womanly. Nor would I have you hurt her, even if she provoke you; for she is a hostage even as I myself, and hostages in a besieged place have been found to abate the eagerness of attack, and even to save the holders of them in extremity."

He took my drift as I meant, and played moodily with his sword-hilt as we walked from the hall. "Think you then," he said, with something of anxiousness, "that we shall be besieged here?"

"Unless the King's party recover beyond all likelihood," I answered him; "the Parliament generals will assuredly hear of us and send against us."

"Against us!" he repeated. "You are not of us, but rather of their faction, and have nought to fear."

"Your pardon," I said, laughing, "I have never heard that a cannon-ball had any niceness in choosing where and whom it should strike, nor that hostages have grown fat when the garrison starved. Rather do I look to be eaten the first when provisions fail. Nor am I of the Roundheads, for that Cromwell himself has asked me to serve with him, and I would not. He would let me perish here, and show his friendship to me by devising new deaths for you and your men."

"There is something in your words," said Gulston, as he turned to the door of his quarters. "I must speak with you again, but not now, for Pompey is yet at the hall door, and he is a spy for my lord on the Signora and the rest, and for the Signora on my lord and the rest, I know not which. Give you goodnight!" and with that he was gone, and I to my lodging, well pleased that I had won some ground, and fondly hoping that I might yet save Mistress Rosamund and myself in spite of my cousin, and my cousin in spite of himself.

So I came to the door of the keep, where a cresset burned to light the stair, and was passing in when a voice called me softly from the shadow of the wall, and I knew it was Mistress Rosamund.

"We have but a moment, for the watch will be coming soon," she whispered quickly. "Did I not play the shrew well to your pedant, cousin? Have we put the Swede off the scent?"

I told her, Aye, so I thought, and that there were factions in the garrison, as it seemed, and hope of working some good; and then I asked her of how the Earl used her, and whether there were any way of escape from the castle.

So she said, hurriedly, and looking for the guard, that she was not ill-used, and had the girl to wait on her that was the blacksmith's daughter of Marsham, but that she went ever in fear of my lord and of the Signora, but rather of the woman, that dealt in witchcraft and perchance in poison also, and had assuredly wrought the death of the Countess through her own craft and the violence of the Earl. "They told me," she said, sobbing through her speech, "that she died of a flux of blood, and indeed she was ailing long; but how she ended I saw not, yet if she were not murdered, why should my lord be taken with madness at the sight of spilt wine or a blood-red shadow on her chair? Cousin, if you take me not away from this house of evil, I shall go mad."

"Alas!" I answered her; "the boat I came in is cleft into kindlings by now, and we should be mired and lost were we to strive to swim to land; but I look to make a party among the garrison, or to find someone that for promise of money or life will help us to a boat. Other hope see I none, save in the hand of the Lord and our patience."

"The hand of the Lord!" she said, rather in sadness than in mockery. "Nay then, if we must wait till the heavens open and fire fall on the wicked, we may die first of old age. Preach not patience to me, that have seen the end of my cousin's piety and endurance."

Now I was grieved to hear such rebellious words from her, and was minded to bring her to a better way of thought; but ere I could think of aught to say, I heard the clash of weapons and the tread of heavy feet across the court.

"The guard comes!" she whispered, "and they must not see us together. Goodnight, cousin!" and catching at my hand, she dropped it again and fled up the stair silently, and I followed more slowly, feeling my way to my chamber.

When I had struck a light and looked around, I noted that the key was gone from my door, and there was no means of shutting it from within. Yet I remembered that there was little safety in a lock, when all the household save one might be counted enemies. So without more ado I made ready for bed, and before I had lain down, I heard the tramp of feet on the stair, and saw torches through the crack of the door, and then a key was set in the lock and turned, and I knew that I was a prisoner indeed till the morning. Yet I went to the window and opened it, to see if by chance there was any way out; but the bars were over close for a man to slip between, and though eaten by the sea-wind, they were great and strong and sealed fast into the wall. For a season I lingered, looking out at the night; but the stars were veiled by a mist, and a breeze was blowing cold from the land, till I shut the casement, for meseemed that I could smell the savour of the slime in the water of the Hole, though more like, it was some seaweed or dead fish cast up on the castle wall.

CHAPTER VI

Of the End of Master Eldad Pentry

I have ever been an ill sleeper in beds that were strange to me, and my first night in Deeping Hold was but troubled, though of noise there was little save the wash of the water at the foot of the wall, and now and then the tread of the sentinel on the rampart. Yet could I not compose myself to rest but that a sound would set me thinking, while half asleep, that men came to murder me, and I would start awake and catch at my sword, that hung on the bed-head, before I knew that there was no cause for terror, for that my cousin had no need to deal stealthily if he had a mind to take my life. Also when at last I slept, the horror of a dream would come on me, so that I wakened crying out, yet could I not remember what had affrighted me.

Yet in the end I slept soundly, nor waked till the sun was well above the sea to eastward, and the morning was still and fair, and as I clad myself hastily, the world seemed goodly to dwell in. Also, when I tried the door of my chamber, it opened readily, and I came to the court, no man saying me nay. Men were going to and fro, bearing wood and water, or sallying forth to catch fish or shoot wild-fowl, and methought they seemed less ill-looking than yesterday; also, if they marked me at all, they made no jest on me, wherefore I judged that either the Earl had bidden them show me civility (and they feared him greatly), or the man I had foiled overnight had told a drunkard's tale of my skill at the sword. So I walked to and fro for a space in the court pleasantly enough, till Gulston, spying me there, came out and bade me to breakfast in the hall, where was none but our two selves and Pompey to serve us. We spake but little in earshot of the black, and when we had finished we came to the court again, and I would have sounded the Swede as to my plan for making treaty with the men of Marsham, but at the first word he winked at the hall door, where Pompey was sunning himself; and raising my eyes from the boy, I saw a curtain drawn and the Signora's face against the window, who, noting that she was seen, smiled on us and nodded her head.

I judged, therefore, that I might wait till a fitter season to confer with Gulston, if so be I could trust the man; and we spake of things indifferent, till he turned the talk on matters of fence, asking me of the Italian that was my master, and would have me show him some of the devices of the school with my sheathed rapier; the which I was fain to do, for that no suspicion should fall on us from the Italian. After I had shown a pass or twain, my cousin himself came out to us and greeted me kindly; and when he saw our play, nothing would serve him but that he should have out a pair of foils and try a bout of friendship with me, Gulston standing by for judge. The Earl's sword-play was well enough for a soldier, but showing more of strength than of art, and more reckless than the Swede's, who was ever cool and watchful; while my cousin grew easily heated, and would seek to beat down my foil and waste his strength on the air. But he was apt to learn, and took delight in the exercise, and I taught him a cunning parry and return or two; only the favourite thrust of my Italian master, that I had been at great pains to perfect myself in, I told not to the Earl, deeming it fit that I might have somewhat yet in store to defend myself when the Earl was possessed by his devil.

In no long time he tired of the game, for he was ever restless, and went off to his apartment, and I to mine, being somewhat heated, to rest, and perchance to catch a sight of Mistress Rosamund; but I saw her not till dinner-time, nor could we speak freely, being ever under the eye of my cousin and the Signora, or a servant of theirs. So I was fain to speak of the pictures and poetry of Italy, and then of the secrets of nature and the subtleties of alchemy, though in this I have rather curiosity than knowledge. And so the day wore on, and the Earl's troopers came back with their fish and wild fowl, and nought happened, nor was I one hair's breadth nearer my aim. Only at supper-time we came to talk more freely, and my Lord speaking of our play with the foils that morning, and desiring me to do the like on the morrow, Mistress Rosamund was pleased to make light of my skill when the Earl praised it, the better to confirm him in his error that his two cousins were at variance between themselves; and she saying that it was but folly in me to teach another my secrets of defence, I laughed, and answered that I had yet a thrust or two that could save me at the pinch; and at the word I looked up and caught the Signora's eyes fixed on me strangely, as though she were revolving in her mind some subtle device. Yet she said nought, and the evening passed off with no quarrel, my cousin being merrier than his wont. Also, when Mistress Fanshawe was gone to her room, and Gulston was about some business of the garrison, the Earl would have me in to play chess with the Signora while he also was busy. Between the moves we fell to talking, and she asked me of the Lord General Cromwell and his friendship for me, and other questions that I answered truly, or perchance with some over-rating of the general's friendship for me; for indeed, in all his after greatness, he found never occasion to remember my name, which hurt my self-conceit, but was to my advantage when King Charles, now reigning, was restored to his father's throne. We played not long, for my cousin, returning, said that he must rest early; so I went to my room, and this night none locked the door on me, nor were the garrison making their wonted noise, so that I slept soon and soundly.

But about the first beginning of the dawn I awaked suddenly, for my door was open, and half-a-dozen men armed in breast and backpieces, with swords and musketoons, were round my bed, who bade me rise and come with them. Wondering much what this boded, I arose and clad myself in my travelling suit, making what speed I might by the light of the torch one of them bore. When I asked them of the purpose of this haste, none would say a word; only when I made to gird on my sword, one of them clapped the mouth of his piece to my breast and bade me leave my rapier, the which I did, for it had been of no use to dispute with them. So I put on my cloak, for the air was chilly, and came down into the court in the midst of the men, and there saw the more part of the garrison gathered, and my cousin the Earl in buff-coat and cuirass ordering them.

The thought passed my mind that perchance he meant to fulfil his threat of shooting me for a traitor, though I knew not what fresh grudge he could bear me; and it was an ugly thought that I should presently be facing a row of ruffians with lighted matches. But my cousin's first words scattered my fears.

"Good morning, Cousin Hubert," he cried to me. "I must crave your pardon for breaking your beauty-sleep, but time and tide wait for no man, and we must catch the tide to go and deliver our answer to King Eldad the First of Marsham and his loving subjects; also you, being his ambassador, must be at the conference."

Now when I knew his purpose, I began earnestly to remonstrate with him, but he cut short by bidding the men set me in the barge, so that I went out at the barbican rather than be roughly handled by his troopers.

In the grey twilight of the hour before the dawn I could mark the two barges swinging at the quay, and a man or two in each; and into one of these I stepped and sat in the stern, wrapping my cloak round me. The oars were ready set on the tholes, and at the fore-part of either barge were a barrel or two and a truss of straw, also a basket of food and bottles of liquor. In no long time out came the men, some two dozen of them, and took place in the barges, with no word spoken; and lastly Gulston and the Earl, whereof the first sat in the stern of the other barge, and my cousin leapt in last by me and bade push off, and presently we were out of the harbour, and the rising tide swept us landward under the wall of the keep.

    I sought to speak to my cousin, but he answered not, except to bid me hold my tongue, for he needed his wits for steering; and indeed, it was no easy task to keep a heavy craft from the mud-banks and shallows; and the Swede, that knew these waters less than his chief, grounded his barge more than once, though he soon got her off again. So with tide and oars we were not long in coming within hail of the shore, and I could see (for the light was growing fast) that we were making for the horn of the ruined castle that overhung the Hole.

    Now at this some murmured, for a few of the troopers were of the country, and had heard of the story of that place from their mothers, and had told it to the others; but the Earl held on his way.

    "Have you heard the old wives' fable of this place, cousin?" he said to me softly, as he set our course for the round black space of water.

    "Surely I have," I answered him; "and a strange spot it is, and fit to put fear in men's hearts, as I can well say, for this way came I to the castle."

    "And saw you the monster?" he jeered.

    "Nay," I said; "somewhat strange I saw, or thought I saw, like a grey snake winding up from the deeps, but I took no harm save an ill odour, like this" — for we were now in the midst of the Hole, and I could snuff the salt foul smell of the slime, but fainter, by reason of the cold.

    My cousin answered me not, but cried out to the men in the boats to cease rowing, and set them to muffle their oars that they might not be heard. When this was done, the men were eager to push on, for the smell of the place and the terror of its blackness had daunted them. But before my lord gave the word, he spake in the ear of one of the men by him, who suddenly threw a belt round my arms and buckled them tightly to my side before I knew what he would do.

    "Why is this, cousin?" I asked him, being angered at this indignity.

    "To save your life, man," he answered grimly; "for fear you might be minded, though a man of peace, to strike on one side or the other, and so either meet with your end from a bullet or lose the favour of King Eldad for taking part with your own kin. Now, shall I muffle your mouth, or will you give me your word as a gentleman not to cry out or warn the Marsham men? But if you promise to me and break your word, I swear by my sword that I will fling you into this Hole with mine own hands."

    I bade him rather stop my mouth, for I would be no helper in his enterprise, even under a constrained promise; and he took off his scarf and tied it round my mouth so that I could not cry out. Then he gave the word to row on, but stealthily, and in a stroke or two we were out of the Hole, and making for the basket of the beacon that showed black against a grey cloud. So we came into the river and felt the tide, and were borne up towards the village. Yet was all my cousin's care vain, and Master Pentry was a warier man than he deemed; for as we came near to the village, the prow of the first barge struck on a rope stretched beneath the water, and dragged it some way, and forthwith a bell tolled from a tree by the bank. The Earl swore a great oath, and bade cut the rope, but it was too late.

"Curse on the crop-eared knaves!" he cried; "they have taken a bell from the church and hung it in yonder tree to give the warning! Row on, men!" and with that he took the scarf from my mouth and bade me bellow my fill if it list.

"Were it not better to go back, seeing we are discovered?" I said.

"No!" he roared. "A thousand times, no! Give way, men! Catch them before they have their doublets on!"

All thought of stealth was now cast aside, for after the bell we could hear dogs barking and men shouting in the village, and lights showing confusedly in the windows. Therefore the men bent to the oars as rowing a race, and we came speedily to the landing-place under the church. There they made the boats fast, and my cousin leapt out the first and led the one half of his men up to the village, Gulston fetching a compass round the houses to take in the rear any who fought; me they left in the barge, charging the men of the guard to keep me safely, but show me no discourtesy.

Now this command they obeyed, being of that country and holding our house in honour, and one of them proffered me a drain of Hollands, and held the bottle to my mouth; nor was I sorry to be warmed in that chilly dawn. Yet could I not rest, but gazed on the village to see what would hap; for it might be that some of the Parliament soldiers had come to these parts, and then might my cousin find more than he looked for. But it was soon plain to me that little fight, if any, was made, and indeed, as I heard after, Master Pentry's device served only to give the more part of his flock time to flee to the woods. When the Earl and his company ran up among the houses, shouting, the doors stood open, and neither men nor women within; and Gulston and his band, though they made haste to intercept the fliers, could but catch one old crippled woman, that they let go again. The Earl was (so Gulston said after to me) as one beside himself that his devices had failed, and would follow the Marsham men into their refuges; but the Swede withstood him, saying that they would lose the tide and have to stay half a day while the others raised the country on them, and overwhelmed them with numbers. Therefore he gave his word for plundering the place and coming back.

To this counsel the Earl must needs yield, for it was manifestly wise, and the men fell to plunder; but their harvest was small, since some of the cattle and sheep had been kept in the fields, and others had been driven into the woodland. Some bread and bacon they found, and the troops had sport with chasing of fowls; but there was little to reward any. Thereat the Earl fell again into a frenzy, and swore that they should pay for cheating him of his dues, and so took straw from the barns, and wood and pitch that his men had brought up from the barges, and to make an ill story short, fired every house in the place and so left it burning.

Now all this was reported to me, but the rest I saw. First a feather of blue smoke and another sprang out against the clear sky that was now growing of a yellow colour. Then the smoke grew thicker and blacker as the thatch caught, and flames leaped above the trees, and I heard the crackling of the rafters like a tight of musketry. And then came my cousin's men disorderly, by twos and threes, laughing and jesting and carrying their poor plunder.

The sight of their homes burning may well have moved the Marsham men to madness, for the most of them had ventured back as they saw the troopers leaving the village, and doubtless they came among the houses as the flames broke forth. While the more cautious of them strove to quench the fire, the bolder thought rather of vengeance, and fell on the rear of the Swede's party that came last, with stones and scythes and pitchforks. At that the soldiers faced about, and with a shot or two kept off the villagers, that had but rude weapons; and thinking they had scared the countrymen, they came on carelessly to the boats.

But as they passed a close thicket by a hollow lane hard by the church, there arose a puff of smoke and the sound of a shot, and a man rolled over, clutching at the ground; and ere he lay still, men came running from the thicket and set furiously on the robbers, that were daunted by this sudden onslaught. Foremost of the party was a strange figure that was like an ancient warrior from his tomb, for he was clad all in mail of plate from head to foot, and wielded a great sword, and after him followed others with scythes and sickles; and before any order could be taken, they had slain one more of the Earl's men and wounded three, so that the rest gave back. Only Gulston, crying out on his troopers for cowards, snatched a musketoon from one of them and shot down a great fellow with a scythe as he fetched a blow at him, and made at the leader with his sword; but the blade glanced from the armour, and the other dealt him a blow that had been his end had he not worn an iron plate in his hat, and sent him to his knees half stunned; where he had been thrust through, but that my cousin, who had leapt ashore again at the sound of battle, struck up the sword and engaged the man in armour. For a time they stood striking and thrusting and parrying, unable to hurt each other, for that the Earl was the better swordsman and the other was armoured in proof; but in no long space the armoured man wearied of the weight of his harness and the labour of wielding his great sword, and my Lord, seeing this, put aside the blade and came within his guard and tripped and threw him, and the Marsham men, or such as were left, fled back into the lane.

My cousin bade bring the wounded and dead to the barges, and bind the prisoner with ropes and carry him thither also; and when the valiant fighter was set in the boat where I was, they lifted the visor of his helmet, and I saw the face of none other than Master Eldad Pentry, flushed with fighting and sore spent, but without shadow of fear.

"Master Pentry," I said, "I grieve to see you thus when I have no power to help you."

"Grieve not, Hubert Leyton," he made shift to answer between his gasps; "of a truth it was written before the foundation of the world that thus and no otherwise should I end, and I need not that any should say a word for me. Peril not thy life, for I have taken the sword, and I must perish by the sword."

As he spoke thus, the Earl leapt into the stern of the barge where we were, and bade push off; then his eyes lightened as they fell on his enemy.

"By God!" he cried, "we are well met, Master Eldad. I had not thought you could handle so long a needle as yonder sword; and where found you your iron doublet and hose? Stay — I have it — the knave hath stolen the armour of the third Earl, mine ancestor, from the vault of the church. Lo, mine own arms wrought on the breast-plate. Was there no meaner coat that would serve this dog of a ranting tailor?"

Master Pentry did but smile, and his fearlessness was a marvel even to me. "Aye," answered he, "it is easy railing on a bound man, well-nigh as easy as to slay an ailing woman"; and at that word the Earl sprang up with his hand at his dagger, but sat again, as he saw that Master Eldad was nowise moved.

"I will not soil my steel with base blood," he said, grinning on his prisoner. "What say you, cousin, what death shall we choose for King Eldad? The axe is for men of gentle birth, like the Earl of Strafford and the Archbishop."

"Aye," said Master Pentry, "and perchance for their master —" whereat a trooper smote him on the lips, but he did but laugh.

"Shall we hang him in the armour he has usurped?" went on the Earl. "Or shall we roast the hog in armour till he crackles?" whereat Gulston assented with his great laugh, and so did the foreigners of the troop, but the Englishmen of the company murmured.

"Since you ask for my judgment, cousin," said I, hoping against hope that if I saved not Master Eldad I might yet respite him for awhile, or at the least win him an honourable death, "I have ever read that in a war of two states, such as this has become, though a civil rebellion in the beginning, it is the custom to spare the life of a prisoner taken in fair and open fight, and hold him for ransom or exchange by cartel, according to the law of nations."

But at that my cousin cried out on me for a pedant, nor would Master Pentry himself accept my advocacy, for his fanatic doctrine was dearer to him than life.

"Nay, Hubert Leyton," he said, turning in his bonds, "between true men and traitors is no quarter given or asked, and thy kinsman is an open rebel to the Parliament of England; nor would I have spared him for thine intercession, if he sat bound as I now."

The Earl laughed at that speech, and bade the men cease rowing, so that the barges drifted side by side; and looking round I saw that we were come again to the black circle of the Hole.

" 'Fore God, I like thy spirit, man," he cried; "tell me what death thou wouldst deal me if I were thy captive."

Master Pentry looked around him, and marked the spot where we were, and his eyes were great and shining, as though he saw somewhat to us invisible.

"Methinks," said he, in his harsh and jarring voice, "the place itself might teach thee, Philip of Deeping. Here, if the story lie not, is the tomb of thine ancestor, to whose name and wickedness art thou heir, and I would but send thee to join him."

"It is well spoken!" cried out my cousin, pulling at his beard; "and so shall it be done to thee. Ho, two of you, take him up and fling him into the midst of the pool."

But the twain that sat on either side of Master Pentry shrank back murmuring, not that they loved him or were unready to slay him, but that being of those parts, they knew the ancient story of the Hole, and feared to awaken the monster that dwelt therein; which terror they made shift to stammer out, being pitiably divided between dread of the Thing in the pool and of the wrath of their master. Yet would he not listen, but signed to other two, who, being ruffians from the German wars, and fearing neither God nor man, made ready to take up the prisoner. But first he craved leave to speak, the which was granted him jeeringly, and he turned to me.

"Hubert Leyton," said he earnestly, and as though there were none by but us two, "fear not for thyself, for it hath been revealed to me that thy life shall be given thee for a prey; nor seek to take vengeance for my death, seeing that, as thou knowest, it was foredoomed from before the beginning of the world. Surely vengeance shall be upon the man of Belial, and that by no help of man. And for thee, son of perdition, get thee back to thine harlot, and make merry with her, for the time is short."

But when Master Eldad spake of the Italian woman, the Earl could endure no longer, and shut down the visor of the ancient helmet, so that we saw the face of the man no more; and thrusting me back (for bound as I was, I had attempted to make in to aid Master Pentry), he gave the word to the two troopers, that lifted the iron figure by the shoulders and the feet, and swung it three times, and at the last hurled it into the midst and darkest of the Hole, with a great splash of the water, that fell on all in the boat, and smelt salt and foul of the slime.

When the trouble of the waters was abated, I looked eagerly over the side of the boat, for it was in my mind that some strange manifestation might be shown to us. But there was no sound or sight, nor indeed could we look for any; for no man, though a strong swimmer and unbound, could think to rise again in such a weight of armour. A bubble or twain rose, and no more; so that at the last my cousin bade loosen my bonds, and gave word to row homewards, ere we lost the tide.

Now as the men set the oars ready, the pool, that was still and black with immeasurable depth, grew troubled, and it was as if a fountain of grey slime were breaking upwards from the pit, with a great and evil smell, and lastly somewhat black like a man rose from the mid-most of the Hole, and sank again, and rose again higher, like a ball dancing on a fountain; so that Gulston, that was nearest, thrust at it with a boathook that he had caught up, and drew it to him, and we could see that it was of iron.

"As I love," cried my cousin, "it is the knave come back to us! Have him in, Eric, and let us see if he be yet alive." So the Swede, helped by the two men that had cast Master Pentry in (for the others dared not lay a hand to the work) hauled in the thing, that was smeared with the grey slime. But when they raised the visor, the face was gone, and only empty blackness within; and looking into the hollow of the body-armour was there nothing but water and slime. So they cut the straps of the armour with their daggers, and opened the cuishes and greaves, and still was there nothing; till they came to the steel boots (for it was a full suit of plate), and in the right shoe was what had been a man's foot, but the ankle-bones gone, and the flesh shredded out like the claw of a lobster that a man has sucked for the meat. At that sight a great sickness and shuddering fell on us all, and my cousin fell back in his seat like a dead man; but I only, perchance because I had no part in that murder, had strength given me to spring forward and heave that loathsome heap of iron and slime and human flesh over the side into the water, that was now still again, and clear of the slime, and I cried out to the men the while to bend to their oars and escape from that accursed place.

But ere we could win clear of the Hole, for the men were weak with fear at the first, one of our wounded men, methinks Giles Warner, that had beset Mistress Rosamund before, and that had now been sore hurt with a scythe by the man that Gulston slew, sprang up in the barge, screaming out in terror like a beast, and with that the bandage round his thigh slipped, and his blood brake forth in a spout, and so he fell and died, no man marking him save I.

CHAPTER VII

Of our Returning and the Burial of our Dead

The sight of that which had befallen left my cousin's crew, and even himself, with little thought of what was to be done, or will to do it; and indeed, it hath been often found at such times, that men, otherwise bold and apt enough, are as puppets, ready to work the bidding of any that has kept his wits. So it was here; for the rough troopers that were wont to scorn me for a scholar and half a Roundhead, now bent to their oars as I bade them, and let me steer them whither I would; till it came into my mind that if I commanded them to set me ashore, they had no power to say me nay. Yet would not I make the venture; for what was there left for me to do on land? Master Pentry was dead, and the smoke of Marsham village went up great and black over the hill. The poor men whose unlucky ambassador I had been had now suffered all the ill that their tyrant could do to them, and there was none left to help but Mistress Rosamund; and she to be helped only by my continuing at Deeping Hold, whereas by my escape should I advantage none but myself. Therefore I made no delay, but set the boat's head right for the castle; nor did I count myself any hero for so determining, for the strange fulfilment of Master Eldad's prophecy concerning himself had wrought me to a strong belief that his other words would not fall to the ground, so that my life should be given me for a prey.

In no long time, the chance of escape that I had forborne to take was no longer mine; for the Swede, being hardened to dangers, nor apt to be moved greatly by aught that he could not see or handle, recovered his wits speedily, and began to swear at his crew for a pack of quaking cowards. At this my cousin stirred in his place, and shook himself like a dog coming out of water, as though to empty his ears of the curse that clung in them. Then, with no word spoken, he snatched the tiller from me, and so steered us homewards;

and I, rising, bent over Giles Warner, that lay in a puddle of his own blood, strangely mingled with that slime. Yet was there nought to do, for the man was stone dead; so I made shift to close his eyes, that stared horribly at the sky, and then sat me down in the bows, that I might look back on the land, where the smoke of Marsham village yet went up in a cloud.

But when I cast my eyes shoreward, it seemed as though the smoke had spread abroad over half the heavens, till I knew that this was no smoke, but a storm-cloud drawing up over the land, the blacker for the morning sunshine around us; and as I yet looked, a crooked fork of lightning leapt out in a gap in the hills, and a mutter of thunder came to me.

The suddenness of the storm, and the strangeness of it in time of autumn, moved me to imaginations, and I came nigh to believe that here might be the vengeance of the Lord on murder and robbery. The men also, that could see the growing cloud as well as I, had the same thought, and began to labour at the oars with the strength of fear. So we made good speed to the Hold; and as we rounded the rampart on our way to the haven, the handful of troopers left behind shouted to us and ran to open the gates; also, as we passed under the keep, a casement was opened, and Mistress Rosamund Fanshawe thrust out her pale face, that flushed suddenly as her eyes fell on me, and she drew back her head, leaving me glad at heart, though I knew not why.

So we came to the harbour and made fast; and first, the Earl giving short command, our dead men, being Giles Warner and the two that were slain in the fight, were borne in and laid in an empty store-chamber, till we should take order for their burial. Then the rest of us followed, and my cousin, with no word to me, went up to the door of his hall, where the Signora stood wrapped in a great Eastern cloak, and Pompey by her with a flagon and goblets. The Earl, stumbling for weariness and haste, drained a cup of wine and filled again, nor thought of offering the draught to me that stood apart, or to Gulston, that poured out for himself, asking leave of no man.

The Italian woman spake low and whispering in her own tongue, asking (as I conceive) of the fortune of his enterprise; and he raised his head and answered wearily, "*E morto!*" speaking, I doubt not, of Master Pentry. With that a flush came on her face, and her eyes opened and shone green as a cat's. "How died he?" she asked, smiling as though for pleasure; but the Earl was past the joy of vengeance. "He is where we shall soon be," he muttered, yet not so low but that I heard him. "The curse is loose, Fiammetta, it is loose!" and at his speech her eyelids fell again, and her face was drawn with fear; yet she mastered her dread, and was at point to speak, when the heavens brake open above us in blue flame, and there followed a crash as though the sea and sky were coming together in ruin.

Now the suddenness and greatness of the flash and thunderclap daunted me, though I had marked the black cloud climbing over us; but to the others it seemed as though the day of judgment had come on them. Some of the ruffians fell down for fear, and the foolish maid of the Apple Tree Inn at Marsham, that was chattering with some of the troopers, ran about shrieking that the end of the world was come. Yet was none hurt, nor was this the Lord's vengeance, as we came to know afterwards; for while the most of us stood waiting for some fearful judgment, the next flash shone great and bright but further to seaward, and the thunder was long in breaking, and rather heavy than sharp. With that the rain began to fall in great plashes, growing thicker till it hissed on the stones, and drove all to shelter, myself among the rest; and I had much ado to come to the door of the stairway and climb to my chamber, for I was weak with the weariness and horror of that morning's work, insomuch that I had no thought to shift my clothes, but sat by my window looking into the grey veil of rain that blotted out the hills, till the storm passed suddenly as it had come, and there was sunlight on the land, where a thin feather of steam rose yet from the black scar that had been Marsham. The air that had been sultry with the coming storm was more cool, and a wind blew from the landward, striking chill on me, so that I remembered that I was wet, and changing my garments, came down into the court and walked there, choosing my way between the pools of water, and seeing no man, for no sentries had been set.

I paced the court for some half hour, keeping close beneath the wall, for indeed the air was chilly and damp after the rain, and the wind to my fancy had a savour of the slime of the Hole in it; yet the breezes died away, as I could see by the flag on the turret, that drooped round the pole, and I went up on the rampart to see if Marsham yet smoked. But when I looked over the battlements, I could see no whit of the village, or of the hills behind it, for a mist had risen on the marsh, and was slowly drawing nearer, though wind was none, and the air was dead and damp and chilly, and methought the salt charnel savour was stronger than before; also the sunlight was veiled in white cloud, and the marshes looked more lonely and desolate than was their wont.

Now, as I watched the mist stealthily drawing onward, I heard the sound of feet on the stair of the keep, and presently came Mistress Fanshawe, with a hood drawn over her head, and her maid, the blacksmith's daughter of Marsham. So I made haste to descend to the court, and putting off my hat, greeted her. She hardly answered my greeting, but asked me of the happenings of that morning, the which I told her as I have set them down already, save that I would not speak of that which followed on Master Pentry's end; for when I thought thereon, the dreadfulness choked me, and the savour of the Hole was yet in my nostrils, whether in memory or in the air. Only I took heed to tell her of my will and endeavour to save the man, and how he himself chose his death and the manner of it; for I would not have Mistress Rosamund account me a coward, or slow to help my friends. Yet, need I not have feared, for she herself, as she hath told me afterward, was fain the rather to praise me for my boldness, but forebore, for that she knew brave men to shrink from hearing overmuch of their deeds; though belike I had been as greedy to take her praise as I knew myself unapt to deserve it.

Also I remember that the maid, a well-favoured girl, but ever glancing this way and that for fear, asked me of the villagers; so I told her, thinking to comfort her, that none were slain but Master Pentry and the tall fellow with the scythe that gave Giles Warner his death wound. Thereat she asked me earnestly of the man, but I knew nothing more save that he wore a cap of blue, so far as I might see him from the barge. But as I said this, the maid gave an exceeding great and pitiful cry, and called on the name of a man, and so fell a-sobbing; and when Mistress Rosamund would have cast an arm around her to comfort her, she brake from us like a hurt beast and fled to the door of the keep; nor was it hard to tell that the dead man had been dear to her, her lover perchance.

Mistress Rosamund gazed after the maid, with her eyes full of most sweet compassion, and would have followed, but I stayed her, saying that in such sorrow women were best alone; also I was loth to lose the chance of seeing Mistress Fanshawe. So we spake of this and that, that I remember not, till I saw her of a sudden turn white, and stagger; and had I not thrown an arm around her, she would have fallen in a swoon. She recovered herself, and craved my pardon for what she called her foolish weakness; but she had felt a sickness and faintness come over her heart with an ill savour in the air. Of a truth the smell of the Hole was stronger than aforetime; and as I looked up, I could see the first wreaths of white mist coiling through the battlements like the arms of a ghostly monster, and wrapping the castle in their dank vapour that grew thicker without breath of wind. Soon the mist had filled the court, growing thinner or denser in turn, and the breath of it was a sick loathing and a shapeless fear.

" 'Tis but the marsh mist," I said, though mine own voice sounded hollow and meaningless; and Mistress Rosamund nodded her head, and spake of the fogs that would ever beset the castle when the air was suddenly chill. Yet we both knew that this was no common mist of the river or sea; and when we heard a strange wailing in the air to landward, a great fear fell on me of what might be approaching, for it seemed like the voices of the ghosts that were fabled to flutter over the marshes of Styx. Yet when somewhat white rose above the ramparts and wheeled round our heads, I could see that it was no spectre, but a seagull, and many others following it, till the court was full of birds, circling round the turrets and wheeling above the walls, yet never settling, crying out very mournfully the while, as though in warning and sorrow for somewhat that we knew not and they would fain tell us. For the space of some minutes they continued flying and lamenting, the mist growing thicker the while; then one took sudden flight, and all the rest after him, as though by word of command, and we could see them in a cloud going seaward, for the mist on that side was thinner, till they vanished, still screaming, nor was there a flutter of a wing to be seen in air or on the water or marsh, where commonly were many birds quarrelling and crying over their food.

Now the wailing of the gulls and their flight, as though before some coming peril, moved us strangely; and though we spake it not, one thought was in the minds of both, that these wild creatures, that are nearer to the secrets of the earth and water than we, had come to warn us to flee from somewhat dreadful, or to lament over us if we fled not. But Mistress Rosamund, that was ever brave beyond the wont of women and even of men, shook her shoulders as though to throw off a load of fear, and said lightly that perchance somewhat to landward had frightened the poor gulls, and so went up to the rampart to look, I following. Yet naught was to be seen but the white mist slowly drifting over the marshes, and the dull water lapping at the foot of the wall, with here and there coiling streak of grey slime.

As we stood gazing, not finding aught to tell us why the birds should have fled, there arose a stir and clashing in the court, and looking down, we saw some of the garrison come forth, talking among themselves, yet soberly and in low voices, with less of swearing than was their wont. After them came Gulston, who hallooed to me and asked me what I did there; and when I told him I had seen a great flight of gulls, and was seeking what had frightened them, "By Bacchus!" said he, "as the Signora might say — I have heard tell that these birds are spirits of drowned sailors, and perhaps they were singing a dirge after their fashion for our soldiers. We are a burial party to bear forth the bodies of the men your friends of Marsham slew, and it were but charitable for Your Solemnity to be our chaplain; for we left our parsons to Noll Cromwell at Naseby field, as being too heavy baggage for our haste."

I had wellnigh told him to take the bodies of his men to the devil that had their souls, so did his fleering jar on me; yet would I not yield to anger before Mistress Rosamund, that had heard all. So I was but turning away without answer, when she laid her hand on my sleeve, and I saw her eyes darken and then glisten with tears.

"Will you not speed these poor dead with a prayer?" she said. "They did wickedly, but they knew not what they did, and if we forgive them not in death, nor pity them, how shall we look for mercy? Go with them, and I will stay and pray for their souls," and at that word she caught herself up, and a shadow of a smile was on her lips. "Oh, cousin!" she said, "I forgot that you are a Puritan, and will count me a mere Papist. Yet think you that it is wrong to pray for the dead?"

I shook my head, for there was no time to answer; and indeed it has ever been my belief, since I thought deeply on these matters, that the former ill-practices of certain Papists in making a market of the mercies of God have led us Protestants to be over stern in denying a place of repentance after death to such as by youth or ignorance were unable to find the way of salvation. So I turned to go with the men, and when I looked again at Mistress Rosamund, she had bowed her head in her hands over the battlement, and (I doubted not) was praying for the poor wild souls of these three men.

By this time the troopers had brought forth the bodies of the dead, and wrapped them in old sails and cloaks for shrouds; and so, laying them in one of the barges, we pushed off, and rowed through the mist, that was not so thick but that the landmarks were to be known at times. Also the vapours shifted strangely, so that at times we could see down a clear reach of water, like a grey road between white walls, and again we were shrouded in white darkness, and breathing the cold savour of the Hole. So, by lying on our oars when the mist was too dense, and taking our bearings when it lightened, we made towards the land. Yet it was not the purpose of Gulston to bury the bodies on the mainland, which had been perilous, for the countryside was now roused against us, but we shaped our course for a knoll of the marsh, that had been thrown up a few feet above high tides by some old storm, and was now covered with harsh grass and samphire. Here we landed, and some of the men laboured with spades to dig a grave in the close grey shale and sand; and being apt at digging from practice of throwing up forts in the wars, they had soon made a hole, wide enough for the three bodies to lie side by side, but not deep, for in that ground we had soon come to water. Here then the men laid their dead fellows solemnly enough, and stood by while I spake some of the Service for Burial of the Dead, that I knew well, having been bred for the Church; save that, seeing the manner of men they had been, and the business in which they met their end, I could not bring myself to speak confidently of their lot at the Resurrection, but rather commended them to the infinite mercies of the Lord, that are beyond the bounds of our creeds and controversies.

Methought that some of the men were moved by my words, though they understood little; and one man, a Spaniard, with a face tanned like leather and seamed with scars, muttered his prayers in haste with much devotion. When I had done, the men began to fill in the trench above the bodies, and the Spaniard busied himself with binding together two staves he had brought with him, thinking to make a cross.

While they laboured, I stood by the boat watching them, and now and then turning to look at the marsh, when the mist thinned. As I looked, a wind began to blow from the land, lightly at first, but strengthening, and the fog drifted in strange shapes like ghosts, and the smell of the Hole came on the wind, growing stronger, till my heart was sick at the foulness and the chill of it. With the wind, the dull grey water that had been lying still at the edge of the knoll, began to lap at the bank; yet through the sobbing of the water I seemed to hear another sound. At first it was a whisper, far off, but it grew into a noise of sucking, as when water is drawn into a whirlpool or a pipe, and the mist now being in part blown away by the wind, I could see in the channel that led landwards to the Hole, a whirl or funnel of water here and there, that eddied and vanished and then appeared anew, growing slowly nearer, so that I wondered what this might be, and spake to Gulston, that was urging his men to finish and begone from this stinking marsh. But when he turned to look, the whirls in the channel were gone, and naught to be noted save the smell and some streaks of slime that floated past us; whereat he laughed, saying that those waters were full of eddies, and then spat and cursed the stink, and taking a flask from his pocket, proffered it to me; and when I would not drink, he tossed off a dram, to wash his throat clean, as he said. By this time the mound was finished, and the Spaniard, taking the rough wooden cross he had fashioned, and doffing his hat, planted it at the head of the grave, and we were about to go, when the Swede remarked that the end of the grave had crumbled and sunk somewhat, and catching a spade from one of the troopers, heaved a shovelful of the shale and sand on the mound, and slapped the earth with the side of the spade to make all smooth, as children do in building castles in the sand.

Now even as he smote the mound, the end of it crumbled away with a loud sucking sound, and where the hillock had been was a yeasty whirl of grey sand and water and slime. So Gulston gave back with a cry, and leaned on his spade, and we all gazed, while the whirl grew larger, and the mound crumbled away before our eyes, and the cross that was but just planted rocked to and fro and went down with the rest. At that the Spaniard made forward as though to save his handiwork, and I to hold him back, and only in time; for the mound we had reared and the bodies under it were gone, and nothing but a whirling funnel of water and sand. As we looked over the edge, the Spaniard staring as one distraught, and I behind him holding his arm, the whirlpool seemed to open down black to the very deeps, and then filled again with a spurt of slimy water, and in the midst of it one of the corpses, with the shroud gone from it, and the dead hands turning as though in strife to escape. The body was wound, as it seemed, with streaks of grey slime, but the face was bare, and I knew it for Giles Warner, even as I had seen him dead, save that the eyes I had closed were open, and their look was ghastly, so that I could not have borne it, yet might not turn away. Yet, as I gazed, the body was drawn down slowly into the water, the tendrils of slime seeming to tighten around it like cords; and when I looked back, the men were stumbling into the boat, cursing and crying out for fear; and had it not been for Gulston, that kept his wits, they would have left the Spaniard and me on the crumbling remnant of the knoll.

In good time we gained the side, and none too soon; for as I heaved the Spaniard over the gunwale, he being palsied with fear, and got my knee on the boat's side, the hold melted from beneath my other foot, and I was fain to cling to the nearest man to clamber in; and where we had made our grave was nought but a grey eddy and the Spaniard's cross tossing in the waters.

No more I saw, for Gulston bade row, and the men bent to their oars, caring not whither they went so it was away from that accursed grave; also, the wind dropping, the mist closed in again, and folded us in a white shadow, so that we went at a venture, grounding in shallows, and feeling for channels with our oars; and mazed with fear as were the men, we might have wandered long in the marshes, had not Gulston bethought himself of his pistols, and firing one of them, in no long time came a musket-shot from the castle, that was nearer than we thought. So we made harbour again, and the troopers crept to their quarters as men broken by fear; but Gulston stayed with me, talking of the strange whirlpool that had swallowed up our dead, and would have it that this was but a sudden sinking of a quicksand, whereof there were many in the marshes. I feigned to assent to his speech, even as he himself feigned to believe it; yet as he went in at the gate and I was following, I looked back on the little port, and as the mist lifted somewhat, I seemed to see a tendril or streak of grey slime coiling round the arm of rock that shielded the harbour, and feeling at the edge of the quay like a finger searching for us blindly. Yet even as I looked, the appearance vanished, nor might I be sure if I had seen aught but a trick of the tide.

CHAPTER VIII

Of my Talk with the Italian and of certain Men that went a-fishing

As we came to the court, the Signora was standing on the steps of the hall door, with my cousin at her side, both silent, and, as it seemed, ill at ease, for the Earl's brow lowered as though he were in one of his black moods, and her face had something in it of anger mingled with fear. Yet as the Swede and I came nearer, she lifted her eyes on us, and passing Gulston over as of little account, she smiled on me and greeted me with her foreign courtesy, asking how we had fared. For a space I spake not, finding it hard to choose words to tell what I had seen; and the Swede thrust in, as was ever his wont.

"A fool's errand we have been sent on, to bury men in these cursed marshes of my Lord's," he said, pulling at his beard. "We might have spared our trouble, for when the grave was well dug and filled, a damned quicksand must needs open and suck all down, and like to swallow us too, had we not been speedy. God bless the land and the sea, say I, but the devil take this puddle of slime that is neither."

At that the Earl muttered somewhat in his throat, and smote his hand on the side of the door; but the Signora, letting her green eyes rest on the Swede for but a moment, fixed them on me again as though to draw out my very soul.

"Of a truth," I said, stumbling in my speech, "all went much as he saith; the grave, and the knoll whereon it was digged, crumbled away before our eyes, after a strange fashion, and we were fain to flee or be sucked down ourselves. Nay, so sudden was it, that the dread of it yet abides with me."

"Saw you or heard you anything else, sirs?" asked the woman sharply, though courteously.

"Nay, I saw and heard naught," muttered the Swede, shaking his head; "but Master Leyton here spake somewhat of eddies in the water, and I know not what else."

Thereat the Signora looked at me again, with her eyes wider than their wont, as though eager for what was to hear. So I answered her, telling of the strange sucking noise that I had heard, and of the moving whirls in the water; and when I had ended, she dropped the lids over her eyes and bent her head in thought, speaking not, and we all stood silent, till my cousin lifted his head and pushed back his hair in his wonted way, and laughed loudly, with a desperate and false mirth.

"Why, so it is!" he said, clapping Gulston on the shoulder. "They are gone, and we have the fewer mouths to feed when Old Noll comes to smoke us out. Of a truth," he went on, "we are like to need all our store of victual, for our fishermen have caught not so much as a sprat this day, nor seen a fin. Perchance these shiftings of the sands have frightened the fish."

At this the Italian lifted her eyes again. "The fish gone too?" she said. "You told me not of that, *Filippo mio*."

"Why, it slipped my mind," said the Earl, with his mirthless laugh. "Never fear, Fiammetta, we shall see the fish back again in time for your Friday dinner, or I will send further to seek for some. But it is dry work talking. Come and taste my fresh cask of Spanish, that was broached this morning. If fish fail us, we have store of wine and powder in the cellars, and what more does a soldier need?"

Gulston was never backward in answering a challenge of that sort, and I myself was about to accept my cousin's courtesy, when the Signora looked at me with her narrow eyes, that spake plainly, though without word, that she would have me stay. So I excused myself, answering, as was indeed the truth, that his wine was like to be too noble for my poor brain, and the Earl, waiting not to hear me out in my excuses, took Gulston by the arm and went in, calling for Pompey to bring the flagon. When the sound of their feet had ceased on the flags of the hall, the Signora slipped down and sat on one of the steps, beckoning to me to take place at her side, the which I did. For a space she looked earnestly on me without speaking, then asked me suddenly:

"Signor Uberto," she said, "these are strange happenings in land and water. What make you of them?"

I was fain to answer that I knew not of these parts, and of the currents and quicksands of the marshes and channels, but she took me up with a certain scornful impatience. "O aye," she said, "all that is good enough for Signor Erico, or Signorina Rosamunda, but you believe it not yourself, nor does Filippo. Tell me what is in your mind. I am no English girl, to be scared with tales of warlocks, and, scholar as you are, belike I could teach you somewhat of curious arts. Have I not the name of a witch in the countryside?"

I answered something to the purport that peasants were ever prone to think a stranger to be witch or wizard, but she cut me short again.

"Here are we talking follies," she said, with an angry scorn of herself and of me, "and the time is flying, and it may be too late. Tell me what you know and what you fear."

"There is an old tale," I answered her, "of a Thing that bides in the deep pit of water they call the Hole; and but the other day, as I was ranging the books in my library, I came on a book of our family, wherein the rhyme was written —" And so I told her the verse, and she would have me say it over twice or thrice, till she knew it herself. But when I would have gone on to say that this was but an old woman's fable, she stopped me again.

"Do not lie to yourself and to me, signor," she said. "There are strange things in this world we see, and in the world unseen, and yet stranger, perchance, in the world of the border. We are in the fall of a heavy peril, and my Lord's great guns and the muskets of his rascal troopers are as straws to ward us, and a straw is your own pretty rapier, though it be good Italian steel, and you have the right trick of using it, signor —"

She had been so scornful of our wasting time in compliments, that when she quitted the business in hand to praise my skill of fence, I could but stare at her in amaze, till she laughed daintily.

"Nay, I am straying from the matter in hand," she said. "Pardon me, signor, but I have grown up among swordsmen, and it is a joy to me to see you playing with our good Filippo as a Spaniard fights with a bull. Had you been an Italian, you had entered into your inheritance long ago; an angry word from my Lord, coats off, a pass or twain, a turn of the wrist, and Signor Uberto is the Earl of Deeping."

I marvelled the more that she should talk thus idly; for I was yet to learn later that the Signora spake no word without a purpose below it and, perchance, a darker purpose or two hidden behind that. So I did but tell her that I was no such master of fence as she would have me, and that I looked on the duello as barbarous, and no more to be accounted civil than Christian, wherefore the Swedish King Gustavus had rightly forbidden it among his officers. As I spake, the Italian woman opened her eyes as though coming back from a dream, and broke in on my homily, waving her hand as if to brush away my reasons.

"Enough, signor," she said; "I am partly of your mind. The rapier is a pretty tool, but there is overmuch chance in the duello. A loose shoestring, a mote in the eye, and where is your artist? Nay, a scholar such as you has apter weapons. Signor Uberto, there is upon this house the shadow of a great fear, and the malice of a nameless adversary. What can you do to save yourself and us?"

"I know of no arm but prayer, and no help but the Almighty," I said, doffing my hat.

"I knew you would say that," she answered softly, yet with a scornfulness in her voice. "You Puritani are ever in one story. But the Almighty is far away, and I have seen the good man cry out for help and perish as one of the wicked. There be other spirits, not almighty, yet assuredly potent, that are nearer to help, if one knows their speech."

I was about to tell her that I had no faith in the invocation of saints, but at that word she caught me up scornfully.

"*Dio mio!* What pedants are you English! Nay, I speak of others than the saints, though perchance they mask themselves saintly. Think you that I could pray for help to the rotten bones of a stupid friar, that would rub out the wisdom of the ancients to have parchment for the jargon he called Latin? I have better helpers than saints, as you shall yet see — if you be not afeared."

"I will have no dealings with devils," I said shortly, rising from the step.

"Who spake of devils?" she answered, looking up at me with narrowed eyes. "To the wise there is no devil and no saint, but powers and intelligences that are mighty to help or hurt, perilous to compel, and deadly to fools and cowards, but answering to the right word. Much can I do alone, but not enough. Uberto, wilt thou dare to help me?"

As she spake, with more of passion than I had known her to show before, she fixed her eyes on mine, and caught me by the wrist, and it was as if a fetter was laid on my hand and my will. Nor know I how I should have answered her, had not my cousin smitten open the door and come on us, and, at the clash of the lock, the woman dropped my hand, and as it were a veil of grey came over the green light of her eyes. Gulston followed the Earl, and both were flushed with the Spanish wine, and laughing loudly.

"Why, Fiammetta, what hast been babbling so long?" he asked, taking her under the chin and turning her face up, but she writhed away from him like a snake, and looked at him smiling.

"We were but talking of sword play and tricks of fence," she answered, "and I was saying to Signor Uberto that were he of mine own country, he might have won himself a goodly name and heritage by his mastery of the sword."

At that my cousin laughed harshly, and Gulston made an echo. "Of a truth, cousin," the Earl cried, "I had not taken you for so worshipful a sworder, though you are apt at your weapon for a Puritan. And pray, Signora, what name and fortune should my kinsman have won by his rapier? I knew not that titles and estates of nobility came to masters of the sword, even the greatest."

The Italian's eyes grew narrow like mere slits for malice as she answered him, "Nay, my Lord, what say you to the name and estate of the Earl of Deeping?"

My cousin stared, and then laughed again, but not as one well pleased.

"Oh, aye, I take you," he said. "A right Italian plan, too. What say you, cousin Hubert? Shall we play a match with the buttons off the foils? You stake a book of sermons, and I this ragged Hold and the rents that none will pay me. Nay, the wager is not fair; shall I throw you in Fiammetta for the prize?"

He spake jestingly, but I could see that in his desperate mood he defied me to take him at his word. But the Signora, having proved her power, was loth to drive him further, even though she was angered at his slighting manner. "Nay, *Filippo mio!*" she said softly, "the match were unfair. Signor Uberto is a man of peace, and his tricks of fence would serve him little with the bare weapons. And little as I am worth, I am too good to be the wager of a bout of fence." So the Earl's mood passed, and he turned to Gulston, that had stared on us blankly the while.

"Eric," said my cousin, "the men tell me that they can take no fish with their lines, nor is there any fowl to be seen on the marshes. Send a half-dozen of them forth in a boat with nets and guns, and see that they come not back without a cargo."

The Swede's face changed, and he shifted from one foot to the other.

"My Lord," he said, "I would bid you consider that the men are sore tired with the day's work, and some are feared of the marshes, for the strange quicksands and the evil smell. Also the mist may close in and leave them astray in the channels."

The Earl's brow darkened, and he swore an oath. " 'Sdeath!" said he. "Am I captain of a troop of old wives? I know what you would say. Here have some cowardly fools been stuffing the knaves with old fables, till they are afraid of their own shadows. Send forth some of those that were not in this morning's business, and bid them make no more words, or I will flay the hide off them with my dog-whip."

Gulston shrugged his shoulders, and left us with no more ado; and presently I could hear him routing the troopers from their quarters, till some five of them came forth grumbling, two carrying fowling-pieces and the others fishing-tackle and bait. They were wont rather to take these fishing and fowling cruises as a holiday, yet now they went sullenly, and had they not felt the eye of their master, and known that he would be better than his threatenings, belike they would have let who would go a-fishing. One of them, I remember, turned at the door of the guard-room and went back, as though he had forgotten somewhat, coming out presently with a great sword girt to him, whereat my lord laughed, and would ask the fellow whether he would play at cut and thrust with the cod-fish, but the man answered not. Yet a breeze sprang up and drave the mist away seaward, and a gleam of sun gilded the belfry, till the afternoon looked fair again, so that the men pushed off their boat cheerfully enough, being reckless rascals all, nor apt to mope; and thus they set forth, the Earl crying out to them that if they brought home a full load, fin or feather, they should not lack for ale nor strong waters to wash down the catch.

So we parted, each to his quarters; but, before I sought my chamber, I walked on the rampart for a space, and could see the boat making good speed seaward with oars and a small sail, till presently a shift of wind brought the mist landward again, and I could scarce see the boat, that was dwindled to a black speck on the grey water. Yet I heard no shots, so that it seemed they had found no wild fowl.

Wearying of the grey flats, I sought my room, and cast myself on the bed, for I was sore weary, meaning to rest for a half-hour; yet my head had no sooner touched the pillow than I fell into a deep slumber, that must have endured for hours, and at the first dreamless; but at the last, as I conceive, I had a strange dream, born, as is the way of these visions, of that which I had seen and heard, strangely entangled with other fantasies. Methought that I was at the sword-play with my cousin, and at either elbow of me was a hooded and shrouded form, that I could see, yet I knew, how I cannot tell, that the Earl could not; and as he grew angry and rough in his fence, as was his way when I was too hard for him, the shape on my left hand stretched an arm forth and took the button from my fencing foil, and pointed a long sharp finger at my cousin's breast, saying, in a woman's voice, and that the voice of the Signora, "Strike! Stone dead hath no fellow!" as my Lord of Essex spake in urging the death of the Earl of Strafford. And at that it seemed that the other figure threw back its hood and showed the bare skull of a man with Master Pentry's eyes glowing in the sockets, and spake in his harsh voice, "Vengeance is mine, saith the Lord!" and would have stayed me, but in my dream I drave my cousin's blade aside with a sweeping parry, and springing forward, thrust him through the breast with the favourite stoccata of my Italian master, and methought the Earl fell with his breast spouting blood, that changed presently to red slimy tendrils creeping over the stones to fasten on me, till I cried out in fear, and then came a great peal of thunder, and I waked with the sweat streaming down my face, and the echoes of the thunder yet trembled in the air.

Now, when I was well awake, I saw that it was dusk, and the dark mist was rolling through my window, bearing the faint foul smell that I knew too well, yet mingled with the reek of powder, whereat I wondered, but not long; for presently the dusky court was lit with a red flash, and there came the great crack of a culverin from the gate, and the smoke mingled with the mist and drifted across the court in strange shapes. So, much marvelling what this might mean, I cast my cloak round me and made haste down the stair, and as fortune would have it, I chanced upon Mistress Rosamund Fanshawe, that was bound on the same errand. She put forth a hand and caught my cloak, asking what this might be, yet could I not tell her, till presently a tall shadow brake through the rolling mist, and I clutched at it, and knew that it was the Swede; and to my question he answered shortly that the fishers had not come back, and the Earl was firing his cannon to guide them through the mist. So I let him go, and went up to the rampart with Mistress Rosamund to listen, and in no long time we heard the sound of a musket-shot, yet far off and muffled as it were by the mist, whereat I rejoiced that the men were returning safe; for in that lonely and fearful place, the worst ruffian seemed a friend, as being at least human. So we stood shivering in the chilly mist, that increased in thickness; and at last came another shot, somewhat nearer, but far off still, and then two or three thick together, and a stillness, and last of all a faint cry of voices, wailing or shouting, that fell suddenly silent, and nothing more.

Presently I could hear my cousin's voice bidding men set a blazing cresset on one of the turrets for a torch to guide the boat homewards; also he bade toll the bell of the hall: but no shout or shot answered for an hour or twain, till the mist lightened somewhat, and the watch on the barbican tower cried out that they saw the boat. So all crowded to the port, and Mistress Rosamund and myself with them; and indeed the tale was true, for we could see a spot of black slowly drifting out of the night towards the quay, till it grew greater, and yet no sign of oar or man. Lastly the boat drave heavily against the quay, and men ran out with torches to see how their comrades had fared, and called to them.

There was none that answered, and the black hulk drifted in till the wavering light shone down into the boat, and we could see that the craft was half full of water, streaked with glistering slime that shone like blood in the red torch-light. Of the men, of their tackle and weapons and the fish or fowl they had taken, was no sign; only in the side of the boat was sticking a broken blade of a broadsword, sunk deep into the wood as though by the frenzied stroke of a madman, and we knew it for the weapon of the man who turned back to fetch his sword, that had profited him little. Other sign to tell the end of these men, there was none.

CHAPTER IX

Of the Sacrifice of the Black Fowl

Now when my cousin had looked upon the boat, and upon the shard of the sword that was the only sign of his men, he was as one distraught, crying out desperately to launch all the barges and set forth to take vengeance on man or devil. Yet did none stir to do his bidding, and when he would have leapt into a boat, the Signora plucked him back by the cloak and whispered to him, so that he forbore, and she, turning to Gulston, bade all within, and to bar the gates. The which we did, and when we were girt round by the great walls, the fear of the garrison somewhat abated. Yet still they stood huddled and muttering, as if afraid to be alone; till the Italian spake to them smoothly.

"Here is an ill business," quoth she. "Surely these men were maddened by fear or liquor to set on one another. Doubtless the shots we heard were of the fight, and any that were left alive have cast themselves overboard. Think you not so, Filippo?"

At that the Earl nodded his head, but spake not; but the Swede, falling into her story, sware many and great oaths that he had known such madness to come on men oft-times in the wars, and in wrecks at sea; so the others taking heart somewhat, a double watch was set on the walls, and we went to our quarters. For myself, I cast myself on my bed as I was, with my sword ready to my hand, and so lay uneasily, running to the window at first when the lapping of the water grew louder, and seemed like to the sucking noise that I had heard in the morning, till for very shame I must lie still. Also in the hour before the dawn one of the sentinels loosed off his piece, and brought the more part of us to the walls, with a tale of a black bulk of somewhat that he had seen heaving above the edge of the quay. Yet when we kindled torches and looked, was there nothing; so Gulston put the fellow in ward, with a promise that he should ride the wooden horse on the morrow. Nor were we troubled again, so that toward morning I fell into a doze, nor wakened till the sunlight was bright on my face.

When I looked forth, the day was fair and still, and the mist hung only in the fold of the far hills, also I could hear the men stirring, and one struck up a song. When I came to walk in the court after my wont, all looked to go on as aforetime, nor did the happenings of yesterday seem other than an ugly dream. But presently, as I walked, I heard the sound of groanings from a chamber hard by the guard-room, and it came to me that here was one of those hurt in the fight at Marsham; so when the Swede came forth, wiping the froth of his morning draught from his beard, I asked him how his wounded did.

"One is nigh sound again," he answered me; "but the other doth but ill, seeing that his sword-hand was cut through by yonder rascal's scythe, ere I could shoot. We have bound his arm, but I look for him to die, for we have no surgeon among us. Well, it is one fewer for our victuals and a day longer life for our chickens."

As he spake, I heard a noise of cackling, and a few fowls that were kept at the castle came forth into the court, as the blacksmith's daughter of Marsham, that was maid to Mistress Rosamund, called to them from the door of the keep, and scattered crumbs and broken meats from a basket on her arm. Truly it was a pretty sight and a peaceful one to mark the hens pecking between the stones, their lord and master Chanticleer strutted in the sun like a young gallant in his holiday clothes. So thought Gulston, for he sighed once or twice, and laughed as one ashamed.

"Zounds!" said he, "I might dream myself at my mother's house by Upsala, fashioning a wooden sword to lead the bonders' boys to war, while the maidens cast the broken barley-bread to the fowls. 'Tis a fair hall, and before the hearth is the skin of the first bear I killed — shall I ever stand thereon again?" and with that he sighed again, and swore, and strode away with his long scabbard swinging against his legs, leaving me to divide the lordship of the court with the fowls.

But when I had walked a turn or two, I marked the Signora put her head forth of the hall door, and seeing me alone, she came stepping daintily to give me greeting, and ask me what I did; and when I answered that I was but watching the chickens fed, she was pleased to ask me in jest whether I were practising divination by fowls after the manner of the ancients.

"Nay," said I, laughing; "I have no skill of augury, and fear that I might be counted a scoffer with Claudius the Consul, that cast the sacred chickens into the sea, bidding them drink if they would not eat."

"Aye, and thereby brought his ships and himself to miserable ruin," answered she, "as a warning to all that despise divinations." At that she broke off suddenly, and gazed earnestly into a corner of the court, where I, for my part, could see naught save a little black hen picking at the stones apart from the rest. Presently the Signora turned to me again, and her eyes were shining as though she had found a treasure.

"Signor Uberto," said she, "you remember how yesterday we talked of the unseen powers, and of curious arts that might compel them? Was it not so?"

"Aye," said I; "yet have I ever accounted but little of magic."

"Therein are you right foolish for all your learning," she answered me scornfully; "yet if you fear not, you may see somewhat ere long" — and with that she looked again earnestly on the black hen. But while I marvelled what she could see in the pecking of poultry, the wounded man groaned again and called on his Saints, being a Southerner, and she asked me who was sick. I answered as the Swede had told me; and when I spake of the manner of the man's wound, her eyes widened again and grew brighter. "*Ah, povero!*" said she, yet her voice was less pitiful than her words; "his right hand nigh cut off? I will see the man, and perchance lighten his pain by what of surgery my father taught me. But first — tell me who cares for yonder fowls?"

Methought that she would take a fowl to make broth for the sick man, so I told her that Mistress Rosamund's maid tended on the poultry, and the girl came forth even then with another basket of crusts; but when she saw the Italian's narrow eyes fixed on her, she grew pale and made her reverence, and so stood.

"Hither to me, wench," said the Signora, and the girl came slowly, dragging her feet as one in fetters. "What is thy name?" and when she heard that it was Elizabeth — "It is well, Elisabetta," said she. "See'st yonder black fowl? Take her up and go to my chamber and wait till I come."

At this the girl hung back, and began to stammer out that she was Mistress Rosamund's maid, and had no leave to go on other errands; but the Italian cut her short.

"Who art thou, and who is the Signorina Rosamunda, to say what shall or shall not be? Do as I have said, or thou shalt taste the whip!"

Now it moved me to loathing to hear this stranger speak so to a free countrywoman of mine own, belike no worse than her in birth, and surely better in virtue, so I told her plainly that the wench was no bondslave, nor would I hear such words to an Englishwoman. Yet the Signora did but laugh, looking at me with her eyes narrowed to slits.

"Nay," said she; "I forgot that here is the land of freedom, where Jill is as good as her mistress, and Noll Cromwell better than the King. I will use no violence, neither compel anyone. Look on me, Elisabetta, and thou shalt see that I mean thee no hurt."

Her voice was smooth and sweet as honey, yet hissing somewhat as a snake's; so the girl took courage to look her in the face. But when their eyes met, the wench trembled sore, and writhed her body as though she strove to break away, but was fast held; and I looked on the Italian, and her eyes were green and steady, and her lips sucked in as though she were drawing the life from the other. So they stood for a space, till the Signora stretched out the forefinger of her left hand and pointed it at the forehead of the girl, who shuddered with a great sigh, and without word walked slowly, dragging her feet, and took up the black fowl, and so went in at the great door, looking back piteously at the Italian as though for mercy that she found not, and then at me, that would have helped her, but knew not how.

"Now must I within, to see if I can help yonder poor man," said the Signora, yet smiling, as though her meaning were other than her words; but even then Mistress Rosamund called from the stair of the keep, "Bessie, Bessie!" and when none answered, she ran forth to seek her maid, and so came on us together.

"Your pardon, Signora Bardi and my cousin," she said, with a scornful reverence to the Italian. "Have you seen my maid Bessie?"

"I have need of Elisabetta for today," answered the Signora; at which Mistress Fanshawe's face flushed, and she beat her foot on the ground.

"Why is this?" she asked. "Methinks the girl was given to wait on me. Surely, if you have need of a woman, there is the maid from the inn, that is as fit to serve you, aye, and fitter perchance, seeing that she loves to company with soldiers."

Now I feared what the Italian might say or do, as I knew the hatred that was between these two. Yet did she but smile again, and wave a hand after her foreign fashion, as though to put aside somewhat too slight to hold her.

"I cannot stay to bandy words," she said, "seeing that yonder poor man needs me. Suffice it that the wench came willingly, nor will she take hurt with me, if she be a true maid. Will you have the other in her place?"

Mistress Rosamund shook her head with no word, and the Signora left us and passed into the chamber where we heard the groaning, and presently came out a trooper to the hall, whence he returned with Pompey the black, that bore a box and some vials, also a chafing-dish of charcoal; and we talked the while of things indifferent, for that the casements of the chamber were open. But when Pompey had entered with his burden, and the windows were shut, I began to tell Mistress Rosamund of the strange talk of the Signora, when there came from the sick man's room a great shrieking cry, and then a babbling in a foreign tongue, and again screams and foul oaths, so that we were fain to stop our ears. Yet in a brief space the cries turned to groans, and fell silent, and presently the Italian came forth smiling, bearing somewhat wrapped in a napkin, that dripped red on the stones, and Pompey followed with her other matters; nor did she waste a look on us, but passed to the hall, as one steadfastly making for a goal. Yet could we well guess what had happened; and also the trooper that had gone in came forth, swearing under his breath as one affrighted, and told me, when I asked, that the Signora had made no ado, but sliced off the man's hand more deftly than any surgeon, and dressed the arm, and so left him asleep with some secret drug from one of her vials. With that he went about his business, and Mistress Rosamund looked on earnestly. "It is passing strange," said she; "a black fowl and a man's hand, and a murderer's, I doubt not! Savours not this of witchcraft, cousin? And what would she do with my poor Bessie?"

I strove to comfort her, saying that I would speak to the Earl that no hurt should come to the girl; and so we went up on the rampart to look abroad. The tide was now full, and the more part of the marshes was a sheet of grey water, darker in the channels, and quiet enough in the pale sunshine; yet was there somewhat amiss in the stillness, where aforetime we had heard fish rising and leaping, or sea-birds crying over their food. Presently Mistress Rosamund grew deathly white, and would leave me, for that an ill savour was in the air; and indeed there was a breath of the smell of the Hole, that I had come to know and to fear. So she went down from the wall, and I continued walking for a space, but marked naught but that a good way from the castle there seemed a whirl of eddies moving swiftly in the water, which passed, and the smell with them; but in some quarter of an hour came the savour again, and the whirls in the water, going the same way as at the first, and so yet other times, till the tide ebbed and I marked the appearance no more, and the day passed wearily.

Now at supper-time we were all gathered together save Gulston, and as I had promised, I spake to the Earl my cousin of the wench Elizabeth; and he, that knew naught of the matter, asked of the Italian what she would with the girl, thinking it but a women's quarrel, and somewhat angered, methought, that the Signora should take it on herself to command his kinswoman's servant. But the Bardi did but smile after her wicked fashion, and answered him smoothly that she needed the wench for a matter of curious arts that should do her no harm and might be greatly for the advantage of us all; also she bade us come and see for ourselves that very night what she purposed to do, if we had the courage; for that as the business was of great moment, so it was not without danger to herself first, and also to others.

Now when she spake thus, we were all silent for a space, for this matter savoured to us of sorcery and the black arts; also my cousin, whose right it was to speak the first, frowned and sat sullen, as is the wont of violent men that are faced with a danger that they understand not. But Mistress Rosamund, that was ever of a high courage, seeing that no word came from the Earl, leaned toward me over the table and spake earnestly.

"I partly conceive of the nature of tonight's business," she said; "nor will it be without peril of our souls as well as of our bodies. Yet is this girl given into my charge, and how can I draw back? Signora, I will come."

The Italian spake not, but smiled as a man will at the boldness of an enemy; and indeed, though she was an evil woman, she had a man's relish for bravery and learning wheresoever found. Seeing this, I could no longer hold back, and for very shame must make one; and the Earl, awaking from his sullenness, drank off a full goblet and vowed he would be with us. "We four and the wench," said he, "and belike the devil to make the half-dozen — or shall we bid Gulston also?"

The man came in as my cousin named him, and sat down in his place, seeming much distempered. Nor would he answer wherefore he was late, till he had eaten and drunk; when he pushed his platter away, and looking in the Earl's face, "The man is dead," says he. "I have seen him passing and heard his confession, for he took me for a priest in his fever; and an ill story it was, with a dozen murders or so for the best of his deeds."

"A murderer, and worse?" said the Signora, "Ah, *povero*!" but her eyes shone strangely as though with a secret gladness.

"Well, I'm for sleep now," said the Swede; "I go on no more burial parties, day or night. Methinks, signora, your surgery profited him little?"

"I did what I could," she answered him, with her eyes cast down as in sorrow; "and sad am I that I could not save him." The Swede grunted for all answer, and so flung out of the hall; and as he went, my cousin asked of the Italian with his eyes "Shall I bring him tonight?" and she shook her head.

" 'Tis a good soldier," she said scornfully; "but with wit as leathern as his sword-sheath. Signorina Rosamunda and Signor Uberto, I will send for you."

So we went to our rooms, and I to watch at my window, for the fear of what was to be kept me from sleep; also once or twice the smell of the slime was strong in my nostrils, and a strange sucking noise, that was more than the wonted lapping of the waters, made me look sharply into the night, that was black and moonless. Yet saw I naught till, a half hour or so before midnight, the black came for me, and I did on my sword and went out; yet looking back to see if I had forgotten aught, mine eyes fell on my little Bible in the Greek tongue, that I ever took to read on journeys; and I thrust it into my pocket with little thought. On the stair was Mistress Rosamund, muffled in cloak and hood, and we followed Pompey to the door of the hall, and up a little stair where I had not before been to a door, whereon he knocked, and so departed in great fear, waiting not till it was opened to us.

The chamber whereunto we came was of a fair bigness, and panelled in oak darkened by age. The floor also was of oak and polished, nor was there a cloth on it, nor any hangings on the wall, nor chair nor other garniture, save one little table curiously wrought of brass after the fashion of a tripod of twining snakes, whereon were two candles lighted, and somewhat covered with a black kerchief. On the floor were four circles drawn with red chalk, or some such thing, of which one was larger, and in each the figure that is called the pentacle or Seal of Solomon; and characters written therein that seemed in the scant light to be of Arabic or other Eastern tongues. Yet though I knew these to be but the customary baggage of sorcerers, I was feared of them as I looked not to be, and more of that which might be under the black veil on the brazen altar, for such it seemed. My cousin was there waiting, but spake not; nor did any word pass before the Signora came to us, strangely habited in a long black robe, and with her hair unbound, and a garland of leaves round her head like an ancient Sibyl.

"You are here," said she; "now listen! Stand each of you within one of these figures, nor go out for your lives, whatever you may see or hear, till I bid you." And when we were set within our pentacles, "Elisabetta!" she called, "come hither to me." At that the girl came forth from the inner chamber, clad in a black robe of strange fashion, and barefooted, with her hair loose, and her eyes staring as though she saw naught, and the Signora set her in the greater circle over against the table. This done, the Italian threw the casement wide open, and the smell of the Hole came in on a little wind, and the candles flickered. "Ah," says the Signora; "it is there, it is there, but we may yet escape—" and she came to the brazen table and twitched off the veil, and there lay, as I half looked to see, the severed hand of the dead trooper, long and lean, and strangely swarthy, with dusky hair on the back, that lay uppermost. By the fingers of the hand she laid a candle that she took from her bosom, and on the floor between the girl and the tripod, a lighted brazier; and so, standing herself in the great circle with the girl, she cast on the coals a double handful of somewhat like incense, that burned with a wavering flame of green and a strong smoke that made mine eyes wink and water, and my head swim as though I were drunken with wine; nor do I know if what I thought I saw after were not in part the work of that devil's incense.

"Now," says she, "is it high time for the sacrifice," and at her bidding the girl laid somewhat black on the brazen table before the hand, and I saw that it was the black fowl that had been chosen in the morning. The bird struggled a little, but made no sound; and the Signora gave to the girl a great knife or short sword bent as a half moon. Even then the clock of the belfry struck the hour of midnight; and on the last beat of the bell, the Italian cried out "Strike!" and the maid cleft the fowl asunder with one blow, so that the blood of it spurted on her gown and on the dead hand, and hissed on the brazier. So throwing down the knife, she came back into the circle, and standing as one tranced, began to chant a strange song or incantation in some jargon that to my ear savoured now of the Hebrew, now of the Chaldee, now of the Latin, and anon was like the barbarous chatter of black slaves in the plantations. Now when the girl had chanted for a space, there came a puff of air through the window and blew out the candles on the table, so that there was no light save the green flames of the brazier, that the Signora fed ever from a box of her incense. With the wind the fire leapt up, lighting the whole chamber, and I looked toward the brazen altar where the halves of the stricken hen and the hand of the slain man lay.

While I gazed, it seemed to me that the hand was other than I had seen it, being darker of hue, and the nails long and hooked as a bird's claws; also the hair on the wrist was much increased in thickness and blackness, as on the hand of an ape. And whereas the hand had lain flat, it was now bent as though leaning on the table, yet could I see no arm pertaining to it. But presently in the flickering lights and shadows, there seemed to be somewhat moving like a strand of black hair blowing in the wind, that increased in bigness and blackness, yet all disordered and shapeless; and when I looked on the hand again, the fingers of it clutched the strange candle, that came alight without touch of fire, and burned with a green flame; and with that the semblance of the hair writhed about the table and hid the body of the fowl, that we saw no more, only a whirl of wind blew feathers about the chamber, like a flight of black snow, and a savour of burning mingled with the incense. And now the Signora first uplifted her voice in a strange singing manner, and I could tell well what she spake, for she used the Latin tongue, yet rather monkish and barbarous than as the Romans talked. "*Cibum potumque tibi dedi,*" said she; "I have given thee meat and drink, even flesh and blood of a black victim. What wilt thou give unto me?" Then, whether it were the disorder of mine own senses, or the girl speaking in trance, or verily the voice of a demon, it seemed as though a shrill, chattering voice, as of an ape that could speak, answered her again out of the shadow that had the appearance of hair, saying, "*Quid vis, domina?*" or "What wilt thou, mistress?" and the green flame of the candle bowed before her.

She stood still for a space before she answered, and the green lights flickered on her face from the brazier and from the candle that was held in the dead man's hand; also it seemed to me, and (as I have heard) to Mistress Rosamund, that in the shade of the Appearance there was a green glowing light as of eyes that turned this way and that. In the stillness that fell I could hear the clapping of the little flames leaping in the brazier, and far out on the marshes, the whisper of the tide, mingled with the strange sucking noise that I had heard before. Lastly, the Signora spake in a tongue that I knew not, pointing to the window, and the Appearance moved somewhat the way she pointed, but, as it were, unwilling; and when she would speak again, and stretched out her arm beyond the ring where she stood, the shadow grew higher, and a long strand of hair lashed back like a whip, so close to me that I felt the wind of it on my cheek, and it was burning; yet did the Signora draw back in time, and the Appearance flickered halfway to the window and then back, as I have seen a wild beast that the tamer would have to do some leap or trick. It was of the bigness of a mastiff dog, but I saw not how it was shapen, nor what limbs it had, other than the hand that bore the candle. Only I could note that as it moved to and fro it ever shunned the rings of the pentacles wherein it stood, even as a cat picking her way daintily among pools of water. Also the dread that I had of this Appearance was somewhat lessened, for that it moved sullenly and as in fear.

Yet was this stillness but for a moment's space, for the Signora signed to the wench that stood tranced, and by some art would make her speak the incantation that was (or so it seemed to me) to compel the evil thing to do her bidding. Now when the girl spake certain strange unknown words, the Appearance passed toward the window, and again hung there; till at the last the Italian woman beckoned to the girl, that took up a little rod or wand that I had not noted, and pointed toward the window, and so made after the thing as if to drive it forth. But of that which followed I cannot speak but confusedly, for it seems like the ill dream of a fever, or the vision of a madness. Yet it was to me as though when the maid came from the ring on the floor and approached the Appearance, that it swelled to a huge bigness and blackness, hiding the window, and so flapped and roared like a great sail torn loose in a tempest, and wrapped itself round the wench, that screamed but once and so fell, and all we stood struck still with fear. Only Mistress Rosamund, that till now had turned away from the evil thing, hearing the girl cry, leapt from her place with no fear for herself, and ran to the window, where in the green flicker was a writhing blackness. And I, though I feared greatly, made in to help her, seeking to draw my sword; yet as I felt for the hilt, my hand struck on the Bible in my pocket, and I caught it out as a fitter weapon than steel against the power of Satan. Even as I ran forward, could I see the blackness and the appearance of hair shrink and dwindle, and draw back before Mistress Rosamund, till I could mark the wench lying senseless; but at the window it grew great again and hung over the enemy that did not fear it, being secure in her own purity. But I, that feared for her as she could not for herself, cried out on the name of God, and moved by some spirit that I knew not, flung the book at the blackness and the green glare that had the likeness of eyes; and with a flash of fire and a great noise, whether in mine own eyes and ears only or in very deed, I know not, the brazier was hurled over, so that we were in darkness; and when the Signora found flint and steel and lit the candles, was there nothing but the girl Bessie lying on the floor, and the hand of the dead by itself, and my little Bible. But when we went to take up the wench, she was dead, and her face strangely blackened; also on her throat were marks as though she had been strangled with fine cords. At which Mistress Rosamund fell a-weeping, and the Earl, my cousin, was moved; but the Italian woman broke out into a passion of scorn, with many ill words in the Italian that none noted but I, on the village slut that had lost her own life and the lives of all by her folly. Nor did I know then what she meant; but I have read since in old books of magic, that none can defy the malice of the powers of evil save those that are pure, as is set forth in the stories of the saintly virgins that were beset in vain by dragons and devils; and of a surety there was such a strength of innocence in Mistress Rosamund. Of all this I then thought nothing, but bade the Signora leave her foul speaking of one that she had done to death with her sorcery; and her passion being somewhat abated, she left raving, and stood sullen for a space. Then, as she marked Mistress Rosamund rise from kneeling beside the body of the girl Bessie, she went to her and caught her by the sleeve eagerly.

"Signorina Rosamunda!" she called to her. "Will you not help us in our need, and save yourself from the doom that is upon us? The spirits fear you, and you only, of our company. I will teach you the word of power, and perchance it will avail, for I have seen none that had so high a courage as yourself."

Mistress Rosamund answered not at the first, but gathered my Bible from the floor, and held it to her bosom ere she spake. "I have lent myself too much to your evil arts in being here," she said, gravely; "and the guilt of this maid's blood lies partly on my soul. If I could save the lives of you all by giving mine own life, without sin, freely would I do it. But I will have no more dealings with the enemy of man. Let me fall into the judgments of God, though they be terrible, and let me not lose my soul to gain a few days of earthly life." With that she opened the door and left us looking one on another.

The Italian smote her hands together in anger, and turned to my cousin, that had stood the while without word or motion. "*Filippo mio!*" she cried; "will you suffer us to perish for the pride of this cold girl? You are master here; give command and I will make her say the word of power, if I scourge her to the bones!"

At this I laid my hand on my hilt; and assuredly if the Earl had spoken to do the Signora's bidding, he should have uttered no word more on earth. Yet need I not have feared for him, for in all his desperate wickedness was some spark of honour, and yet more of pride in his house; and now he lifted his hand and spake more nobly than I had yet heard.

"Surely," he said, with a heavy scorn in his utterance, "the world is turned upside down indeed when a quacksalver's daughter of the scum of Italy shall talk of scourging a kinswoman of mine own and my dead lady's. Go!" — and here he gave her a foul name in the Italian, that I will not set down — "and take thy carrion with thee, ere I send thee to join thy devils in hell!"

But at this she fell down before him, clasping his knees and crying out for pardon, in that it was but her great love for him and concern for his safety that had made her so desperate; and his mood lasting not, as was his wont, presently they were friends again.

But when we came to lift the body of the wench, it was already blackened and corrupted, so that we cared not to handle it; yet need urging us, the Earl and I made shift to thrust it through the window, the tide being at the full and the current strong. For a while the body floated on the dark water, till there came a breath of the slimy smell that I knew, and a sound of sucking and a whirl in the waters, and no sign more of the dead. So we went forth; but first the Signora cast out from the window the man's hand, that was charred like a coal, and the brazen altar and her other matters of sorcery. "I have done with curious arts for ever," says she; "yet have I mine own self left!"

CHAPTER X

Of my Sword-play with the Earl, and of the Night After

Surely is there sooth in the old proverb that tomorrow is another day, and wisdom in the way of old men that will forbear to judge of a matter till they have slept on it; for the new dawn often brings new heart to endure, and a few brief hours of sleep avail to carry away the darkness of the soul and mind.

On the morrow of that ugly night of death and devilry was the morning fair again, and clearer than the wont of autumn; and to me, looking from my window at the growing dawn, came the thought that perchance, if the putting off of clothes and lying down to slumber can wipe our hearts clean of so much ill and sorrow, the doffing of our worn and tattered flesh, and the falling asleep that is called death, may lead to an awakening to a new day clearer than the last, yet not unlike, rather than to a glory or a torment too great for our little deeds. Nor have I ceased to comfort myself with this thought, though I have found no divine of any church to hold it other than heresy; so that I have kept my fancy for myself and for one other that will never account me heretic.

When I turned my eyes from the morning to the court of the castle, I could gather that somewhat new was afoot. The troopers were gathered in knots, talking eagerly, some laughing and some sullen, though all cursing; for in the King's army oaths were as many as texts among the Ironsides, yet rather from the fashion of the time than from wickedness in the one host or godliness in the other. One or two of the men were on the rampart, peering eagerly under crooked palms to landward; and as I still looked, came my cousin the Earl with a perspective glass in his hand, and all made way for him to go up and behold what might be toward.

Therefore I clad myself in haste, and went down into the court; and my Lord, turning from the land, saw me and called:

"Hither, cousin, and see where your friends come!"

Now when I was on the platform by his side, I looked landward, as I had marked him spying, but nothing was to be seen save the marshes; so I asked where these friends of mine might be.

"Why, up in the hills, as far as thou canst see," says he, laughing. "Hast left thine eyes in thy books, man?"

I strained my sight on the hills, as he bade me, but vainly; and I was about to ask him the answer to his riddle, when I spied a little feather of smoke over the edge of the furthest hill, and told him.

"Aye, that is they," said the Earl. "They have lit their fires for breakfast, and a plenteous one, I warrant them. Many is the time I have seen that smoke over the hills in Bohemia, and known that Piccolomini or Gallas was on the road to fight us."

"Then you think that yonder smoke is made by soldiers?" said I.

"Think? Nay, I know," he answered. "I give them for a troop of horse, with Noll Cromwell's orders to knock all on the head that will not take quarter, and hang all that surrender."

Here one touched him on the shoulder, and he saw the Signora.

"Ah, I forgot La Fiammetta," he went on. "For her no steel or hemp will serve, but another puff of yonder smoke."

She smiled on him with no kindness, and her eyes grew narrow. "Are the Parliament soldiers come then?" she asked of me.

"We can see the smoke of fires in the hills," I answered; "and it is most likely that they are made by soldiers of the Parliament. They should be at Marsham by noon."

"And at Deeping Hold by Doomsday," quoth the Earl laughing. "I am sorry that I beat in the boats, for I would love to fight with somewhat in the likeness of a man. Now I see not how they are to come at us."

The Italian woman shook her head in impatience. "What need for them to do aught?" said she. "What need for us to care whether they come or go?"

"Why," says my cousin, "surely you should not ask that when you have followed our camp over half Germany and all England." And with that he turned to the troopers, who were looking up at him. "Men," he goes on, raising his voice that all might hear, "these are the Roundheads come to make an end of us, if they can. Here is no flight, nor hope of escape save in fighting. If they promise you life, they will keep their word with a halter. Look to your arms, then, and if we must sleep in hell, let them go first to find us warm quarters."

He ended, and they gave a great shout and went to furbish their weapons and armour, and the Earl to gaze landward again; but by now was there no smoke to see, the Parliament men being on the march again; so he came down into the court, where were none but the Signora and myself. Now she had not said word again after he put her off, save that while he spake to the troopers methought I heard her mutter "*E matto!*" under her breath. But now she was all smiles, and taking him by the arm, "Well, *Filippo mio*," says she, "if you must needs fight the Roundheads, it behoves you to be apt with your weapon. Will you not have another lesson from Signor Uberto?"

Now these words of hers, perchance so meant, jarred on my cousin's temper, as reminding him that I was the better at sword-play; but he laughed harshly, and bade Pompey bring the foils and other matters, adding that a bout of fence would serve to pass the time, though of little use for battle. "For," says he, "your Roundheads are no nice duellists, cousin, and they will have my head cloven while I am studying in what eyelet-hole to pink them."

With that Pompey brought us the foils, and I took one and did off my coat; but when the Earl would have done the like, the Signora came before him, and catching up his foil, fell on guard prettily, saying, "Nay, Filippo, let me have the first bout, for I would fain see if I can handle so long a needle" — and he laughed and bade her go on.

So for a little we were at thrust and parry, and I wondered not a little at her skill thereat; for she seemed to know all the tricks that my Italian master had taught me, and more, and once or twice had well-nigh mastered me, so that I was fain to keep off a thrust rather by strength than art. Yet did she soon tire, or seem to tire; her play grew slower and less artful, till at the last, fetching a lunge at me, her foot slipped and she well-nigh fell forward, and her foil, catching between two stones, snapped short. Thereat she threw down the hilt, laughing at her own discomfiture, and would have the Earl take her place, and he, being nowise loth to show her that he could do better, called for another foil, but Pompey, stammering with fear, told him that none remained unbroken. At that I was fain to give over, but the Italian would not have it so, and would have my cousin take his rapier to my foil; "For so," says she, "Signor Uberto will not hurt you, Filippo, and I am sure you cannot hurt him."

At that the Earl's brows drew together, and I, fearing lest his rage should take him, made haste to decline so strange a match, for that I was unwilling to set my skin on the hazard of such a bout; and indeed, though I had little fear that the Earl could hurt me by his fence, I feared the chances of the game, wherein I had known men hurt grievously even by the breaking of foils. But the Earl's blood being heated, nothing would content him but a bout with the bare swords; and when the Signora spake against it, he snatched up the unbroken foil (for I had cast it down) and brake it across his knee, and so drew his rapier, and bade me do the same or be called coward. So, as there seemed no way out of it, I drew out my sword and fell on guard, with a great resolution that I would not hurt my cousin, and still less would let him hurt me.

So we fell to at this dangerous play, and at the first the Earl was wary, and I for my part did rather make a show of fighting than fight; for when I thrust, I ever drew back ere I could have hit him, and gave him time to guard; and so did he also at the first. But as he warmed to the work, moved by his temper, and by a mocking word or two of the woman's, his fence grew to be more than play, though still less than cruel earnest, and I had much ado to escape a scratch or worse. So that I cautioned him between thrusts, saying that we should do well to cease, or one or both might take hurt; and perchance he had listened, had not the Signora laughed at my words. At that he came at me the more madly, till I had need of all my skill to keep him off, and of all my patience to refrain from hurting him.

He was swordsman enough to know that I spared him, and grew the more furious, laying himself open as he thrust, and taunting me with my forbearance, till I was angered out of patience, and after my next parry thrust swifter and touched him on the arm, so that a spot of red showed on the sleeve of his shirt. With that the Signora laughed again, and he, either at the smart of the scratch (for it was no more) or at her laughter, was as one possessed of a devil, and made at me so that I was sore put to it not to slay him or be slain, till his breath was spent, and he stood panting and grinding his teeth. This rest I took first to get my own breath, and then to crave his pardon for hurting him, thinking to call him back to the manner of our fight at the beginning. "For surely, Cousin Philip," said I; "I am sorry that I hit you, and you will believe that it was but by chance and not with my will."

"And wherefore not?" he cried out. "Why should you not thrust home, if you can, and end all? You have your Roundhead friends to please, and I know not what devils beside, and Mistress Rosamund with her white face, and the canting knave Pentry to avenge. I am one against you all, and I bid you do your worst. Make this a duello to the death, if you will, and be damned for it!"

Now as he spake, panting between his words, and leaning on the wall, and I waited for him, the thought came swiftly on me that here was a man doomed and desperate and desirous of death; a man for whom no mercy would be asked or given from heaven or earth or hell, a man outlawed by God and men and devils. He was past saving; what mattered whether I or another should end him? Whether one of Cromwell's troopers, or a traitor of his own men, or a monster of the great deep, mattered little; his slayer was but an instrument in God's hand, as my sword was in mine, and they that strove to help him would be but partakers in his doom.

So thinking, I made ready to meet him as he took up his weapon and came towards me, his eyes shining with hate and madness; and so sure was I of the secret thrust that I had kept from showing him, that I marked the very fold of his shirt over his breast where I should thrust him through after a pass or twain. And surely (since the best of us have the leaven of Cain in our hearts) I had taken him at his word, had not the Italian woman that watched us, smiling, looked but once into mine eyes, and pointed her forefinger at the Earl, saying, "Guard yourself, Signor Uberto!" The words were harmless, yet there was that in her voice that said "Kill him!" and the pointing of her finger called back to me the ill dream wherein I had done in sick fancy the deed that now I would do in truth, and I remembered how in a vision I had thrust my cousin through the heart, and his blood became a nest of red snakes to coil around me. On the instant was my mind fixed, that I would do no evil that good might come; my sword, that was to guard mine own life or quell the public enemy, should be no dagger for the plots of this devil's daughter. Therefore, as my cousin got his breath and came at me again, I dropped my rapier on the stones and so stood, saying, "Cousin, I am to blame that I hurt thee; and I will not hurt thee further. Thou and I are the last of the house of Deeping; I will not slay thee, and if thou slayest me thou shalt slay a man unarmed."

For a flash methought that he would thrust me through as I stood, and a horror came over me as he drew back his hand; yet did he but offer his point at my breast, and so stood wavering, for his frenzy was yet strong upon him. Nor do I know what would have befallen us, had not the Swede Gulston come hastily upon us, saying that the Parliament men were to be seen riding over the hills to Marsham. After he had said this the second time, my cousin, as one awaking from an evil dream, ran his hand over his eyes once or twice and fell shuddering; then, with no word to us, he went on up the ramparts, catching up his coat and scabbard as he went, and left the Swede staring at us. To whom I excused myself as best I could, saying that we had been trying tricks of fence with the bare rapier, as our foils were broken, and that having by mischance hurt the Earl, I had ended the bout. With that I also took my scabbard and my coat and went to my chamber, leaving Gulston, that was apt enough at stratagems of war, but in other matters of small quickness of apprehension, yet perplexed. And perchance better had it been for him that I had remained to enlighten him further; but I was weary and spent with labour of body and mind, and thirsted to be alone. Nor did I think aught of it when from the turret stair I glanced in the court and saw the Swede deep in talk with the Signora; I but hastened the more to be out of sight and sound of her, nor rested till I sat on my bed and felt the wind blowing chill at my window, with now and then the sick savour of the Hole.

I stayed thus till the bell rang to call us to dinner, and so to the hall; nor was there aught to mark the rest of the day, save that the Signora was more pleasant and courteous than her wont, and the Swede more sullen and silent. Mistress Rosamund I saw not till supper-time, fain as I was to have speech with her; yet as we rose from table at nightfall, and my cousin gave us brief goodnight and passed to his rooms, I made shift to whisper to Mistress Fanshawe that I would walk in the court when the guard had been changed. Nor was there aught else to note, save that with the darkness and the rising of the tide the smell of the Hole increased, till it had been grievous to us, had we not become accustomed to the savour. For the troopers, the coming of their enemies to Marsham had driven their late terrors clean from their minds, that were too narrow to hold more thoughts than one; or if some of them had not forgotten their fear, they made haste to cast it from them, and bend their wits to a new battle with their old enemies, the Roundheads. My cousin, though of a surety he must have known how vain was his care against an adversary that could not well come at him, was eager in setting a watch, and in telling off his best gunners to the culverins on the barbican. Also he was careful, as befitted a captain, to guard well the points of the wall where an escalade might be easiest. Now not far from my turret the wall was somewhat lower than elsewhere, and the shale of the marsh was heaped against the rampart in a mound, that seemed to me, idly looking upon it that day, to be higher than I had seen it aforetime. On this spur of the wall was a little guard-house of stone, with a narrow loop-hole bearing on the marsh, and here were set two sentries to fire on any seeking to climb the wall.

So soon as the watch had gone their rounds, and new sentries were set, I went quietly down the stair of my tower, nor was it long before Mistress Rosamund came from the door of the keep. The night was still and chilly, and the mist had risen from the marshes. No sound was there but the lapping of the tide, and the clanking steps of the sentinels, till presently I seemed to hear the sucking noise that I had noted before, but faint; and the two men in the little guard-house striking up a rough soldier's song, I noted other sounds no more.

While we walked in the mist, then, I told Mistress Rosamund what had been that morning, but doubtfully; for I could not be fixed in my mind whether she would not think I had been weak in sparing my cousin, when one thrust had gone far to save us all from siege and famine, or I knew not what other worse doom. Yet might I have spared my fears; for when I had told her all, but haltingly, she stood and looked on me for a space, and then said earnestly, "You have done well, cousin, and better than I should have done in your place" — the which when I could in no wise allow, she went on, "He hath deserved death many times, it may be, yet could you not be his hangman, even to save us all."

"Had I thought more of your danger," I said, for I would not have her hold me better than I was, "I might have slain my cousin. I fear it was but pride and kinship that kept me from revenging the innocent, and I am little less ashamed of forbearing him than I had been of killing him."

"Well," says she, with a catch in her throat that was between a laugh and a sob, "be ashamed of yourself if you will, cousin, but I will be proud of you for both of us."

At this I was gladder than I had thought to be of aught that I might hear, and caught her hand, that was cold in the wet mist, and had kissed it, but that a puff of wind came in our faces, and she cried out softly and drew back, snatching her hand from me, and yet, as I think, not meaning it; for the wind was filled with the deadly savour of the slime, that made her faint, and I myself was near to stifle with it. Also the men in the little room on the wall must have smelt the like, for I heard one cry out on his fellow, "Reach me the jack, Tom, else I shall poison with this cursed stink" — and so he drank noisily and cleared his throat with a great hem, and struck up his song again:

> 'We'll hang up Noll with his crop-eared poll,
> And the hounds of his canting pack;
> By one, two, and three, they shall dance on the tree,
> When we bring our good King back —
> With a hey derry down—'

And the other chimed in with the burden that neither of them was to end in this world; for while they sang, I had marked the sucking noise that I had heard aforetime, growing louder, till it was as the wash of a whirlpool, and looking to the wall, where was a battlement hard by the guard-room, I could see no more the white glimmer of the mist through the break in the coping-stones, but all was black and humped in a mound that grew higher, and with that one of the men brake off his singing and gave a great shout of fear, and the other, as it seemed, sang on for a note or twain, and changed suddenly to a horrid strangling cry, mingled with a grating and cracking as of rock crushed in a miner's mill. A moment I stood tranced with the horror of these noises, and then my manhood came again, and putting aside Mistress Rosamund that would have held me back, I whipped out my sword and made up to the rampart, and as I went, came some of the soldiers running from their quarters, and Gulston doing on his buff coat as he ran, with a dagger between his teeth. But ere I could be at the door of the room, had all cries ended, and only a mumbling voice and the sound of laughter, that daunted me the more; yet I made haste to open the door of the guard-room, where the torch the two men had with them burned yet on the wall.

Well nigh had I fallen as I entered, for the floor was reeking with slime; but naught else was there to see, save one of the men leant against the corner of the wall and laughing softly to himself, as one demented, and then muttering somewhat. Of the other man was no sign save his musket and pike on the stone floor, and the loophole in the wall was scored and jagged at the edges, and dripped with slime. So I stood and stared at the fellow, that gazed on me and laughed and mumbled, twisting his fingers together like a little child; and after me came in the others, yet hanging back, and huddling in the doorway, with wild eyes rolling in the red flicker of the torch. Only the Swede thrust the others aside and took the man by the shoulder, shaking him and bidding him tell where was his fellow.

But he went on twisting his fingers and laughing to himself, and then between his chuckles as it were singing, "Tom's head's a rotten apple! Tom's head's a rotten apple!" — and naught else, and so laughed again. Nor would he say one word of reason, though Gulston fetched him a great blow on the cheek, that he seemed not to feel, for he left not laughing nor twisting of his hands. So we had him thence to his bed, where he lay laughing and singing of his foolishness till cock-crow, when he shuddered and so died, with no word to tell what he had seen.

CHAPTER XI

Of the Quarrel of the Earl and the Swede, and its Ending

As we bare the crazed man to his quarters, came the Earl from his door, with a furred nightgown cast around him, and his naked sword in his hand; and when he heard what I could tell him, he went up to the little guard-room, and thence on the rampart, and I with him; but nought was to see save that which I had seen already, and the slime on the battlements, and the white mist hanging over the black waters, and a silence of death. What my cousin thought I knew not, nor belike did he, for his face was desperate, and he stood by the wall a long time, till he stretched out both arms to the sea, crying out as to some enemy, "Take me then, if you will!" but there was none that answered, and no sound save the washing of the ebbing tide on the rock. So he turned to me sighing as one wearied beyond endurance, and spake strangely.

"Cousin," says he, "why didst not thou thrust home this morning? Thou wast at point to do it, and all had been better for thee and no worse for me."

I scarce knew how to answer him, for I would not speak of the Italian woman, partly that I was loth to accuse any without strong proof, but rather that I knew her power over him, and feared that she might move him to fasten a worse quarrel on me. So I did but say that I had grown heated with the play, and done foolishly in hurting him; yet had I come to my senses ere worse befell, and craved his forgiveness. "For," said I, "it is written, 'Let not the sun go down upon your wrath'; and though it be too late for us to say this, yet let not the sun rise on anger between us twain."

"Thou art ever a Puritan," he answered me, laughing with no mirth, yet not unkindly; "but thou art better than Noll's saints yonder by Marsham, that will knock a man unarmed on the head to the glory of God. If God take pleasure in such villains, let me serve the devil still."

I answered him that I for one could not hold that the Lord had delight in the violence of men, though oft-times He might work out His purpose by such tools; and thinking that in this mood I might perchance move him to repentance (his evil genius also being away from his elbow), I said further that it behoved us rather to doubt our own ways than the goodness of God, and that when we had amended ourselves even a little, we should see clearer into His will. "Even," said I, "as we see the stars now, that have been shining all the while, though we marked them not for the mist." For indeed, while I spake, came a shift of wind from the sea, and the mist rolled away from the marsh, and the night was fair and quiet, with the little sparkles of the stars dancing on the ripples.

Methought I had moved him, but he showed no sign, but turning away from that fair night, "Well," says he, "the tide is ebbing fast, and none can come within a mile of us unseen. So to bed, cousin!" And so he strode off, bidding the sentries in the towers keep good watch; for none would come near the guard-house, that yet reeked of that charnel smell.

So when I had paced the court once or twice, and heard nothing but the call of the watch, and when I came by the troopers' quarters, the babbling of the crazed man (for he died not till dawn, as I have said), I must even betake myself to my chamber with a heavy heart; for I had supped full of horrors, as the play hath it, and but for the thought of Mistress Rosamund (that was with me oft-times now) I had gone near to think the earth a foul and friendless place, and to love life hardly more than did my cousin.

Yet on the morrow, when after a brief and troubled slumber, I awoke to find my window a blank of mist. I remembered rather the fear that hung over us than the hope of converse with another that lay under a like peril with all of us; for though there was at that time no ill savour in the mist, it seemed the cover for I knew not what enemy to come upon us. Yet because there was naught else for me to do, I came down and walked in the court after my wont, and marked naught save the passing shadows of the men; and stopping one of them I asked of the madman, and was told he was dead, and it seemed a little matter to me. So I walked, till the mist lightened somewhat, and I was aware of the Earl coming to me.

"What say you, Cousin Hubert?" says he. "Shall we have our bout again?" To which I made answer that we had no foils left, else was I willing.

"Why," says he, smiling, "let us take our rapiers, but sheathed, cousin; for I would but kill time today."

So, as I had naught against his wish, I bound my sword sheath to the hilt that it should not fall off, and he doing the like, we were at fence for a space, but idly; and thinking to please him, and also to take away the temptation that had gone near to make me a murderer, I asked to show him a new device of sword play, and he being ready, I taught him the trick of the thrust that I had been minded to use on him, and the ward for it; and as he was apt at arms and quick of sight, it was not long ere he learned it nigh as well as myself, and could tell how to prepare for it with a cunning feint that led another, if he knew not its meaning, to bear his hand too low and lay himself open.

Now while I showed him, was the mist still hanging around us, so that none could see what we did; but now the wind freshened, and the vapours thinning, the court was plain in a pale sunlight, and the Signora looking on us from the doorway, and Gulston standing by her. So I ceased, and gave them good morning, and the woman nodded her head, and the Swede came lounging to us, with a swaggering manner that methought sat but ill on him.

"So you will take your lesson with the sheathed swords today, my Lord?" he said, grinning in his yellow beard. "It is right prudent of you."

Now at this my cousin lifted his brows and pressed his lips together; for the man's words were naught, but there was an insolence in his voice, that made me marvel. Yet I wondered more at the coolness with which the Earl took it.

"Why, surely," answered he, smiling at the Swede. "Even I am not a fool two days together," and with that he unbound the handkerchief from his hilt, and put his sword at his side, and I was about to do the same when Gulston stopped me.

"Will you not spare me a crumb of your learning?" he said, smiling with a show of a soldier's frankness. "We could not well see you for this cursed mist, but you seemed to be teaching my Lord a pretty trick of fence. Could you not of your bounty show me it again?" As he spake, he looked askance at the Signora, that glanced back at him; and I stood perplexed, thinking that there lay some purpose behind this request, and looking at my cousin for guidance. But he laughed and answered me, "Aye, show him, Hubert, show him!" and so leaned on the steps and watched us.

Now I could no longer delay, though my mind misgave me that here was some fine plot of the Italian's. So I showed Gulston the thrust I had been taught, and he seemed apter at learning than my cousin, as even the Earl owned. " 'Swounds, Eric!" he cried; "you are a better fencer than I thought you. I could not master these Italian tricks in a week of learning. I am but a blunt Englishman, as Madonna here will certify. To it again, Gulston!" And at his word the Swede lunged so aptly with his sheathed rapier that I was over late in my ward, and took a sharp touch on the breast, and the Earl and the Signora clapped their hands. Then I ceased, telling Gulston that I would teach him no more, and feigning a hurt to my vanity; also I was purposed in my mind that I would in no wise show him the parry of the thrust, though I knew not what harm might be therein.

So when my cousin had broken a jest or two on me for my defeat, and the Signora had done the like, but more subtly, and I had answered as best I could (for indeed my wit was never nimble), we stood talking of this and that, till a trooper came from the men's quarters asking what should be done with the man that had been crazed overnight and was now dead.

"Why," says the Earl, "Gulston, you will take a burial party in one of the boats, and see that the poor fellow has his rights. Pick me a pair of men, and see it is done ere dinner time."

At that the Swede's face turned red under the burn of sun and wind, and he pulled at his moustachios, as was his way, and stood a while before he gave answer. So my Lord spake more sharply again. "You understand?" says he. "This is no strange thing for soldiers to do in the wars."

"Aye, but it is a strange thing here," answers the Swede, getting his speech at last. "For Mr. Leyton here can bear me out that when we buried the men that were slain at Marsham we were like to be swallowed of a quicksand, or what else I know not, but perchance you may. So I sware, and he heard me, that I would go on no more buryings."

Now I looked for my cousin to break out into one of his rages; for here was not only flat disobedience, but the manner of the Swede's speech was worse than its matter. Yet if the Earl was possessed of devils, as he seemed full often, this was the cold devil's day, or his pride, which was great, would not let him show that he was moved.

"Well," says he to the troopers that stood by (for a few more had come forth while he spake); "if your cornet cares not for catching of a cold, will you bury your comrade, and you, and you—" and he called some of them by name. But they all hung back, divided between their fear of the Earl and their greater fear of the peril on the marshes; nor could I blame them when I remembered what I had seen.

"Nay then," said my cousin; "I will never send another on an errand that I fear to go myself. Cousin, will you come?"

Now the Italian had stood silent while Gulston had bearded his officer, and had but glanced up from narrow eyes; but now she brake in, counselling the Earl and myself not to go forth, for that assuredly there was danger to us both. Whereat, as even I could have guessed, my cousin was all the more fixed in his purpose, and I, for very shame, could not leave him to make his venture alone. So he called on the men to make the body ready for burial, and bring it to the harbour, with a pair of spades, the which they did, and laid all in the smallest of the boats, and so stood looking on us as we sat down; and the Signora and Gulston came also unbidden. But when we were at point to push off, first one and then another of the soldiers that were the Earl's own servants came into the boat with us, and took the oars from me as I settled myself to row; and the Swede, seeing this, and bethinking himself (as seemed to me) that he might be counted coward, or belike moved thereto by a look of the Signora, sware an oath and leapt in with us. "Well, sink or swim," says he, with a wry laugh, "I am with you for this bout," and the Earl, with no word to any, pushed off.

Nor did it seem that any peril would come to us in our errand; for the air was clear, and the sun shone on the marsh, whence the tide had fallen some space, and even the grey flats and stretches were less desolate than their wont. This daunted me the more, for it looked to me as though some ambush lay under the brightness of the day; yet to the men, that were rough and simple of nature, there seemed no cause for fear, and had it not been for the corpse we carried, they had even laughed after their wont.

Not a word did my cousin vouchsafe, but set our course for a wide stretch of shale that lay somewhat to the landward, smooth and grey, with no hollow where an enemy might lurk, and no channel to break the plain; only a space away was a long shadow, marking, as I thought, the course of some ditch or channel like a seam across the marsh. The Swede also sat sullen, playing with his sword hilt, but speaking no word, till we ran the boat up at the edge of the flat, and my Lord giving command, the two troopers carried their dead fellow up to a place where the ground was even and hard, and began to dig a grave; and the three of us sat and watched them labouring, shewing darkly against the sunlit marsh, that was broken only in that place by the shadow of the channel. I looked around sometimes, and listened earnestly, but no swirl in the water was there, nor yet the sucking noise that I had heard; nor did aught strange appear, till the men beckoned to us that they were ready, and my cousin nodding to me, we went up, Gulston following us, and left the boat swinging with a rope to the boathook that we had planted in the ground.

So we came to the grave that was dug for the dead man, and again I made shift to play the chaplain, and with more readiness than the former time, for the soldier that we were burying had perished in no murder or rapine, but in his plain and daily duty; also the extremity of that terror that had reft him of wit and life might be counted by some a fearful retribution for what sins his had been. So I prayed, and my cousin and his men stood with their hats off and waited, and the Swede covered, and aloof from us, till I had done, and the two men filled in the sand and earth above the body; and still the sun was clear and the air calm and still, and no sign of life stirring on the marshes, that were pale in the sunlight, save for the dark streaks of the channels, and chief of these the long shadow that I had noted before to landward, and methought (but I put the fancy aside as idle) that it was somewhat nearer than I remembered.

All being now decently done, I looked for my cousin to bid us go, and the men shouldered their spades ready; but the Earl stopped them. "Nay, leave them as yet," he says; "Maybe you shall need them anon." And while the men stared on him open-mouthed, and I wondered what this might mean (for he spake quietly, as one that had a purpose), he went up to the Swede, that stood sullen a few paces off, and tapping him on the shoulder — "A word with you, Eric Guldenstierna," says he; "have you forgotten that you dared to disobey the order of your officer but now? What is that but mutiny?" And with that he whipped a pistol from under his cloak. Gulston started, and laid a hand on his hilt; but my Lord saying, "Draw and you die," he took his hand away and so stood.

"Had you been Noll Cromwell's man and not mine," said my cousin; "you had been pistolled in the castle court, on your first word of mutiny. But we of the King's side, as our cause is the less holy, are less apt at slaying men defenceless. Nor would I risk bespattering a gentle lady like the Signora with your brains, though she has seen worse things perchance. But one of us two goes not back to Deeping Hold."

"And what will your Lordship do, then?" asked the Swede, sneering. "Will you have your worshipful cousin and your two men to dispose of me, and save yourself the slaughterer's work?"

"Why, no!" answered the Earl carelessly. "You shall have your fair chance, little as you merit it; our swords are of a length, and Hubert here shall see fair play, and be priest to the one that dies and ferryman to the other. How sayest thou, cousin?"

But to this I would in no wise consent, for that I held the duello as little better than murder at any time, and most of all when we were in deadly peril, and should hold together for defence rather than turn our hands against one another. Somewhat of this I said; yet could I not move my cousin.

"Thou art no coward for a scholar," says he; "but thou hast little knowledge of wars, else thou hadst known that in peril mercy to a mutineer is death to true men. Either I give the dog a chance for his life, or I shoot him down as he stands. Choose thou which it shall be."

"I will have no part nor lot in the matter," said I. "With my will shalt thou neither slay nor be slain."

"Why then, stand and look on and keep thy conscience warm," answered my cousin; "and if he win, let him go free of vengeance. Come, sir, shall we walk?" and as the other nodded without word, the Earl laid down his pistol and did off his cloak and coat, and left them by the boat with his scabbard, and Gulston did the like. Then each with his rapier under his arm, they went back to the place where we had buried the man. "This place will suit as well as any," I heard my cousin say, as they came on a bare stretch of the sands beyond the mound that marked the grave. Gulston answered not but by deed. He took his sword in hand, saluted and fell on guard, and the blades clinked together.

Now I had not followed them, nor had the two men, for I would have no share in this quarrel, and the soldiers dared not move without a word from their head. So we stood by the boat, on the shelving bank, and looked at the two that were, it might be, an hundred paces from us, and showed dark against the pale marshland, and beyond them was the dark riband of the channel I had noted, that seemed to have water left there, for the sunlight flickered on a wetness in it here and there. But in a minute or twain I had no eyes for aught but the two that were fighting to the death.

Yet at the first it seemed no more deadly a game than our bouts in the castle court, for that both were wary; and the clinking and grating of the steel as they thrust and parried was like the beat of some strange great clock. The Swede was careful, as I had known him; and my cousin was no whit behind him for coolness. So even a match it seemed that when they ceased and took breath, I had hope that the quarrel might end without blood. When they were breathed, they fell to again, and now grew fiercer, till I heard Gulston vent an oath, and guessed that the Earl had touched him; but he fought on none the less stoutly, and I looked for this duello to last yet a good while, and withdrew mine eyes from the flash of the swords for a moment, resting them on the shadow of the channel, that was grown somewhat wider, so that methought the tide must be flowing. Then, as I looked on the two again, suddenly came the end. I saw Gulston giving back a little, and the other pressing him, and they wheeled so that the Swede turned his back on us; then I marked his blade sweep round swiftly, and he lunged forward in the thrust I had taught him but that morning. I shut mine eyes for a flash, for I deemed my cousin but dead; but when I looked, he stood black against the grey marsh, and Gulston reeled, clutching at his side, and fell, and so lay, and his slayer looked on him for a space, and then came to us slowly, with his sword stained to the hilt.

Truly, if one had to die, I would not that the fight had gone otherwise; yet it sickened me to think that the life of a man could be so ill used, and so lightly lost, and I could say no word to the Earl as he began to do on his coat. Then as he wiped his sword and sheathed it, "So, cousin," says he, "thou art sad that the dog has died a man's death. Yet what does it matter if he has gone first, or I? Hadst thou taught him the answer as well as the thrust, he had been standing here now in my stead. Well, I would I may end no worse than Gulston. Let us go now and do him what honour we may."

So the men bent down for their spades, and we turned again to the place where the grave had been made, and the Swede had fallen a few paces beyond. But when I looked for the mound and the body, naught could I see but the grey space of the marsh, and no sign that man had been there alive or dead. Then methought that I had turned to another quarter, and I cast my eyes over the plain of grey, but still was there naught save a glistering of the ground, and colours as of a rainbow, as I have seen them on a puddle of slime in the sun. Also the channel beyond, or what I had held to be such, was gone utterly like a smear of chalk wiped from a slate; and a little wind blew to us over the marsh, and the breath of it was salt and foul.

At that a great fear fell on me, and I clutched my cousin by the arm, crying out to make homeward; so he caught up a cloak from the ground, and muffled himself in it, and so came to the boat, and we were with him as soon. The men rowed fiercely, though sight and sound of danger was there none; so in no long time were we at the quay, and all the while my cousin sat with his hat pulled over his eyes and the cloak drawn close round him, and shivered once or twice, as if from cold. And looking at him (for there was naught else to do) I marked that he had taken the Swede's cloak for his own as they lay together.

Now as we drew near the harbour, it seemed to me that I saw a woman on the barbican gazing on us; yet as I looked was she gone, and none but the sentinels to meet us till we came to the court. There stood more of the men, that asked no question of their two fellows, but drew apart from them. At the door of the hall was Mistress Rosamund, and her eyes lightened on me, and her lips moved without sound. Then came the Italian forth, and Pompey bearing a flagon and goblet, and she looked on my Lord that was yet muffled in Gulston's cloak, and his hat pulled over his eyes; and the twain being of a like height and bigness, he seemed the counterpart of the man he had slain. The Signora spake no word, but filled the goblet with wine, and stood waiting and smiling strangely, till the Earl came nearer to her, and threw back the cloak. "Well, Fiammetta," says he, "thou art not rid of me yet."

Now when he spake thus, her face changed and was convulsed, and she cried out sharply and threw out her arms, marking not the goblet, that flew from her hand and shattered on the stones, and the red wine oozed in the chinks like blood. Also she reeled as though in a swoon, and called on Pompey to hold her; and he stretching out his hands to her, the flagon went to join the goblet. Yet did she recover herself and cast her arms about the Earl, laughing and sobbing as one distraught, and so remained till he shook her off and went in heavily, and the rest of us to our quarters.

Yet must we meet again at dinner presently, and make a show of eating, and speak words that none noted; and the Swede's chair was empty, but Fear sat at the board in his stead.

CHAPTER XII

Of the Pool that Crawled

Of that which we spake at dinner-time, as I have said, I have no remembrance, nor did any say much; also, though I held my cousin's cause to be the better in his late quarrel, and would not have had the fight go otherwise, if fight there must be, I had more sorrow for the death of the Swede than I had thought to feel for a mere sworder. We were a little company, beset with many dangers known and unknown, and prisoned on our rock, that was like to prove but a sandy refuge; and sudden or lingering, the end of the leaguer seemed sure. Also from some words that passed between the Earl and one of the men that served us, I gathered that our store of victual was dwindling, nor was I surprised thereat, for it had been as wastefully spent as it had been hastily and wrongfully gathered; and indeed, I remembered that Gulston, in the days when he was yet loyal, had spoken thereof to my cousin, who (being in one of his reckless moods) would take no order, saying that the food would last our time.

Therefore, as soon as we had eaten, I rose from the table, asking leave of the others, and getting a nod from the Italian woman, and went down to the great gate, and finding it open, with a watch set at the side and men in the barbican tower above, I walked on the pier, part of masonry and part of the rock itself, that sheltered the little port, where the barges swayed on their chains with the little waves of the tide, that had risen to the full while we dined, and was now falling, leaving wet stones and shallow pools towards the sea. As I went towards the water's edge, the rocks and stones were slimy, as is the wont after an ebbing tide, so that I had nigh fallen once or twice, and turned back to the drier footing, and went not down to the spot where there lay a larger pool, near to the waves, like a sheet of lead on the grey stone and green weed.

As I came to the gate again (for the mole was but a little one) I was aware of Mistress Rosamund within the gateway, and seeing me, she came out and walked with me, whereof I was glad, for my thoughts were but ill, and it heartened me to see the one face that I knew to cover no memories of bad deeds, nor plots of worse things to come. So as we went to and fro, she asked me of that morning's happenings, and I told her of the fencing bout, and the Swede's disobedience, and the story of the fight; and ever as I told her, she would say, "And what spake the Signora?" or, "How looked the Signora at that?"

When I told her of the strange vanishing both of Gulston's body and of the grave of the other dead man, she fell a-shuddering, and gripped my arm, not knowing, as it seemed, and murmuring to herself, "And it might have been he!" and it gladdened me, though I dared not guess at her meaning.

But when I came to telling of the Earl's catching up the Swede's cloak for his own, and muffling himself in the dead man's apparel, Mistress Rosamund drew in her breath sharply and leaving my arm, smote her hands together, and "Ah!" says she, "now I see it all!" At which I was amazed, and asked of her meaning.

"Why, cousin Hubert!" she said quickly, "you a scholar and know not what this means? Did you not see, when my Lord did off the Swede's cloak and showed his face, how that woman cried out and dropped the goblet of wine, and called on Pompey to help her, that let fall the flagon, as well she knew he would? Can you not see it now? The wine was for Gulston, if the Earl had been slain, and belike for you also. Me she might have spared for a space to sacrifice to her devil, if he be not sick of a greater wickedness than his own!"

Her words affrighted me, as when I had seen the first grave we digged melt away from under our feet into a whirlpool of slime; and though her meaning was clear to me now, I would not let myself believe in such a black deep of iniquity. "Nay, nay!" I answered, too roughly, I fear; "This is surely madness! I love not the woman, nor have cause to; but anyone in her place, good or bad, would have gone nigh to swoon and cast away whatever she held, noting it not. Nay, cousin, give the devil his due!"

Mistress Rosamund turned and smiled on me, but sadly, and somewhat pitifully, as a mother on a child that speaks foolishly.

"Ah, Hubert!" she said, and neither she nor I then marked that she left off calling me 'cousin'. "Thou art no woman, else hadst thou known all this and more long ago. Where are thine eyes? Canst thou not see that behind her cat's eyes there is ever a plot, and behind that another, and behind that again a throng of stratagems, one blacker than another? I tell thee, she eats and drinks and breathes treachery, and plots in her sleep. Nay, see where she stands and murders us with her looks!"

As Mistress Rosamund spake, she waved her hand a little towards the barbican, and there indeed stood the Italian woman, with her hand on one of the culverins, that were ever trained on the mouth of the harbour, that they might be ready against an attack by boats. As I looked up at the Signora, she signed to me, as though in mockery, saying somewhat that I knew not. Then I heard heavy feet on the stone stair, and the Earl's hat and then his head and shoulders rose above the battlements, and he spake to the trooper by the culverin, and looked to his musket; for indeed the sentries were bidden to have their matches ever burning, as is the custom in a leaguered place.

I could see naught clearly of their faces, that were between us and the sky, and showed black against the white blankness; for the sea mist had come up, but thinly, with the tide, and hung in wreaths over the grey shores and leaden ebbing waters. Also I seemed to savour the smell of the Hole, but hardly noted it, for my nostrils had grown used to the odour, when hardly a day went by without some breath of it. Yet, though I marked not her face, nor the Earl's, I saw her lean towards him, and heard her speak in the Italian, what I knew not, save that I caught the word 'drudo', that signifies a lover; and it came to me that she might be speaking of Mistress Rosamund and myself, for her voice was scornful. Also Mistress Fanshawe seemed to catch that word, and having some knowledge of the Italian, knew the meaning of it; for a redness came into her face, that became her mightily, though I cared not to tell her so for fear of angering her, and she drew hastily away from me, and began walking seaward from the barbican, and I after her, divided between my desire to be near her, and a wish to give no colour to the ill supposings of the Italian; for indeed when a man and a maid walk close together in privy talk, the first fool that sees them can laugh at them for lovers.

Methought that Mistress Rosamund was (as is the way of maidens) more moved by the other's spite than myself; for when I followed her, she did but quicken her pace till she left me some ten paces behind; so, as I would not vex her by a forced companionship, I halted and let her go whither she would. But even as I stood, came a breath of wind from seaward, and with it the cold foul savour of the slime, that was ever a token of danger, and forgetting all else but the peril, I made towards her again, calling on her to turn back. As I spake, she had come nigh to that deeper pool toward the end of the mole; and turning to hear me, she slipped on the stones, that were slimy with weed, and fell with half her body in the water. Yet she seemed not to be hurt, and began to raise herself, and by then had I come to the edge of the pool, and stretched forth my hand, and she doing the like, I looked to help her up. But as I caught at her hand, it was drawn away from me, so that I clutched but the air; and looking again to know wherefore I had missed my hold, I could see a space of wet rock between my feet and the margin of the pool, though I had sworn that I stood in the very water when I reached out my hand. Yet thinking that this was but my lack of skill, I stepped further into the pool and caught at her hand, and again missed it; and looking on her I could see that she clutched on a tangle of the brown seaweed, and pulled it out from the rock; yet was she brought no nearer to me, but the contrary. Also her face, that had been flushed with the fall and the labour to rise, was now pale, and I doubt not (as indeed she told me after), that mine was yet whiter; for in one moment were we aware that this that we took for a slimy pool was slipping towards the sea and drawing her with it to destruction. As I looked, I could see the slimy jelly seething through the shallow water, and winding round her like ropes, and oozing seaward over the rocks, with foul bubbles rising on it. Not a word said Mistress Rosamund, nor could I, for my deadly fear; only I could hear the Italian woman laughing on the barbican.

Perchance her scorn saved Mistress Rosamund and me, for my frozen will awakened, and in a very madness I leapt into that living slime and caught her by the arms and so held her back for a space. More could not I do, nor can I tell how, save by the favour of the Most High, my weak arms were strengthened to hold her against the cords of the abyss. Yet somewhat may I have been helped by the rocks, that were here jagged and beset with sharp barnacles and shells, and broken into narrow winding cracks, so that the thing that we strove against was hampered to come at us; else had we both been sucked down in a twinkling. So I set my feet in a crevice of the rock and held to Mistress Rosamund, that her arms bore the marks for many a days, and I remember that she bade me let go and not die with her; and still could I hear the Signora laughing.

But now, by what sense I know not, that which was drawing us was moved to make an end speedily, and with a strange sucking sound somewhat great and grey and slimy began to rise in the mouth of the harbour, and heave itself toward us like a round wave. And I, seeing the fringe of the thing come oozing and twining up the slope of the mole, cried out in the face of death and closed mine eyes. Even with that came a mighty roar in mine ears, and a rush of wind by me, and a great rain of spray; and when I got my senses again I lay in the empty place of the pool, and Mistress Rosamund beside me, and a great cloud of blue smoke curling above us. So I got to my hands and knees and crawled a little higher; and then I made shift to stand and dash the spray from mine eyes, and could see the barbican, and a culverin smoking yet at the mouth, and my cousin standing thereby gazing under his hand, and two or three of the troopers coming from the gate doubtfully, as men in fear; nor was there sight or sound of that which had lain in ambush for us. So with no small pain we won to the gate, though the way was but little; for the men feared to come half-way to meet us, and cared not to handle us, for the slime clung yet to our garments.

When we came into the court, was my cousin standing above us on the stair to the barbican, and his eyes were shining.

"Well, cousins both," says he, "if you will needs play Pyramus and Thisbe, I counsel you to keep on the safe side of the wall. Here be no lions, but worse, mayhap." With that he gave a great laugh, and the Signora after him, like an echo, and Mistress Rosamund grew red again, and beat her foot on the ground for anger, but anon conquered her pride and went towards him.

"Cousin Philip," says she earnestly; "you shall not shame me out of thanking you for my life, that was but lost—" and she had said more, but he brake in on her, as was ever his way.

"O aye," says he; "I need no thanks, and least from thee or Hubert here," — for I was making shift to stammer somewhat of gratitude. "Nay, man, keep thy sermons till they be dry. Go and shift thyself, or I shall regret that I wasted good powder on thee."

"And you, Signorina Rosamunda," says the Signora from the stairs, "shall I send you the maid with a change of clothes? You have the air — what is the English word? So draggletail!" and she laughed again.

"Aye, Signorina Bardi," says the other. "Methinks among the soldiers I might be taken for a camp-follower from the German wars" — and with that she turned to her tower, and I to mine.

But when I had shifted to my other suit, I was fain to cast my hose and boots away, for the smell of the slime clung to them, and made my chamber like a charnel of drowned men. So I flung them from my window and watched them fall on a point of rock some yard or twain from the water's edge, for I had misjudged in my cast. Then I turned to go, but ere I was at the door, I heard a plashing in the water, and went back to the window, but naught was to be seen, only that the bundle of my matters was gone.

CHAPTER XIII

Of the Path that had no End

Now when the horror of that escape had somewhat lifted from my mind, and the savour of the Hole was gone from me, was I of a better courage than before, seeing that the thing which beset us might be but mortal, and subject to fear, if not to wound; also my cousin the Earl was merrier at supper than I had seen him, for that he had at last for once baffled the enemy that beleaguered his castle. But in the hearing of the men that served us, he passed off the whole matter as a slip of the foot on the part of Mistress Rosamund, and would have it that seeing us, as he thought, nigh to swooning with the chill of the water, he had shot off the culverin to shake us out of that stupor, wherein we might well have slidden into the sea and been drowned; and we, catching his meaning, fell into his humour, and took his jests easily, though they were rough, and such as savoured of the camp, rather than of the court.

But when supper was over, and the women had bidden us goodnight and withdrawn to their several apartments, the Earl signed to me to stay; and after the serving men had cleared the platters and gone forth, he locked the door on them, and coming back to the dais where we set, pushed aside his chair, and bade me stand and look on him. So I saw that he stooped to the floor, and taking hold of a ring that I had not before noted, drew up a trap in the boards, that came up easily on its hinges, and without sound. Then he took a candle from the sconce in the wall, and holding it aloft warily, bade me look down. At first mine eyes were dazzled, and I could note naught but darkness; but presently I could see that there was a vault beneath, hewn in the rock, and in it many casks and kegs, big and little; whereat methought that my Lord would show me his cellars of wine and liquors, and I marvelled that he should be so secret, save that perchance he feared that the garrison might mutiny to get strong drink, as hath been known in places under leaguer.

"Truly, cousin" said I, "thou art bravely provided, nor do we risk dying by thirst."

He laughed harshly, and clapped down the door again, and set the candle back in its sconce. "Nay, thou simple scholar," said he; "hadst thou been in the wars thou wouldst know that here is no Rhenish nor cordials. This is one of Noll Cromwell's powder trains, cousin, that I took coming from Naseby field, and have kept safe, all save a pair of kegs that I spent on thy friend Master Eldad to warm his house for him against his coming. If the thing that besets us has dread of powder, as by this day's work would seem, it shall have stuff to stay its stomach. There is enough here to send the canting knaves of the Parliament nearer heaven than they will ever go of themselves. I had thought to baulk Roundheads or monsters of my life, and go aloft in good company when I could no other; but now am I fain to see what my powder can do behind good iron and stone, and feed yonder fiend" (and he jerked his thumb at the windows) "with somewhat he likes less than flesh of men. What sayest, cousin? Will it serve?"

Now while he spake, had I stood in some bewilderment what to answer, for that assuredly his timely shot had scared away the monster, if monster it were, that had been dragging away Mistress Rosamund; yet could I not believe that the judgment of God could be beaten back by mere gunpowder, nor that the Earl's artillery would profit him a second time more than did Satan's engines in the story of that noble poem 'Paradise Lost', but late given to the world by Mr. John Milton. So I thanked him, as indeed was due, for his timely succour, but briefly, for he grew impatient, as though ashamed of his good deed; and then I passed to the matter of our provision, that might well (I said) fail us before the powder. "For," said I, "I have read in the story of the wars that soldiers have salted their meat with powder, but not that it would serve instead of meat; and if we can hold off our enemies, men and worse, from giving us a storm, yet if we starve shall we be none the better."

"Why, so!" says he, clapping me on the shoulder. "We shall make a captain of thee yet, Hubert. 'O this learning, what a thing it is!' as the play hath it. Surely will I take order for our victual, now that we may have time to eat it," and with that he gave me goodnight, and strode off to the men's quarters, and I to my room.

The tide, that had been half-way at ebb when we had adventured on the mole (a thing that we were not like to do again), was now more than half full, and was already lapping on the walls, in those places where they went down sheer; for the island whereon the castle stood being but small, and broken with creeks, the builder of Deeping Hold had been fain to win space by building buttresses down into the holes of the rock, that were never dry save at low tides. Now the great hall of the castle (for though it was of no marvellous bigness in itself, it was yet by far the greatest room there) had been builded out from the rock, to give it what space might be, and the outer wall of it went straight down into the water, with buttresses holding it up; and some way up the wall was an overhanging gallery, where two men might scarcely pass, or one man might walk easily. Now this passage, that led to the rampart at either end, went around the two sides of the hall at a height a little below the foot of the great windows, so that a man standing on the narrow way between the wall and the battlements might see through what panes were of clear glass into the hall itself.

As I think, this pathway was made that the garrison might go round the whole circuit of the walls and see if any foe sought to break in through the wall of the hall, where were no defences, nor could it otherwise be seen from the ramparts save by reaching out beyond the shelter of the battlements. But it was not the custom for the sentries to walk there, there being no turrets for shelter, and also (which perchance weighed more) my cousin had no will for his men to take the excuse of their duty for prying on him as he sat at meat.

As I went through the court to my lodging, musing on my cousin's words, and wondering how so small an advantage as my escape should hearten him so greatly, I was aware of a little sound in the stillness; for of the splash of the waters and the call of the sentries I had ceased to take note, nor did I hear them more than one hears the beat of a clock, so are a man's senses dulled by some few days' use. This new sound was hardly louder than the lapping of the waters, but it was other, being a slow, grating noise, something as of the sea breaking on a beach of pebbles, and rolling stones over stones. So I listened, and judging by the sound that whatsoever might cause it lay beyond the hall, I went up on the wall, and so along the little path whereof I have written, to find if I might see what made that noise, for in our present peril a small thing that was new might grow to a great fear. But as my feet rang on the paving of the pathway (for a footstep sounded hollower and louder there than on the rampart) I could not hear the grating noise for my own walking; nor when I stood still to listen, could I hear it again. Only as I came to the corner of the walk, where it passed to the other side of the hall, could I see that the battlements were somewhat broken and crumbled, as in the way with stone that has stood long in the salt air; nor was there light to see if the breach were new or old. So I turned back, thinking that some pieces of the wall had fallen from decay, and were washing in the water at the foot of the wall; nor did I hear aught but the accustomed sounds of the castle, till I came to my chamber door. Only I remember looking in at the chief window of the hall, where were yet a few embers burning on the hearth, and I saw the shadow of a man going to and fro.

On the morrow I awaked later than my wont, being more weary and shaken than I had thought to be from my yesterday's peril; and the castle was already astir in the mist. So I clad myself hastily, and hearing talk and laughter in the court, I came to the door of my stair and looked to see who might have heart to laugh in our beleaguered place; but seeing only the men of the garrison, I went not out, being unwilling to give them a handle for mirth; though indeed, since our peril and the end of the Swede, their roughness and insolence were somewhat dashed. Yet on this morning, as I judge, the better spirits of the Earl had given them heart to swagger; for it is a true saying, Like master, like man. So I kept myself in the shadow of the doorway, that they marked me not.

As they jested together, some seven or eight of them, and as evil-looking ruffians as you should find in all Alsatia (I mean the part of London so-called), came out the silly maid of the inn at Marsham, that was now the only woman in the castle save Mistress Rosamund and the Signora. So the troopers must needs break a jest or two on her, that she answered foolishly after her wont, with shrill laughter, and such rudeness as she knew, though she was herein far behind the men, that had garnered the foul words of many lands, and knew the harsh oaths of the Germans and Hollanders, and the camp talk of Spaniards and Frenchmen and Italians, that was better for sound but worse for beastliness. So, feigning to be mad at someone of these speeches, that she understood no whit (though had she known the sense of it she had been justly angered) the wench gave one of the men a clout on the cheek, laughing foolishly, and he swearing that he would pay her for it by flaying her face with his beard, that was like brushwood for stiffness, she fled from him in a mock terror, and he chasing her, she found no way of escape but up the stair that led to the rampart. Thither came her rough wooer after her, and the rest, some half-dozen, following to see the sport; and one of the sentries, after she had leapt over his pike that he laid across the way, joined in the chase, and so they ran, she screaming and laughing, and they swearing and hallooing as at a hunt, till they came to the path that led round the hall on the gallery, and there, one by one, vanished from my sight, but yet could I hear them yelling, till the girl gave one dreadful screech, that ended suddenly, whereby I judged that her pursuer had overtaken her, though her fear sounded greater than should come from the rough handling of the soldiers, whereto she was well used. Also I heard no more of the men, that must by now have come round the corner of the hall; but methought that either the house between kept the sound from me, or that they feared to disturb the Earl, for he was an ill man to trouble in one of his black moods. So I looked for the wench and the others to come out on the rampart beyond the hall. But when I had watched a space and none appeared, I feared that there might be some devilry afoot, and though I liked not to thrust myself into so foul a business, it behoved me to see that the girl took no hurt. So I went upon the wall by the stair, and found naught but the pike that the sentry had dropped to run after the rest, and so on to the corner, and still was none to be seen. But as I was at the turn in the path, and was at point to run round carelessly, came a whiff of the foul smell that I knew well, that I sickened and had nigh fallen; so I laid my hand on the battlement and went warily, and well it profited me; for as I came round the corner of the hall, was the path clear gone, battlements and all, save for a ragged stone or two in the wall, that dripped with slime, and of the wench and the troopers was no sign.

Then a great terror and faintness fell on me, so that I could scarce crawl back to the rampart and down into the court; yet I laboured to reach the ground again, thinking myself but lost till I was off that height, and when I felt the rock under my feet, I fell down and so remained for a space, with nothing left in my thought but fear, and a certain desperate wish that that which beset us would make a sudden end and torture us no longer with dread, so that I went nigh to envy the poor wretches that had gone laughing to their death, and had been spared that death in life of terror.

Nor can I tell but that I had chosen rather to follow them, so great a sickness of my life was on me, had not Mistress Rosamund come forth from her stair, and seeing me yet crawling in the court, ran to me, crying out to know if I had taken a hurt. At the which my senses came to me again, and a shame of mine unmanliness, and I put her hand from me as she would have helped me up, telling her that naught ailed me but cowardice, whereat she was astonished. Then I told her how the gallery was broken, so that those who ran round the wall were miserably drowned; for I would not say more of the manner of the end, nor needed further words, in that she knew without my telling. But when I spoke of my coming to the corner and being like to follow those others, she grew pale, and shivered, and caught me by the sleeve as though to be assured that I still lived, and I was fain to hold her up, till she recovered herself and drew from me, sooner than I would. And therewith, as though ashamed of the weakness that she had so readily pardoned in me, she would have me go and tell the Earl of what had happened. So I found him pacing the hall (for he sat not with the Signora so oft as aforetime) and told him the event as I had said it to Mistress Fanshawe.

He was but moody when I came upon him, for his late show of cheerfulness had been as a blaze of straw; but when I looked for him to fall into a fit of desperation, he did but laugh harshly.

"Well, cousin," says he, "a good riddance to the wench, and fair quarters in the warm for my men. A quick death and a merry one is the health we soldiers drink." Then he asked me more closely of the place where the gallery had broken, and I told him that it lay at the end of the hall where we stood, but that the path above the great window yet stood firm.

"Aye," says he, after musing awhile, "I was above, and heard the slut screaming, and came down to bid her be still, and to find if the men were there with her, when I had strictly forbidden them to use the gallery. But when I came was naught to be seen or heard. Well, we are yet enough to handle the guns if need be; but I would that we could turn them hitherward. Duke Bernard of Weimar said to me at the leaguer of Breisach that a corner with no flanking was a door of entrance to the enemy, that could lay his pieces to shoot away the defences sidelong — " and here he took himself and laughed again.

"Look not on me as though I were mad, Hubert man," says he; for indeed I marvelled that he could remember such matters in our present peril. "I will lay my life, that is worth less than a little, that in thy last hour will a scrap of Latin or Greek, or a stave of a psalm (thou being a Puritan) beat in thine ears for no reason. Soldiering is my trade," says he, "and by the tools of my trade must I end, and the cant of the art military is like to be my last speech. So leave me, cousin, ere I weary thee."

CHAPTER XIV

Of the Stain on the Wall, and of the Wave from the Sea

My Lord had followed my counsel, it would seem, and taken order with the victuals; for when we came to supper that day was the fare but scanty and rough, though no lack was there of wine, insomuch that the Italian woman, that was ever dainty in her ways, rallied the Earl on his table, saying that she, for one, was no Puritan, and used to better feeding, even in a camp, and offering as in jest to be our cook. All this she said smoothly, yet her eyes were restless, and answered not to her words, as though the fear that was on the castle had touched her also.

"Why, Madonna," answered my cousin, "are we not in a leaguered fortress, with small hope of relief, and must we not be rationed for a siege?"

"No, no," she broke in, with a feigned petulance, "it is not for the littleness of the food that I mind, but for your barbarous English cooking and serving. Signor Uberto, would you not wish me to dress you a supper?"

Methought that if I took her at her word I might need no more suppers in this world, but I let my tongue say nought of that, but stammered somewhat of being a plain scholar, and used to English fare and little of it, and how I would not have her spoil her hands by doing service for me, and so forth.

"Why then," says she, "and may I not be your camp cook and sutler-woman and cook your meat?"

"Nay, Signorina," says Mistress Rosamund, "nor belike draw us drink."

At that word, whereof the Italian knew the meaning, her brows drew together and her eyes grew narrow, and she set her hand to the breast of her gown as though she sought something. Yet did she say naught, for Pompey, the black, that was bringing a dish, and was coming by the wall, cried out in fear and cast the dish from him, and fell down by the table, clinging to the Earl's knees. This moved me strangely, for the boy's black face was grey with terror, and he held to my cousin, that loved him not, nor would be thrust away, but babbled of a noise that affrighted him. And when my Lord kicked him off and bade him stand and speak what noise he heard, could the lad say naught but some jargon about the devil rolling stones in the wall. So the Earl, being angered, caught the blackamoor by the collar of his jerkin, and cuffed him for a cowardly fool; but when he let him go again, Pompey cried out, "Again! dere he am again!" and so fell as in a fit, moaning and foaming at the mouth.

Now as he fell, were we still for a space, and no sound was there but the gasping of the black; but presently came a muffled noise as of the grating of stone on stone, such as I had heard it the night before. And this grew greater, until it was as if a wave were rolling pebbles on the shingle in the very hall, and yet no appearance of aught; only the sound came from the end of the hall where it gave on the water, and I remembered that outside the wall the gallery had run that was now broken.

All we sat still, and the serving men stood shaking; only my cousin Philip, that was of a high courage, sprang up, and going to the wall whence the noise came, beat on the wainscot, that was old and cracked. And as he smote the wood, he cried out with an oath that he had hurt his hand, for that there was blood on it, and put his fist to his mouth, not thinking, as is the way of all when their skin is broken. But then he spat and swore again, and gulped once or twice as though he were sickened.

" 'Swounds, here is no blood!" he cried, and thrust his hand under a lamp, and it was smeared with gouts of slime, and savoured foully, that he caught up a napkin and rubbed his hand furiously and threw the cloth away; and looking at the place where he had stood, could I see more slime oozing through the cracks of the panels, and crawling down to the floor, and the wood bellying out from the wall.

So I called to him to leave the wall alone, for I guessed full well what was afoot; but he would not. "Nay," says he, "this must be looked into," and catching hold on the edge of the panelling, that was, as I deem, rotted in places, he tore off a great piece of it, well-nigh to the floor, and showed the stone and plaster of the wall, and catching a lamp, he held it up to show what might be under the wood. Then could we all see how there was a great stain on the wall, and the plaster crumbling away from the stones, as is the way in old and ruinous houses when the damp strikes through the crevices of the building; also the grating of the stones went on, and when it ceased, as it did at whiles, could I hear the waves plashing without, and judged that the tide was high.

Now when we saw that the foulness that beset us had found its way into our innermost citadel, the serving-men stood aghast like men of stone, and the black moaned and muttered to his gods, and for myself I was in a great disorder of mind and could think of naught helpful; but the women sate still and gazed with steadfast eyes on the wall, and I saw their lips move, but heard no word of prayer from Mistress Rosamund or of a spell of sorcery from the Italian. Only my cousin, the Earl, shamed me by his readiness that he ever showed in the face of a present peril, for he cried out loudly that the damp had struck through the wall with the high tide, and drawing his sword, bade the men to bring a brazier, the which they did, sweating with fear of their master and of the appearance on the wall. So I shook off my lethargy and helped, and together we took the burning logs from the hearth and laid them on the brazier, and pushed it close against the wall, that the flame licked the stone, and the slime and water hissed as it dripped from the chinks; and ever as the flame fell the Earl called out for more fuel, for the plaster, and the mortar between the stones, crumbled more and more, and the oozings of slime grew, and seemed to me (though perchance it was but the flicker of flames) to be creeping upward and outward like snakes, and the grating sound grew louder, till it was as though that which was without must needs break in on us.

Yet we nourished the fire, nor noted how the hall was blackened with the smoke; and the men brought wood, and the women sat and watched us, and all seemed like some ill dream. For naught visible was there to fight against but a stain on the wall, and the oozing of slime, and no sound but of the crackle of the fire and the grating of stones, and when these ceased, the plashing of the waves.

Whether this were an hour or twain or yet more, I know not, nor did any know. Only I remember that the men came back at last empty-handed and told my Lord that the wood was done, and he flew out at them for unthrifts and fools, and bade break up the wainscoting and cast it on the brazier, but it was damp and burnt ill, and I looked for the end to come speedily, for that once or twice had I heard a rushing sound, and a splashing as of great stones falling away.

Yet even as I awaited the breaking in of our defences, the grinding of stones ceased, and the oozing of the slime and water, and even the plash of waves was less, so that it seemed that the tide was now fast ebbing. Then Mistress Rosamund arose in her place, and her lips moved with no sound, so that I judged that she thanked God for our deliverance.

But the Earl turned and called on Pompey to bring him wine, yet the boy answered not, but lay still under the table, and when his master stooped down and haled him out, the black lay, nor would stir for kicks or curses; and when I felt his breast, was it cold, and his face drawn horribly with fright, and his jaw hung open.

So we judged that he was dead of fear, and hid his body hastily with a cloth, lest Mistress Rosamund should behold it when she came from her seat, for now the table kept the sight from her.

But the Earl went and sat in his great chair, and the Signora by him, and his face was black with the smoke, and he said no word, till he cast his eye upon the eastward window, and marked how the darkness was a little lightened in that quarter. Then turned he to the Italian that sate sullen by him, and spake more softly than his wont. "*Fiammetta mia*," says he, "we have seen a many dawns together, but here is the last, and let us make merry, for another night shall end our trouble."

She wheeled to him, and her eyes were scornful of him. "Why so, Fillippo?" she asked. "We are not dead yet, nor am I one to give up the game till the last card be played. We shall see other dawns yet, and in better places than this kennel in the marshes."

"It is my house and the house of my fathers," says the Earl scowling. "I will hold it while I can, and then go with it."

"Oh, thy fathers, thy fathers, with their barbarous names and their ragged pride!" she flung out at him in a rage. "Who shall know or care when thy castle and thy fathers are sunk in the marsh, mud in mud? Life! Life! That have I yet, and that will I hold! Die like a rat in a trap if thou wilt — I will live! I must live!"

I marvelled greatly to see the passion of the woman, now it brake out at the last; nor was it that she feared death, for she had a courage more than womanly: rather was this a fury of disgust in her that her strength and subtlety of spirit and her curious knowledge and arts should be wasted, and the tale of her life cut short ere she had proved her power to the full; and she rejected the imminent doom as a thing unjust to her sovereignty, even as King Charles denied the right of the court that judged him.

But this vehemence of the Signora lasted but a space, and anon she was pleading to the Earl to escape from this prison ere it fell in on us. So he rose wearily, saying, "Well, Fiammetta, shall we take to the boats and seek to land out of the way of the Roundheads? 'Tis a forlorn hope, yet a hope for thee, and if thou wilt live, why live. Come, cousin Hubert and cousin Rosamund, and let us make a plan ere the tide rises again. But first," says he, "carry forth yonder carrion."

So, begrimed as he was, he did on his cloak and went out into the court, that was yet misty and grey in the first morning, and we after him, and the two serving men behind bearing the dead black, that they bestowed in an empty room of the men's quarters; for indeed there was no lack of such, since our numbers had sore dwindled.

So we came to the gate and the barbican tower, where was yet a cresset burning for the men to watch, and the sentries walking on the walls and crying to one another, and presently were we joined by the two men that had been with us in the hall, but the Earl had strictly charged them that they should say naught of that which had befallen. Some eight or nine of the troopers were at the gate or around the culverins above it, being nigh half of what remained of the garrison, and their faces seemed strange in the red light of the cresset, being wan with fear and weariness, and it seemed to me that we were already like to a company of ghosts among the marshes of the Styx.

Now when the men marked the Earl's face, how begrimed it was, and drawn with care and toil, there went a whisper through them, but none dared speak openly; so he beckoned to them to gather around him under the gate, and the women and I and the two serving men, that were begrimed like my Lord, stood backward from him, and when he saw the troopers nigh him he spake to them.

"Comrades," says he, "this is an ill strait that we are in, and needs must we try a desperate remedy. Of fuel and food have we little left, and there is a troop of rascal Roundheads besetting Marsham village, nor are we enough to face them; and this old castle of ours, I doubt, has served its time, and is rotten with age and saltwater. But this morning the gallery fell with some few of you, and tonight was the high tide oozing through the very wall of my own hall."

Here one of the serving men was at the point to say more, but my Lord, hearing him muttering, turned on him with so fierce a look that the fellow shook and was silent. "What say you, then," says my cousin, speaking in a manner more friendly that he used to his men, and rather as a soldier to brother soldiers; "shall we starve here of cold and hunger, or give ourselves to be hanged or knocked on the head by Noll's saints yonder? Surely if one life might ransom the rest, should they have mine, and welcome; but you know their mercy to such as you."

At that there went a murmur through the men, like the growling of a kennel of dogs; nor could I wonder, for indeed the Parliament men were never tender, even to those that had rendered themselves prisoners.

"Well," says my Lord, "we have yet our arms, and no lack of powder, and barges to hold us all. Shall we not take our last chance, and seek to land somewhere out of reach of yonder dogs? Then, if we may not come at them by an ambush, at least may we win through to those that yet hold out for the King, or at worst find a ship to the Low Countries, where is good pay from the Spaniard or the Dutch, which, we care not. Will you venture it with me?"

Some of the men said Aye, with oaths after their manner, but some hung back, muttering that there was a sea-devil besetting the marshes and the water, and we should but sail down his throat.

"Nay then, what talk is this?" asks the Earl, with a great scorn in his voice. "Are ye my brothers of the sword, or wenches in green-sickness, that ye had rather starve in a rotten hold than take your lives in your hands and sally forth? And what is this fool's talk of a water devil? Here is my cousin Hubert, that will tell you he is a man of peace and no soldier, and he hath ventured forth in a boat with you twice, and no harm come to him, nor to those with him. Shall you be cowards where a Cambridge scholar is bold? Nay, shall you be behind the very women? Wilt thou come with me, Fiammetta?" and the Italian nodded and answered him, "*Si*," and Mistress Rosamund bowed her head also.

So one and then another of the men, taking courage each from the other, gave their word to try the last venture with him, and my Lord smiled on them, and methought, with his blackened face in the red flicker of the cresset, he seemed like Lucifer among his peers; and he clapped one or two on the shoulder, crying out that they were stout fellows, and worth living or dying with; and all now being at one, he bade open the gate and draw up the boats, that were moored to the mole with chains. So they threw open the gates, and went out, the tide being on the ebb and half way down, as when Mistress Rosamund had nigh perished in the crawling pool; and we stood at the gate and watched them, though the light was but small, for the cresset was burning low, and the dawn was yet faint to seaward, and a mist hung over the water. Yet could I see the men on the mole, as dark shadows against the mist and the low twilight, and the boats black on the oily water, and all seemed peaceful and secure, so that I could scarce believe that we had been fighting for life against that terror of the night.

Now presently came a puff of wind parting the mist, and as I gazed seaward, where a riband of clear grey sky lay on the leaden rim of the water, there seemed to be a rising up as of a heap upon the edge of sight, as when one looks through a twisted glass. Yet as I looked, was it gone; but in a short space I thought to see a rising of the water nearer at hand, as of a wave, and I bethought me of the tales of travellers, how after an earthquake, or by some trick of the tides, a great roller has broken in from the deeps and swept the islands of the South Sea, or cities of the Spanish Main. So I pulled my cousin by the sleeve, and bade him look; yet he saw naught, nor could I, when I turned again.

But in a moment or twain after, as the men still wrought in the boats and on the mole, somewhat heaved up the waters in a heap again, and I was aware of a mound of blackness moving very swiftly toward us, with no crest as is the wont of waves, but round and sleek. So I cried out to the men to beware, and the Earl blew on a whistle, but too late; for as the men heard him, and sought to make for the gate, that smooth hill of water, and what else I know not, rolled full on the mouth of the harbour, and engulfed the jaws of the mole, and while a man might count five was there naught to be seen save a bellying surge, streaked with slime, that rolled up to the very threshold of the gate, yet without foam. Then, as we gazed, was the water sunken again, but of the boats, and the men therein and on the quays was no sign, save the broken chains dangling from their rings, and we stood yet with the hissing and grinding of that strange wave in our ears, and all was still again, and the dawn growing slowly over the dull line of the sea.

CHAPTER XV

Of the Business of the Italian Woman

When that strange and horrid swelling of the waters had ebbed, and left naught of boats or men, but only broken chains and puddles of slime on the stones, Mistress Rosamund was the first of us that spake, imploring the mercy of God on those poor souls so suddenly hurried to judgment. For the rest of us, it shames me to own that I was overmuch busied with my own fear to think of others so soon, for I had looked for the ugly heap of slimy surge rolling in on us to make no stay before it sucked us in also. Nor, seeing that I had been bred a Puritan, was I apt to pray for those that were dead, though I was readier to assent thereto than my teachers had thought a good Protestant might be. And with that, like a very woman, she turned from prayer to the thought of the man that was her friend, and (as I may now confess) sought to be more than a friend and "Ah!" says she, "you saved me from that!"

"Nay," said I, "rather my cousin Philip saved us both."

At the sound of his name the Earl, that had stood in the midst of the gateway staring like a man distraught, heaved a great sigh and turned to us, yet saw us not, for his eyes were inward, and he talked with himself or with one that we saw not.

"All my men gone," says he, but so low that we could scarce hear it. "All gone, and yet I cannot go. Truly, Margaret, I was cruel to thee, but thou art more merciless to me. I did but give one blow, nor meant thou shouldest die, but thou hast smitten me daily and nightly. Make an end woman, nor come to me again with the red stain on thee!"

Then Mistress Rosamund looked at me, and I remembered that the dead Countess of Deeping had been called Margaret. But my Lord went on babbling, and now it seemed that his vision had changed, for he spake to Master Eldad, and called him fool and madman to come in his armour, for that he had been sucked out of it long ago, and suchlike frenzies, till the Italian woman, that had spoken no word, but stood with her head bowed in her hands, raised her face up, and it was ghastly in the dawn, but her eyes were green and shining.

"Fool!" says she to him in the Italian. "There is none here but the living, and thy saint rests well where we sent her, thou and I. It was more than a chance blow that rid us of her, and more than grapes that made her wine. Yet I see her not, nor fear her at all."

When Mistress Fanshawe and I heard this, we drew from the woman as though she had been leprous; and surely she was of a whiteness like that of Gehazi. Yet the Earl stood stupid, as though her words were naught to him; till presently, with a great cry, he flung his cloak from him, and plucked out his sword, and was for running at her; nor could I find it in my heart to come between them; but she moved not nor spake, but looked on him scornfully, and he made but a pace or two and stood still, and then, with a great curse, he flung his sword on the stones and set foot on it and brake it, and so put his arms about her and pulled her to him, laughing strangely.

"Nay," says he, "I will not murder more women, so fear not me. Come, Fiammetta, we will revel tonight, sweet one, and our merry men with us. Shut the gates, knaves, and go to breakfast, and then make ready the hall for feast. Ye shall all sup with me and my new lady, and watch and ward may go hang. What is our muster?" and he ran his eye over the men, that were by now all huddled in the court, gazing on him with amazement. "Four — six — eight rascals yet left," says he, "and four here for the high table, and at supper another guest to make the thirteen. Surely we will give him warm welcome. Come, cousin shall we to breakfast? There shall be no rations and sparing of our cheer any more, but we will drink the sun up and drink him down again, and so goodnight!"

Now when he ended, with a great laugh, was I sure that madness had fallen on him, and yet would I not wish him in his senses again; for had I been in his case (which God forbid) could I have done no other, being sensible, than slay the Italian woman first and then myself. But I would not look on the antics of a madman nor hear his ravings; for I have ever thought that they who find matter for mirth in such things are very fiends, whom it were flattery to call beastly, for that the very beasts do fear or pity madness; yet have there been men, aye, and women too in these evil days, not ashamed to make a sport of seeing the wretches in Bedlam. So without word I turned to my tower, to spend the little of life yet left to me in meditation and prayer; for in spite of Master Eldad's prophecy, I looked to see another dawn on earth as little as did my enemies. And the like did Mistress Rosamund, and when the Earl would have had the Signora in with him, she also denied her company, saying that she had business of her own, and I marvelled what this might be, but had no will to ask, for it seemed a little thing to me now what she might be about, nor could I fear her or aught else. Then understood I, or had understood had I cared to think at all, how cowards have been made brave by desperation of their fear. So I went to the stair that climbed to my room, but standing in the doorway and looking over the court, that was empty of men now, and dusky in the twilight of morning and the shade of the walls, it seemed that a shadow came from the door of the men's quarters, and went up to the great door of the hall; and the shape of it was strange, as of a grey woman bearing a huddled black thing on her shoulders, and I thought idly on the Italian and wondered what business hers might be. But the woman and her burden, that I saw not clearly, were shortly vanished in the doorway, and no more saw I, saving that an hour later, looking toward the court, I noted a red flicker of light in the window of a room that I judged to be the chamber where the Italian wrought her sorceries, and a wreath or twain of smoke from the casement.

Now that morning went by like an ill dream, and strive as I would to set my heart and mind on things of religion, could I not quiet myself, but was restless. Also when I sought to read in the Scriptures, were the words empty of meaning as a speech that one hath said over too oft; nor when I prayed was my state the happier. So I fell to thinking of Mistress Rosamund, that was doubtless (or so I held) praying now that we might meet the end with a calm and godly resignation; and she (for so she hath told me since) had the same belief of me, that comforted her in her like restlessness. For be it said to our shame that in that very valley of the shadow of death were our thoughts rather of the creature than of the Creator.

So wore on the day, without sight of the sun, but a grey curtain of misty cloud, and a blackness to seaward; and of our enemies, man or monster, was no sign, and the sea was still and dead. Only about noon I felt anhungered, and sought to see if I might come at any meat; but going to the hall, the door was fast shut, and I could hear a noise of hammering, as though some carpenter were at work, and a voice singing of a camp song, that I knew for the Earl's, though strangely harsh; and the thought of his madness sickened me of my hunger, so that I turned away again and went upon the rampart to walk, for I was weary of sitting still.

Now could I pace my fill, for no sentinels were on the wall any more, and I could nigh make the circuit of the rampart, save in that place where the gallery had been that was broken away. But along the one side of the hall could I still walk, and I looked into the room, that was as a cavern, through a clear pane of the great window; yet was there naught to see but the firelight flickering (for they had found fuel, whence I know not) and no sign or sound more of my cousin and his labours. Little could I see, for that though it was not long after noon, the blackness in the sky to the seaward gathered and rose higher, and though I have small skill of the signs of the weather, yet I augured of a storm at hand, although wind was none, nor foam on the water, but a steady rolling swell that rose and fell against the stones with no sound.

Then as I turned back to the ramparts over the court, came a gust of wind, that moaned through the loopholes, and died suddenly, and the breath of it was faint with a salt foulness; and looking forth to the quarter whence the wind blew, could I see a streak of paler grey on the black waters, and I marvelled foolishly wherefore, if the thing that beset us were indeed there, it had not will or appetite to make an end of us, where were too few now to keep it out. But the patch of grey lay still, wherefore I judged it to be the shadow of some cloud; and indeed the blackness as less above us. Then, hearing steps on the stone, I looked again to the court, and saw the shadow as of a ghostly woman coming through the gloom with huddled black burden on her shoulders, and as she came near I knew that it was the Signora, and she panted under her load; so, not that I would help her in her business, but for that I could not stand idle and see a woman bear burdens, I came down and made to lend her a hand. Yet when I took hold of that load, I left it again hastily, for I had touched the cold hand of a dead man under the black cloak that was cast over it; but she did but laugh, and casting off the cover, showed me that this was the body of Pompey the black, that I had seen with mine own eyes dead of fright in the hall.

So I was ashamed of my terror, that had been rather of what devilry the Italian might have wrought, than of handling the dead, for this had grown to me a matter of daily use; and judging that she had but been opening the body after the manner of a chirurgeon, to surprise some secret of nature (though I wondered that she should think of her art in that extremity of danger), I asked her what she made with the black.

"You shall hear anon," says she, yet panting with her toil, "if you will but aid me to heave this up to the rampart and cast it forth, for I have done with it now."

So I did as she asked, for I could see no guilt therein, though a labour I liked not; and with no great pain we brought the body up on the wall, and rested it between two battlements. Then the Italian waited and drew breath, and gazed outward a space, till again came a brief gust of wind, and the savour that I had noted before, and I deemed that the greyness of the sea was yet visible, though from the gathering blackness could I not be sure. But the woman snuffed the air once or twice like a hound, and turning to me, "*Sta bene,*" says she, "it is well; now fling him out," and without more words we took up the body, and swung it back and forth once or twice, and lastly cast it out as far as we could into the water, and it went splashing as a boy falling into the sea for sport, and sank, but rose again and wallowed on the waves. So it lay for a space floating idly; but in no long time began the body to drift slowly toward the quarter where I had seen the greyness. Then presently the dead boy went swifter, as though the current carrying him waxed stronger, and lastly rose upright on a swell with the black head and shoulders showing like a swimmer's, and then vanished as though drawn under, nor, if the body rose again, could I see it for the gloom.

So I turned again to the Italian, that had been gazing earnestly after the body, and asked her of her purpose in dealing with the dead black.

"Why," says she, "you will be ready to cry out on me and yourself that I thought not of this before, nor you at all. Signor Uberto, when you are beset with rats, do you not lay baits for them with poison? Well, Pompey must serve for our bait today, and we have yet hope to win free, if yonder sea-devil have a stomach like other beasts, and be not immortal. And even if our enemy be more than man, may we hope; since my poison, though not blessed by any Holy Father, hath been used by one belike, for it is a right recipe of the Borgia."

I knew not whether more to admire the courage of the woman or to reprobate her impudence; so I asked her, thinking to shame her, whether this were the poison she had mixed for the Swede, and for aught I knew, for me and others.

"Nay then, Signor Uberto," she says, "you know little of me if I would be so ill-mannered as to use that poison on people of quality like you and the Signorina Rosamunda," and she lengthened out the name as in scorn. "For you yourself," went she on, "never would I seek to poison you, save as a last chance for life, if then. You are a scholar, signor, and a pretty swordsman to boot, and I would be loth to lose two such rarities in one. Truly, Uberto," and here she leaned towards me a little, and looked in mine eyes, "there is a brave conspirator wasted in thee. Thou canst see, canst understand what is to do; and then comes in thy cursed religion or duty, or I know not what empty words, and the deed goes by undone. Oh, if thou hadst but taken the chance I gave, and thrust home a day or twain, ago, thou hadst then been Earl of Deeping, lord of all in it, men and women, with Mistress Rosamund for the Countess till thou wert tired of her, and then" — and here she drew her lips close together, but her eyes spake for her, and promised I know not what.

Now I could not answer her, being daunted by the naked wickedness of her plotting, and yet mastered by the subtlety and cunning of the woman, and the coolness that could tell all her own devilish deeds as though she had been Machiavelli writing of the deeds of Caesar Borgia, and marking how and where each plot had worked or failed. So anon she spake again, but with no passion.

"Then I took the Swede, as a man might use a club when his rapier was denied him," says she carelessly; "and you foiled me again, not meaning it, and the club brake in my hand."

I marked not then how she had thou'd me for a little and then left off, as though she had come near to me and then drawn back, but after, I remembered this and many other things.

"It was by no will of mine, indeed, that they fought," said I, "as you know well; yet if fight must be, I would not have had it go otherwise." But at that she brake out in a passion.

"Oh!" she cried, with an Italian oath of the camp that I set not down, "that thou shouldst not be a wiser man or a greater fool! A touch more or less wit than thou hast, Uberto, and the Swede had slain Filippo, and come home to my welcome and his cup of wine —"

"And therewith died," said I, for I remembered what Mistress Rosamund had guessed.

"Nay," says the Signora frankly, like one in hell that has no need to feign virtue any more, and finds a pleasure in that; "that were too plain and open. He had died in two days at the least, or I had moved the soldiers to slay him as he lay sick, and charge thee to make their peace with the Parliament. And for the thing out there — who knows if it had not left us, when it had swallowed its dearest morsel? Or we could well have tried my device of today —" and here she brake off and clutched me by the sleeve. "Perchance it has worked by now! Look forth, Uberto, and see if there be any sign on the water!"

So I looked, but the blackness of the sky was now well-nigh like night, and nothing was to be seen save the long smooth waves rolling out of the gloom and lapping up and down without foam.

"If it be dead!" she whispered in mine ear. "If it be gone away! if it come not tonight, what then? Uberto, what then?" and her breath was hot on my cheek. But I would not see her meaning, or so much as answer her temptation. Nor, truly, was it a temptation to me, though haply in my younger days, when I had gusts of ambition, and thought of myself as having in me the stuff of Plutarch's heroes, I had listened more eagerly. So I but spake to the plain meaning of her words and no more, drawing a little away from her.

"Why," said I, "then must we adventure what we were at point to do this morning, and since the boats are gone, must we build a raft and sail under cover of night like shipwrecked mariners, and land in the safest place that may be, leaving Deeping Hold to whoso cares to dwell therein."

She laughed, mocking me. "Oh, the wise scholar!" cries she. "Of a surety that is what we will do, and if the Earl choose to stay here for his life, or longer, shall we pleasure him, thou and I? Nay, say nothing. Even the fool, when he holdeth his peace, is counted wise, which is one of the few sayings of thy Scriptures that I have found worth the remembering. We shall meet at supper, Signor Uberto," and with that she was gone, leaving me to ponder on what ill meaning her last speech might hold.

So I walked yet on the walls, but nothing was to be seen save the gloom and the swell, nor heard but the fitful gusts and flaws of wind; and I felt a pinching of hunger, for that I had not broken my fast that day, yet could I not bring myself to go and ask for meat. So I paced up and down the wall awhile, and wearying of the darkness, went down into the court, and presently came out Mistress Rosamund, bearing somewhat between her hands.

"I saw you parleying with her," says she, and methought with some coldness. "What had she to say that you were so close with her?"

"More wickedness than I looked to find in man or woman," I answered in a weariness, for it hurt me that she should think I had friendship with the Italian, "and more subtlety than I might hear from the Fiend himself. What matters it, Rosamund? Surely we are but dead, thou and I, and if we be no saints, as I know full well of myself, yet shall we be rid of her and her like on the other side."

But when she saw me weary and faint, she forgot the little thorn of jealousy that will gall the kindest of women at times, and came to me, holding out her burden, and it was a piece of bread wrapped in a napkin. "Forgive me, Hubert," says she very sweetly, "though I may not forgive myself that I spake so to thee. Thou hast not eaten today, and art weary, and here is somewhat that I have saved for thee, for I am no such hermit as thou, and could not fast so long."

I looked on her, and her face was pale and weary in the gloom, and her eyes circled with a shadow, and I knew that she had fasted too, and had saved for me all that she had.

"Nay," said I, "thou shalt eat too, else I touch nothing"; and with that I brake the bread in twain, and bade her begin. Yet for a time she would not, saying that she had eaten enough, and felt no hunger, and other sweet lies that the best of women are aptest to tell. Only when I made as though to cast the bread over the battlements, she yielded, and then with pretence that I had given her the greater share; so we sat under the walls in the shadows and ate together, and talked of this and that, and forgot the danger and the darkness that brooded closer, and none came to mount guard, or to trouble us; only now and then could we see lights in the guard-room or the hall, and we judged that the men were drinking, for at whiles came a quavering snatch of song, as though some poor wretch were striving to cheat himself into merriment, and forget his fear. And of what we said to each other remember I no whit, nor assuredly was it worth the treasuring; only I was comforted greatly, and it seemed that the bitterness of death was past, and peril and wickedness but vain and little things, like the foolish flaws of wind that now and again beat against the battlements over our heads.

CHAPTER XVI

Of the End of Deeping Hold

In this talk, or more often in silence, we sat, for how long I know not, till a rain began to fall on us, and I bade Rosamund rise, for I would not that she should be chilled now, though we both might look to be under the waters ere the morrow dawned. So we came under the shelter of a turret, and stood a little. But presently the great door was cast open, and I heard my cousin's voice calling for me; so, being unwilling that he should see us together and perchance break a jest on us in his wildness, I left her in the shadow and came forward to the door, telling him that I had been walking in the court, and asking what was his need of me.

"Why, man Hubert," says he, with the boisterous mood still on him, "I would have thee make thyself brave for tonight, for it is nigh supper-time, and we have a guest coming. I will be as gay as I may, and Fiammetta here, and if thou meet Rosamund, bid the wench wear her best also."

Now this she heard, standing in the dark, for he spake loudly, so I but told him that I would see to it, and when he had shut to the door again, I came back to her and asked her what she thought, saying that in my mind we were better spend our last hours in prayer and repentance.

"Nay," says she, "I have said my prayers by now, and I would fain die without thinking that I denied my cousin his last desire. Foolish it may be, but no sin; and since I heard him cry out on his dead wife this morning, have I forgiven him, as doubtless she hath, and repented of many ill thoughts of him. He knew not what he did, nor knows now; and if our folly can help him to end the easier, why not be fools together?"

It warmed my heart to hear her speak thus, and without thinking that I had spoken no word of love to her, I caught her close to me and kissed her; nor did she struggle, but presently she put me away, saying in a voice between tears and laughter, "Nay, Hubert, thou shalt see me in bravery for once, if no more, and judge if I cannot ruffle it as well as even Her Highness the Signorina Bardi!"

With that she sped to her room, and I to mine, though since I had come with but two suits, and the commoner was spoilt with the slime of the crawling pool, had I little change of apparel. Yet I clad myself in my best, with what little of price I had, and came down into the court; and the rain had ceased, but the wind was blowing in unsteady gusts, each stronger than the last, and the tide rising fast, as I could judge by the dashing of the waves on the rock and the wall; for all was now dark as the mouth of hell. Yet I found my way to the hall door by the light streaming through it, when the supper bell tolled mournfully like a knell over the desolation of the marshes and the sea; for the door stood open as at a feast, and two men with torches to guide us thither. So coming into the hall, I found my cousin seated in the great chair on the dais at the head of the table, and the seat by him empty, and he was in his best apparel of war, scarlet with gold laces and broideries; and what of plate he had left (for his wars and revels had melted the more part of it), ranged on the high table, and below sat the troopers, all the eight that were left to us, and each with what rags of bravery he had, and their muskets and pikes ranged against the wall. Also a great tapestry was hung over the wall where the stain was, and all the candles that might be put in the sconces were burning, and strange was it to see how all was set for a feast.

So my cousin called me up to my place, but I lingered to see if Mistress Rosamund would come, and presently she entered, wrapped in a cloak, and cast it off ere she went up the hall; and truly it amazed me to see her so royal. For she had on a gown of green silk flowered with gold, the gift (as she told me after) of the Countess when she grew too pious or too sorrowful for bravery; and she glittered in the candlelight like a goddess of gold. Also in her hair and on her neck she wore old jewels of the house of Deeping, that my Lady had left her, and that the Earl let her keep, though the Italian sought to have them; and the likeness which she bore to her dead cousin, or to what the Countess had been in her happier time, made her seem like the glorious body that the apostle hath promised to the righteous at the resurrection.

So the Earl, when he saw her coming, gave a great cry, and greeted her as his sweetheart Margaret, being distraught; yet was he not wholly beside himself, and soon knew her for his kinswoman only. Yet would he have her to sit beside him in his lady's place where the Italian was wont to sit, and bade all the men rise and give her greeting; and she, willing to pleasure him, sat down on his right hand in the place of honour, and I next her.

In this moment came the Italian through the door, and she also was fine, but after another sort, for she wore a robe of red, with broideries of the East, and figures of strange characters, and stones here and there glowing red like eyes, and her great red jewel bound on her forehead. Now when she came to the high table and saw the chief place taken, she stood still, and her eyes narrowed like a snake's, and she felt with one hand in her bosom. But the Earl marked her, and would make excuse; for he could be courtly when he chose.

"Signorina," says he, "forgive me that I ask you to sit below me for this one supper. This is the last feast of Deeping Hold, and needs must one of the house sit in the high seat with me. Tomorrow shall we dine, aye, and sup together without her, and for many morrows, and belike for longer than we would."

Not a word spake the Italian, but sat her down at the left hand of the Earl, and played with her rings, that were curious, and some over large for a woman's hand. So we supped, if supper it could be called, when the cheer was but little, and our will to eat less; only the men, that were used to living roughly, and to feeding when they could, fell to heartily, yet stopping at whiles to listen.

Now when we had been at meat about half an hour, the tempest that had been gathering all the day brake on the castle suddenly with a great clap of wind, that beat upon the windows nigh the place where the gallery had fallen, and whistled through the chinks of the panes, that the candles flickered; and then came other gusts, and then one constant howling and crying of the wind, as though all the devils were loose around us. Also in no long space could we hear the roaring of the waters, as the waves beat on the rock and the buttresses and the foundations of the wall, till the hall shook with their storming; and yet was no sign nor sound of the enemy that we dreaded worse than any tempest, so that the Signora leaned over to me, smiling, and I knew her thought.

My lord marked her smile, and his madness took him again at her scorn. He cried out that the guest was late, and bade lay his place at the foot of the table, for that he was not of gentle birth, and what more folly I know not. But as he ceased, and the men set the place as he bade them (for they feared his frenzy), came a lull in the storm, and it seemed to me that I heard the grinding of stone on stone that had slain Pompey with the fear of it. Then the wind burst again on the castle, and the waves roared higher, but the grating noise grew greater and nearer; and the Signora left playing with her rings and felt in her bosom again, and her face was white as her napkin.

Only my Lord laughed in his mad mood, and cried out that our guest was coming, and filled a great goblet with wine, and bade all do the like and stand up for a welcome; and by now the noise in the wall was like the grinding of a mill that crushes ore in a mine. Also under the tapestry that hid the wall came trickles of water and streaks of slime, and the stuff blew out like a sail, and lastly came a great crashing, and the tapestry was rent away, and the stones tumbled after it, and a ragged hole was burst in the wall. Then the men cried out for deadly fear, and some grovelled on the floor; but the Earl lifted his cup in one hand and drank to the guest, and as he drank came a mighty surge of the sea against the wall, and the crest of it brake through the hole, and somewhat dark was hurled into the very hall; and when I looked on it, it was the body of the black boy.

With that Rosamund, that had endured till then, fell forward with her head between her hands on the table, swooning, so that I, though I looked not to live, was purposed that we two should die forth from that feast of hell. So I caught her from her seat, and with what strength I know not, threw her over my shoulder and fled from the hall, and some two or three of the men perchance may have done the like, but I marked them not. Only I know that I found myself, yet bearing Rosamund, on the rampart, and it seemed to me that the court was all a plash of water from the spray; also the wind buffeted me so that I was fain to cling to the battlements, and drag myself along till I came on the gallery without the hall window, and the lights within made a glow on the darkness, and a buttress of the wall gave shelter from the wind. So I looked within to see when our deaths might come, and prayed that Rosamund might not waken before the end. And I saw how my cousin sat in his chair, and now was the Italian woman in the place beside him, and he held her there with one hand, and of the men some grovelled, and more sat as turned to stone. Then my lord whispered to the woman, as it seemed, and took a candle from the table, and bent to the floor as though to lift somewhat, and I remembered what he had shown me in his cellar, and knew what he was at point to do. But as he bent, he left holding the Italian, and she caught up a knife from her bosom, and stabbed down at him between the shoulders as he rose, so that he fell back into his seat hurt to death, as I judged, and she brake from him, leaving the dagger in him, and came running down the hall. But as she passed by the body of the boy, came a great heap of blackness through the hole in the wall, and washed round her feet that she fell, but rose again, and would have made for the door, when it seemed as though a band of darkness wrapped round her, and drew her down, and twined higher about her, as she fought with it and tore at it, till I saw naught but the red light of the jewel on her head, and then only a writhing in the folds of that blackness, and I sickened, yet could not look away. Then I saw how the slimy blackness grew, and the stones fell away round the hole, and there rolled in what seemed a wave, but it brake not, but spread over the floor, gulfing the men that lay dead or living, struck by fear, till it heaved at the edge of the dais, and lipped over the step like a living tide of slime, and yet with no form that I could tell. But as that foulness drew nigh to his feet, the Earl rose from his chair, though wounded to the death, as I deemed him, and with one hand holding what seemed like a black cord, he set the candle to it, and forthwith a sputter of sparks sprang out under his hand, and ran downward.

Then my strength came back to me, and power to take mine eyes from the loathly sight, and a fortunate madness, rather than any hope of deliverance, drave me to dare the rage of the storm rather than perish by the madness of man. So I gathered Rosamund, that was yet senseless, in my arms, and setting my feet in the battlement, leapt with all my strength outward, and plunged in the waters. And we sank, but I battled to the air again, and was buffeted by the billows, but strove yet to make away from the horror of the castle; and taking the hair of Rosamund in my teeth as she floated, I swam desperately with hands and feet. But ere I had gone far from the wall, even with the swift current of the tide, came a crack like the blast of the Last Judgment, and a blaze of red fire that lit the sea and the marsh, and then darkness and the roar of winds and waters, and great stones and beams raining out of heaven around us, yet none struck us. Then went we down into the depths, and anon were lifted ever upward on a mighty wave, and whirled onwards like straws, and I caught her body in my arms, and remembered naught more.

Now when I awaked, the first thing that I saw was a clear sky yellow with dawn, and a flash of somewhat white above me, and then another, and it came to me that perchance this was Paradise, and wings of angels over me; yet I sighed for somewhat lacking that yet I could not call to mind. But when I sighed, there came a hand on my forehead, and then eyes between me and the sky, and wet hair cold against my cheek, and lips warm on my mouth, and a voice striving to say my name, and sobbing instead. Then I knew that this was Rosamund, and deemed still that we were in heaven, till she drew back to look at me, and I could see a ragged and ruinous wall of stone closing us in, and samphire and rough grass growing up it; and I felt wet grass and rock under me. With that came back the memory of the night till we had been hurled on that great wave, and I raised myself on one arm and looked around.

First saw I Rosamund, that knelt by me, and her goodly gown was sodden and rent, though gold and gems yet glittered from it, and her hair loose and wet like seaweed; and beyond her was a space of troubled water and grey flats, laced with yellow light in the pools, and white seagulls dotted on the grey, and wheeling over the channels. So I knew that I was yet among the marshes, and a living man, and I looked on Rosamund again, and had no sorrow that this was not heaven, as the divines hold it to be, but rather earth grown a heaven; and she took my hand and fondled it, and for a space spake we no word.

But when I came to my full senses at length, being dizzy and sore bruised, but whole in limb, I asked her where we might be, and how we came there; but indeed, had I thought, I knew the place to be none other than the Hermit's island, where, the story ran, an Earl of Deeping had slain the holy man; for no other rock was in the marshes than the castle and this. So as we sat in the ruin of the cell, she told me how she had known naught after that monstrous revel in the hall, till she wakened in the beginning of dawn on the grass of that isle, and felt my arm yet around her, but knew not how we came there; and thinking me dead at first, she had found my heart to beat, and had dragged me with pain to the shelter of the ruin. So I told her what had happened since her swoon, till the time when that great wave took us both; and we kneeled on the grass and gave thanks to God, that had bridled the sea like an horse, that it might carry us to the place that He had appointed.

Then we went forth, holding each other's hands for fear lest we might not be living in very truth, and looked around, and first could I see the hill over Marsham, and the church tower, and a white patch or two by the river that could be no other than the tents of the soldiers.

But when I carried my eyes further along the shore, to where the wreck of the more ancient Hold of Deeping had stood like a horn on the cliff, was there naught to be seen but a ruinous slope of rocks and stones, that stretched out from the foot of a great fresh rent in the hillside, and nearer to us was no black circle of the Hole, but all brown boulders or grey sand; and marvelling greatly how this might be, we dared at last to turn toward the part where we judged the castle to be, for we had not looked thither at first, for fear of what might be to see. But lo! When we cast our eyes seaward over the marshes, was there no golden vane winking at the dawn from the belfry tower, nor roof of the hall, nor keep nor ramparts, only a grey mound of humped sand and shale in the water, and a spike here and there that might be wall or rock, and naught else to mark where Deeping Hold had been, so that I might have thought that all had been an ill dream, were it not for the drenched rags of golden braveries that clad Rosamund.

So we turned from that desolation and looked again to Marsham, and presently we could tell that we not only saw, but were seen; for there came men down the shore, waving kerchiefs and scarves, and we could hear a shouting afar off. Yet we doubted how we might come to them, or they to us, for there were no boats at Marsham, nor more left of the castle barges than of the castle. But when we looked for a path, we could see that the channels of the river, that lay between the rock and the mainland, were changed, and there seemed a way over the sands to nigh the village. So we adventured, painfully indeed, and stumbling, and with fear of quicksands, but found all firm, till we came near to the shore; nor did the soldiers, that I could now see clearly, come to aid us, for the villagers had filled them with fear of the sands, and also they had seen and heard the flame and the crack of the castle through the strange storm of that night. Only when I came within earshot of them, and named myself, did two or three of the troopers ride their horses into the river and hale us across, else had we been too weak to stand against the current.

Now will I make a brief story of the rest. Suffice it to say that though at first some of the soldiers were distrustful of us (and, indeed, we were strange to look upon), yet when they knew us, having heard of us from the country people, they showed us great kindness, and took us to their tents, where they brought us food and country clothes for Rosamund and for me; and when we were clad and fed, they brought us to their captain. Now when I saw him, I remembered him for the man that had stopped me on the highway aforetime, and gone nigh to shoot me for a Malignant, as the word was; and when I spake of our discourse, he named me, and was the more kind that he knew me for a friend of the Lord General Cromwell. So he would have me tell him all my story, in that he had come to Marsham on hearing of my need by the messenger that was sent on my horse, the which he returned me, and glad was I to have the beast again. But while I rested and ate, had I purposed in my mind that I would say naught of the Thing that had dwelt in the Hole, nor of what of strange and monstrous had happened to our company; for indeed, when I thought thereof to myself, could I hardly believe that all was not an ugly dream, and I looked not for this officer, that was a man pragmatical and set in his own opinion, to give me credit. So I told him, and Rosamund confirmed the tale, of the Earl's cruelty and rage to the men of Marsham, and his murdering of Master Eldad Pentry, which indeed they already knew or guessed. Also I said that many men of the garrison had been lost, and their boats also, by strange accidents, and victual failing and the very walls rotting, the Earl had fallen in a madness of desperation, and had held one last feast, to the which he compelled us to come, and lastly set a train to the powder under his hall, and so destroyed himself and the remnant of his company; from which ruin we alone had escaped, being cast by a great wave on the Hermit's isle. Now to this, being a plain tale and probable, and fitting with that which he knew and had heard of the Earl the captain gave credit, but the people of the village had their own thoughts, and looked on us with fear as more than mortal; and if I were to come there now, under a disguise, and ask of myself, might I find that we had become a legend, other than the truth, yet hardly stranger.

But I had no will, nor have now, to see Marsham again. Ere we rode forth, Rosamund and I, we called together the people, that were rebuilding of the cottages and farms, and made declaration, in the presence of the officer and his troop, that we, as the only next-of-kin to the Earl of Deeping, now dead, renounced his right and his name, and set free his tenants from all service and rent; also we promised to ratify the same by deed, as soon as the country might be settled. So we travelled with the troop of horse, as naught remained for them to do, till we came to a town where we might suit ourselves with apparel more fitting to our quality. And coming to mine own lands, I bestowed Rosamund with the parson of the parish, a good man and a quiet, nor hot for either party of the Church, till such time as we might be wedded.

From that time there hath nothing befallen us stranger than befalls most men, nor do we love to talk of that which we saw at Deeping Hold. Nay, I was moved to set down this story partly, as I said at the beginning, for a warning of the reward of evil, but partly also, as I must own at the last, that having written all down I might the less think on it again. For I am a man that seek not peril nor pleasure, nor am I at home in camp or court, be the camp Oliver Cromwell's or the court of King Charles the Second. Surely in the common things of life, in birth and growth, in love and wedding and the bearing and rearing of children, in sickness and health, in death and immortality, is enough wonder and pleasure and pain and peril to fill any heart; and each man's, aye, or woman's soul is as a Deeping Hold, with its wayward lord, its ill counsellors, and the Adversary waiting in the Pit.

ND - #0495 - 011225 - C0 - 218/144/11 - PB - 9780900891861 - Matt Lamination